THEM

Society Lost, Volume Four

By Steven C. Bird

Them

Steven Bird

THEM

Society Lost, Volume Four

Copyright 2019 by Steven C. Bird

Published by Steven C. Bird at Homefront Books

Illustrated by Hristo Kovatliev

Print Edition 2.20.19

ISBN: 9781795773065

Edited by:

Carol Madding at Hope Springs Editing &

Sabrina Jean at Fast-Track Editing

www.stevencbird.com

facebook.com/homefrontbooks

scbird@homefrontbooks.com

Twitter @stevencbird

Instagram @stevencbird

Them

Table of Contents

Disclaimer 7

Dedication 9

Chapter One 11

Chapter Two 16

Chapter Three 27

Chapter Four 41

Chapter Five 48

Chapter Six...55

Chapter Seven 63

Chapter Eight 79

Chapter Nine 89

Chapter Ten..99

Chapter Eleven..102

Chapter Twelve 110

Chapter Thirteen...117

Chapter Fourteen 126

Chapter Fifteen 130

Chapter Sixteen...138

Chapter Seventeen 143

Chapter Eighteen 149

Chapter Nineteen 153

Chapter Twenty...161

Chapter Twenty-One..166

Chapter Twenty-Two 177

Chapter Twenty-Three 188

Chapter Twenty-Four 194

Chapter Twenty-Five 202

Chapter Twenty-Six 210

Chapter Twenty-Seven 215

Chapter Twenty-Eight 223

Chapter Twenty-Nine 227

A Note from the Author 232

About the Author 234

Preview of Erebus 237

Disclaimer

Them

Dedication

Where do I begin? Them: Society Lost, Volume Four is my twelfth book (counting two novellas), and along the way, I've encountered and befriended many wonderful people. The SHTF/TEOTWAWKI/Prepper/Survival/Post-Apoc fiction crowd is one that generally follows the aphorism - a rising tide lifts all boats. It's a very supportive group of people whom I truly consider to be family. The list is far too long to name them all, for fear of slighting someone who doesn't deserve to be left out, but trust me when I say I thank each and every one of you from the bottom of my heart.

I'd specifically like to thank all the fine authors and readers of DD12 (The Dirty Dozen Post-Apoc Army), founded by L.L. Akers. DD12 is a wonderfully supportive social media group where many of the authors and readers are real-world friends. We don't compete against each other; we support each other.

It's also a way for readers to be able to interact with the authors on a personal level, which is the reason for limiting the official author group to twelve, although all authors are welcome to join the page.

Many of you also may have noticed my shift to a western feel in many of my recent works. Much of that has been inspired by my good friend and acclaimed gun writer Mike "Duke" Venturino. Mike has written for nearly every gun magazine out there throughout the years, as well as having written numerous books

Them

and has appeared both in front of and behind the camera on highly acclaimed movies and historical programs.

Our friendship began as a result of my writing, and since then, I have been fortunate enough to visit him each year at his place in Montana for some outstanding shooting and world-class conversation.

Mike has truly been a mentor of sorts, and for that, I will forever be grateful.

And as for my ultimate motivation with everything I do in life, I thank my beautiful wife Monica, our son Seth, and our daughters Olivia (Livi) and Sophia (Sophie) for being my lighthouse in the storm. You each keep me on track and make me the man I am today. Without you, I wouldn't be me. I love you all.

Chapter One

Bouncing along on an old, unmaintained county road just east of Knoxville, Tennessee, fourteen-year-old Britney Chance looked out the filthy, steel-mesh-covered bus window, and then to her mother and father sitting in the seat beside her, and asked, "How much farther do you think it is? To the new camp—that is."

Patting his daughter's leg with his hand, Bill Chance replied, "I don't know, sweetie. We've been bounced around from facility to facility for so long, I can't even guess what they're doing anymore. We're just along for the ride. But hey, at least we eat. Right?" he said, mustering a smile.

"Something is different this time," Britney's mother, Janice, muttered.

Grasping her hand tightly to signal that he understood, Bill glanced across his wife and daughter, and out the windows of the bus, noticing that the area was becoming more rural the farther they traveled.

Turning off the pothole-ridden paved road and onto a gravel road, Bill saw an International DuraStar single-axle tanker truck with the identification markings on the door painted over with black spray paint. He also noticed that the truck had flammable, hazardous-materials, and no-smoking placards on the back.

In front of the tanker truck was an OD-green-painted Unimog personnel transport vehicle with a U and F painted on the door with a stencil, as well as a six-digit black-stenciled number beneath it. Standing around the truck were what appeared to be fifteen or twenty soldiers or security personnel, wearing a camo pattern he had not seen in the past.

Them

As the bus began to slow, Bill could see a clearing up ahead, as well as a tracked loader and a dozer, both of which had been hastily painted OD green with flecks of industrial yellow showing through the higher wear areas, such as the wheels, tracks, and hydraulic cylinders.

Pulling to a stop, the armed guard who appeared to be in charge of the other security escorts stood, and said, "We'll be changing vehicles from here. This bus requires maintenance. The rest of the men and I," he said, referring to the other armed escorts, "will be returning with the bus. The security personnel at this location will take good care of you until your further transportation arrives. Your cooperation is greatly appreciated and required. Best wishes to all of you."

Stepping off the bus when the door slid open, the man spoke with several uniformed men, as the Unimog personnel carrier that they had passed on the road just before reaching the clearing approached and pulled to a stop. Once the Unimog was parked, its accompanying armed soldiers exited the rear of the vehicle.

As the bus pulled away in front of them, Bill turned to see a large, freshly dug trench behind them. His heart sank in his chest as a fear of what might be transpiring raced through his mind. Bill gripped his wife and daughter tightly as a man shouted something in what sounded like German and the soldiers began to form a solid line in front of them, with the trench directly behind the huddled group of civilians.

Hearing the dozer's diesel engine rumble to a start, the passengers from the bus gasped as the soldiers raised their rifles in the passengers' direction.

The officer who appeared to be in charge stepped forward, took a deep breath, and barked the command, *"Feuer Frei!"*

Upon receiving the order, the soldiers immediately opened fire on the group of unarmed civilians as they began turning to run, screaming for mercy. Bill spun around to embrace his family, shielding them with his own body as he felt several thuds impact his back and his pelvis, sending searing pain through his body before causing him to fall forward and into a world of darkness.

Landing in the soft dirt at the bottom of the trench, Britney felt the weight of her parents knock the wind out of her, nearly smothering her in the freshly dug soil. The barrage of gunshots seemed relentless as the bodies of the other refugees from the bus began falling into the pit around her.

Britney shook uncontrollably as terror swept through her body. "Daddy! Daddy!" she shrieked. Shaking her father, who lay atop her, she felt his warm blood begin to soak into her clothes. "Mom! Mom!" she shouted, shaking her lifeless mother as the deafening sound of gunshots, now including fully automatic fire, surrounded her.

Hearing shouting from the men above, Britney sensed a change in the kinetics of the moment. Something was occurring that she felt wasn't planned. Instead of their all-business approach to following the orders of their commander, the men of the firing squad were now stressed and confused. Gunshots were coming from several directions, not just the location of the line of men who had formed a firing squad.

Maybe others are getting away? she thought. "Daddy! Mom!" she shouted, shaking them both again, to no avail.

As the shooting subsided, with the violence and chaos slowing to merely a random shot here and there, Britney could hear the footfalls of several men approaching the trench where she and so many of the dead lay from the massacre.

Them

Trying to be as quiet as she could, Britney hoped to remain undiscovered. *But what if they start covering us with dirt? What if they bury me alive? Oh, God, what do I do? What do I do?* she thought while nearly hyperventilating from the panic sweeping through her body.

A sound and a thump from the impact of boots jumping into the trench on her immediate left shook her out of her silent panic. Britney focused, remaining perfectly still, hoping the man would pass without noticing her.

She felt the burden of her father's weight being lifted off her, exposing her to the bright sunlight of the day. She covered her face in fear as a man in his early thirties looked at her and with tears in his eyes, and shouted to the others behind him, "I've got one!"

Reaching down to take her hand, the man looked at her blood-soaked clothing, and asked softly, "Are you injured? Are you hurt?"

Shaking her head no, reeling from the shock of what had just happened and too afraid to speak, she watched as he turned and shouted, "Pete! Give me a hand!"

"Sure thing, Nate," Pete agreed, wading his way through the heap of bloody bodies in the bottom of the trench.

"Help me get them off of her," Nate directed. "And gently."

Using care to remove her dead mother and father from atop her, placing them gently and respectfully to the side, Nate knelt down, picked Britney up, and carried her out of the trench and away from the horrific scene.

"Don't look," he warned softly as he quickly carried her into the woods. Nearly tripping on a tree root, he explained, "Sorry. It's a prosthetic leg. It does the job, but I still get tripped up here and there."

Lowering her to her feet, he suggested, "Here. Sit down for a bit while my friends secure the scene and look for other survivors. And don't worry, I won't leave you here alone."

Seeing the emotional pain and confusion on her face, he asked, "Are you sure you aren't hurt? Do you need a medic?" He spoke while looking her over, paying special attention to the bloody area on her shirt and pants.

Seeing her shake her head once again, Nate extended his canteen to her and urged, "Here. Take a sip."

As she reached for the canteen, the sounds of gunfire erupted from behind them, where the massacre had just occurred. Spinning around quickly and bringing his M4 to bear, Nate visually scanned the area, struggling with the decision of whether to run to the aid of his comrades or stay with the young girl he had just recovered from the gruesome scene. Knowing that his mission objective was focused on rescuing and protecting the civilians on the bus, combined with the look of sheer terror on her face, he just couldn't bring himself to leave her.

"C'mon!" he whispered softly, taking her by the hand and leading her off into the densely wooded forest. Hearing the sounds of rotor beats from helicopters approaching from the west, Nate pulled her hand more firmly and insisted, "We've got to keep going! No stopping until I say. Got it?"

Nodding that she understood, the two disappeared into the woods, running as fast as they could, leaving her family behind, lying dead at the bottom of a mass grave.

Chapter Two

Sprinting as fast as possible, Britney stumbled on roots and rocks as her weakened condition from poor nutrition took its toll on her, both physically and mentally. Still, she drove herself, knowing that every step took her closer to safety and farther from the horrors behind her.

Looking back, Nate could see movement through the trees. "They're coming!" he shouted, urging her forward.

As they approached a clearing where a small stream meandered through the woods, Nate looked back to see that their pursuers were rapidly catching up with them. He knew he and the girl couldn't keep up the pace for long, and the threat was gaining ground on them.

Pushing her harder, Nate pointed across the creek and shouted, "Go! Keep going no matter what!"

Splashing as she ran across the slippery, algae-covered rocks, Britney slipped, falling into the shallow water. As she struggled to get back to her feet, Nate ran to her side, grabbing her by the arm to help her up. "C'mon!" he prodded.

Stumbling out of the stream, Nate and Britney ran into the woods on the far side as a lone figure on a horse appeared, raising a rifle toward them. Releasing Britney's arm, Nate started to bring his M4 to bear as the man fired over his head. Watching as the man quickly cycled another round into the chamber of his lever-action rifle, Nate spun around to see one of their pursuers lying dead on the other side of the creek.

Firing another shot, the man on the horse quickly dismounted and ordered, "Help her up!" as he again cycled the lever of his rifle, preparing to take another shot into the woods.

Pausing briefly while he processed what the stranger had asked, Nate reluctantly lifted her into the saddle as the man fired another shot.

Turning to Nate, the stranger said, "Cover her!" Looking Britney in the eye, he spoke with a calm, yet authoritative voice. "Hang on. Hank will take great care of you. Trust him."

Seeing her nod in response, he swatted the horse on the hip and commanded, "Git! Go, boy, go!"

Watching as the horse bolted into the woods, Nate opened fire on numerous targets as more soldiers emerged from the woods on the far side of the creek.

"That way!" the stranger directed, pointing downstream. "Go! I'll follow," he said, just before firing another shot.

Running as hard as he could, Nate was rapidly tiring. Losing his footing on the loose rocks, he fell face first, reaching out with his rifle to catch his fall. As he tried to struggle to his feet, the strange man approached and explained, "It's okay. They've stopped."

"Are you sure?" Nate asked, rolling over and pointing his rifle upstream, scanning the area for threats.

"Yeah. They weren't looking for a fair fight," the man assured him. "I guess chasing after unarmed little girls is more their thing."

Watching as the man walked over to him and offered his hand, Nate reached out and took it. Pulling Nate up to his feet, the man introduced himself. "I'm Jessie."

"Um... Nate. My name is Nate," he answered, stopping short of giving his last name. Looking him over carefully, Nate could see that Jessie was in his mid-forties, with a slim build and a weathered look to him, and a short, scruffy beard that was beginning to show gray and didn't quite fill in all the way.

"The girl. We've got to find her," insisted Nate, getting back to his primary objective.

"As long as she hung on tight, I'm sure Hank took good care of her."

"Hank?" Nate asked.

"My horse. His name is Hank. We'd best go find them, though. He gets bored easily. If he was a kid, they'd have had him on ADHD meds back when he was just a colt. He has to find something to get into when things slow down around him."

Taking a moment to orient himself, Jessie pointed and said, "This way. Let's see if we can pick up his trail."

Working their way through the woods on an angle to intercept Hank's last known path of travel, Jessie observed, "Here we go. He went through here," Pointing down at hoof prints between the rocks and roots in the softer soil. "Hopefully we won't see her tracks, too, which will mean she's still on him."

"How do you know your horse wouldn't just keep running?" inquired Nate.

"Hank's got personality. He acts like he wants nothing to do with people, being an ornery cuss and all, but without people to screw with, he gets bored. No, he'll slow up and wait for me. We've got a pretty good understanding going."

Approaching a clearing ahead, Jessie gestured for Nate to remain quiet while they assessed the situation from the cover of the trees. "There they are," Jessie announced, pointing to his red dun quarter horse who was grazing lazily as the young girl lay forward on his back with her arms around his neck.

With a whistle, Jessie called for Hank, shouting, "Hanky boy!"

Recognizing Jessie's voice, Hank immediately raised his head while still chewing a mouthful of grass. Seeing his master and Nate standing at the tree line, Hank began ambling toward them. Feeling Hank's change in movement, Britney sat up to see what was going on.

When they approached, Nate and Jessie could see her eyes were red and full of tears. She looked pale, and her cheeks were sunken from hunger. Reaching for Hank's bridle with his right hand, Jessie fished around in his pants pocket with his left, retrieving a slice of dried apple. Giving the treat to Hank, he whispered, "Good boy. You did real good, buddy."

Retrieving the girl from the horse's back, Nate lowered her gently to the ground and asked, "Are you okay?"

Nodding in reply, the girl put her arms around him and squeezed him tightly.

"It's okay. They're not following us anymore," Nate whispered, patting her gently on the back.

Regaining her composure, the girl stepped back and looked both Nate and Jessie over carefully. "Who... who are you?"

"I'm Nate. This gentleman is Jessie."

"What... What happened? Why did they do that? Why did they just start shooting us?"

"It's a long story," Nate replied. "But unfortunately, it's not an isolated one."

With a puzzled look on his face, Jessie asked, "What's she talking about?"

"Oh, you didn't know?" Nate replied.

"Hank and I were just looking for a place to stop for water. We were working our way toward that creek when we heard machine gun fire."

"She," Nate explained, gesturing to Britney. "She was with a group of civilian survivors on a government bus. I'm assuming they were told they were being relocated to another government-run survivors' camp. Is that right?" he asked.

Watching as she nodded in reply, he continued, "Anyway, with the limits on resources being what they are at the present time, the UF..."

"UF?" interrupted Jessie.

"Unified Forces," Nate grumbled. "With all the bad stuff going down under the UN flag, the foreign occupiers rebranded themselves the Unified Forces in an attempt to get people who didn't know better to trust them, fooling them into believing they were here to stop the atrocities and abuses that were perpetrated by the blue helmets, instead of having been responsible for them. With no reliable sources of information out there, no TV, internet, or even phone service, all too many people fell for it. I mean, without an avenue for a dissenting opinion, who can tell fact from fiction these days?"

"That's easy," Jessie quipped. "If someone from what's left of the government says it, it's fiction."

Nodding in agreement, Nate fumed, "The UF has just enough Americans on board to make it seem like an American-led organization, too, when it's really the same bunch of globalists. They're basically hiding right out in the open behind a different label."

Shaking his head, Jessie grumbled, "Same filthy bastards, different flag."

"Yep," Nate confirmed. "Control the food supply, control the people. Anyway, the government-run camps, formerly operated by FEMA, can't feed, clothe, and provide medical care for the masses. Illnesses that were once all but eradicated have been making a comeback, and some formerly easy-to-treat conditions have become a death sentence due to the lack of available resources.

"They're slowly but surely filtering out the ones they think can be led or turned, and those who they feel may be threats. The ones labeled as not useful to 'the cause' are told they're being shipped off to a new camp with more resources, but..."

"I get it," Jessie interjected, sparing the young girl the gruesome details. "What's your involvement with all this?"

"I'm with a group that's not putting up with it," Nate responded matter-of-factly.

"Good man," Jessie replied. "What group? Who are you with?"

Pausing before answering, Nate replied, "Like I said, just a group that's not putting up with it."

Smiling, Jessie shrugged. "Good OPSEC. That's smart. You just met me. I wouldn't tell me, either."

Looking around nervously, Nate admitted, "I guess I can trust you. I mean, we wouldn't be alive right now otherwise. So, if you could stay with her for a bit, you know, just in case, I'll be right back. I've got to see if any of my guys made it, and I've got to try and gather any intel I can on the current situation."

Nodding, Jessie affirmed, "Of course. We'll hang tight until nightfall. If you're not back by then, I'll get her somewhere safe."

Reaching out his hand, Nate said, "Thanks. Thanks for everything. I'll be back." Turning to leave, Nate paused, looking back at the girl and then Jessie. Taking a deep breath, Nate turned and darted off into the woods in the direction from whence they came.

Looking at the girl, Jessie asked, "What's your name, miss?"

With her head held low and her eyes looking up at him, she replied. "Britney. But people call me Brit."

Them

"Nice to meet you, Brit. Let's get you something to eat. You look hungry."

~~~~

While Britney rested in the shade beneath a large oak tree, Jessie dutifully stood guard, scanning the surrounding area for potential threats.

Looking her way, he could see the toll the day had taken on her. Her eyes were swollen and red, and the jerky he had given her was still lying next to her, now covered with ants. Not one bite had been taken.

Walking over to her, he knelt down and picked up the jerky, brushing the ants away with his finger. "There won't be anything left for you if the ants eat it all." Placing it in a strip of cloth and rolling it up, he placed it next to her and assured her, "It'll be right here whenever you're ready to eat."

Seeing her eyes pass over the jerky and then away, off into the distance, he empathized, "I know it's not all that appetizing, but once we get a little farther from here, we'll get you some fresh protein to eat. We need to get moving as soon as Nate gets back. We can't get too settled in just yet."

Looking over to the cloth Jessie had wrapped the dried strip of meat in, she picked it up, pulled the cloth back, and took a small nibble. It was more of a symbolic gesture than anything, but it made Jessie feel better nonetheless that she was making an attempt.

Jessie knew all too well the emotional turmoil of having everything important to you stripped away in an instant. He ached in his heart for the young girl, but did his best to conceal his memory-fueled empathy so he could stay strong for her in her time of need.

"Do you think he's okay?" she asked without even turning her head in Jessie's direction.

"Well, he seemed like a capable fellow. I have faith in him."

Just then, Jessie heard a twig snap underfoot in the direction from which they had come. Raising his Marlin.30-30 rifle to the ready position, Jessie saw Nate emerge from the brush, waving his hand to show it was him.

Lowering his rifle, Jessie hurried over to Nate, keeping out of earshot of Britney. "Well?" he asked.

Shaking his head, Nate hesitated. "I couldn't find any other survivors. None of our guys made it out either."

"Who exactly is 'our guys'?" Jessie inquired, still uncertain of who he had been fighting alongside.

"There will be time for that later," Nate maintained, as he looked to Britney sitting under the oak tree in the distance. "How's she holding up?"

"She's quiet and doesn't seem to have an appetite, but that's to be expected, I guess. Do you know her or her people?"

"No. Like I said before, I'm with a group that's just not gonna put up with such things anymore. We'll get her somewhere stable and safe, and far away from the UF. She can start to heal properly then." After an awkward pause, Nate determined, "Well, mister. Thanks for the help, but I'd best be getting back to my unit. She and I will be just fine. You can ride along now."

Taken back by Nate's sudden dismissal, Jessie advised, "There's no need to be in a hurry to part ways. For her sake, at least, let me help you get her somewhere safe, and then I'll continue on as I had planned. But to be honest, I just don't think it's wise to split up just yet. She can ride Hank while we walk. It'll make things much easier on her."

Thinking it over for a second, Nate nodded and said, "We're heading east. What about you?"

"East as well," Jessie responded.

"Where to?" Nate asked.

"I'm not sure exactly."

Shooting Jessie a skeptical look, Nate raised an eyebrow and retorted, "So, let me get this straight, you're not sure exactly where you're going, but you know it's east?"

"My sister moved to a homestead in East Tennessee a while before it all went down. We'd been separated by a divorce early in life and hadn't really kept in touch other than the occasional "like" on a social media post.

"Later on as life got busy, especially when I entered law enforcement and began my political career running for Sheriff of Montezuma County I... I just lost track. Life just got in the way and we drifted further apart."

"You were a sheriff?" Nate asked with piqued curiosity.

"Yeah, for a while," Jessie chuckled as he kicked a stone on the ground. "The wave of organized corruption that was sweeping the nation finally caught up with my little out of the way county and I was forced out."

Getting back on track, Jessie continued, "Then, the attacks began, and the next thing you know, we lost all contact. Since we were mostly communicating via the internet and social media, I never really wrote her address down. I guess, like everyone else at the time, I assumed when and if we went for a visit, we could just ask her for the address and plug it into the GPS. Like many others, we'd gotten out of the habit of actually keeping a paper address book.

"Then, when our online world went dark, it was gone. The few pieces of mail I had received from my sister over the years burned up with the house. I... I wasn't in my right mind at the time.

"I figured I could just make my way to the general area, then start asking questions. That sounds ridiculous, I know..."

"No, that's not ridiculous at all," Nate interrupted, seeing there must be more to Jessie's story that was haunting him so. "Hell, when it all started, and our cell phones went down, even if I could have found a functioning landline, I wouldn't have been able to call my parents back east because I didn't know their number. I didn't even know my own parent's phone numbers! But why would I? It was saved in my contacts under Mom and Dad, right? And my contacts were backed up in the cloud, so what could possibly go wrong?"

Shaking his head, Nate added, "I know exactly how you feel. I think that level of dependency on technology made our nation ripe for the picking. We had lost touch with the basics on almost every level. We were soft. We were weak. And our guard was down, big time."

"Did you find them?" Jessie asked, worrying if such a question would tear the scab off a wound in Nate's heart.

Looking down to the ground and kicking a pine cone, Nate muttered, "One of them."

Replying with only a nod, Jessie looked up at the sun, noting its position in the sky. "Let's put a little more distance between us and... um... the scene," he suggested, gesturing in the direction of the massacre.

Thinking it over for a moment, Nate looked Jessie squarely in the eye and said, "I suppose your horse *will* make things easier on her. For now, at least."

Nodding, Jessie said, "I'll get Hank ready to go. I'm sure he'll enjoy having a thin young girl like Britney on his back instead of me for a while. He deserves a much needed break, too."

"Britney?" Nate sighed as he shook his head. "Is that her name? I... I never even took a minute to ask. Everything was happening so fast."

Putting his hand on Nate's shoulder, Jessie smiled and assured him, "You had your priorities. You did everything you needed to do when you had to do it. A proper introduction would have come in due time."

Chapter Three

As Jessie made his final preparations with Hank, he looked over his shoulder to see Nate keeping a keen eye on their surroundings. "So, do you have a desired course or path you want to follow? I won't ask you for specifics, just give me something to go on."

Removing a well-worn map from his pocket, Nate unfolded it and pointed at their location, saying, "We're currently eight or nine miles west of Dandridge. My goal is to get us across the bridge on TN-92, right there, to get south of Douglas Lake. There's another small road we'll meet up with to head east from there. If we head south through the woods from here, we'll come out in the back pasture of one of the small farms that line the south side of the hills. Once we get there, we'll need to find a place to cross I-40."

Looking over their options, he then noted, "We could go around Douglas Lake by going due south and through Sevierville, but I'd rather avoid the population there if we can."

"Sounds good to me," Jessie concurred. "And I agree. Avoiding population centers is how I've stayed alive while traveling as far as I have."

With Hank tacked up and ready to go, Nate led Britney over to Jessie and the horse, saying, "Jessie and I will walk. You can ride Hank. Jessie will lead him, of course. All you have to do is go along for the ride."

Responding with only a distant gaze, Britney walked over to the eight-year-old lineback dun horse and Jessie reached for her hand. Placing her hand on the back of Hank's neck, Jessie explained, "Put your foot in the stirrup and boost yourself straight up and over. Don't worry, you won't hurt him by hanging onto the back of his neck or his mane."

"Why not use the handle?" she asked, pointing to the saddle horn.

With a smile, Jessie said, "That's for rope. If you use it as a handle while mounting, the saddle will shift toward you. It's best to just place your hand here," he said again, pointing to the base of Hank's neck.

"Now," he continued, looking her in the eye to ensure she was listening. "If, for whatever reason, you and Hank end up away from Nate and me, here's how you can get him to do what you want. To turn left, pull back lightly on his left rein to apply pressure to the bit. Not much, though, as too much pressure can cause him pain and get more of a reaction than you want. He's generally a compliant fellow, so be gentle. If he refuses, he's probably got a good reason. If you want him to make a tight turn, block the side of him where you don't want him to go with pressure from your leg, and open your other leg, pulling it away from his body, on the side you want him to turn. Think of it as putting up a gate on the side you don't want him to go.

"To get him going, just nudge him slightly with your heels. To get going in more of a hurry, use more force. Don't kick him, though. Just think of it as if you're talking to him with your feet. To stop him, start by applying forward pressure to both stirrups as if you're applying the brakes in a car while saying *whoa*. If you need more, pull back slightly on both reins as well."

Looking at the stirrups, Jessie said, "Here, let me adjust these for you," as he loosened the Blevins buckles before adjusting them to match her size. "There, put your feet in now and let's see how it fits you."

Doing as he asked, Britney nodded, indicating to him that the adjustments were acceptable.

"Okay, then," Jessie nodded as he cradled his .30-30 across his chest with it resting in the bend of his left arm. "Come on, boy," Jessie said as he started walking.

Britney was startled when Hank immediately began following along behind Jessie. She gripped the reins tightly and said, "I thought you were going to lead him?"

"I am," Jessie answered with a smile. "He follows me like a dog. Even if you tried to turn him away, he'd protest and try to follow me anyway. Just relax and rest the reins loosely around the saddle horn. Just go with the flow and let him do the rest."

"I'll follow along about fifty yards back, covering our six," Nate called softly to Jessie as he began to slow and fall back.

"Sounds good to me," Jessie affirmed as he turned and focused on the terrain ahead of him.

As Jessie walked through the woods in the direction Nate had suggested, Hank followed along, keeping a keen eye on him just as Jessie had predicted.

Turning to look back, he could see that Nate was dropping back to follow in the distance. Keeping some space between them would allow Nate to both identify and respond to a threat approaching from their rear without immediately endangering Britney, as well as being able to respond to a situation as an independent force if a threat were to emerge ahead of them.

A side benefit of their separation, as Jessie saw it, was to keep the inevitable conversation to a minimum, helping them keep their eyes and ears on their surroundings. After all, they were still relatively close to the scene of the ambush.

After a few minutes of relative calm, Jessie heard the tell-tale thumping of a helicopter's main rotor off in the distance.

Them

That's a big one, he thought as he signaled Nate to take cover in the rear. Turning his attention to Britney, Jessie jogged over to Hank, taking hold of his bridle and quickly leading him and Britney into the thick of the woods.

"What is it?" she sheepishly asked.

When he pointed to his ear, she nodded, noticing the beat of the rotors as the helicopter drew near.

Within seconds, the helicopter flew overhead at a high rate of speed, barely clearing the treetops as it zoomed by at a very low-level.

"Was that a...?" Jessie mumbled aloud as Nate joined up with them.

"Gotta get moving," Nate insisted.

"Was that a Hind?" Jessie stammered.

"Yep. We've dealt with those things before, and I don't intend to again. They'll mess your day up in a hurry. They're also probably dropping off a few hunters on foot."

"Hunters?" Jessie queried.

"Those things can hold up to eight soldiers in the back. My guess is they're responding to what happened back there. They'll drop what they call hunters, which are foot soldiers, trained in advanced tracking techniques, equipped for light and fast movement. They flush out their prey by keeping it on the move, then they radio in and the Hind comes back and rains hell on their prey from above. It's a tactic they employ to keep us insurgent types afraid to make a hit. They come in fast and hard, and more often than we would care to admit, run us to our graves. So, get moving! Get her out of here. I'll throw them off if they come our way. Just meet up with me on the other side of the lake!"

Seeing Jessie mentally processing his demands, Nate reiterated, "Now!"

Pulling Britney's foot out of the stirrup, Jessie muttered, "Slide back onto the saddlebags."

Once she was clear, he boosted himself up and into the saddle. Nudging Hank in the sides, he clicked with his cheek and Hank began moving with authority, quickly disappearing into the woods and out of sight from Nate.

Turning toward the direction of the ambush site, knowing full well that's where the Hind was going, Nate looked around, got his bearings, and thought, "Well, hell. Out of one bind and into another."

~~~~

Running Hank hard through the tight confines of the woods, Jessie took the brunt of the tree branches when he smashed into them, hoping to deflect them away from Britney. Seeing a clearing up ahead, he brought Hank to a slow trot. Nearing the edge of the tree line, he reined back, bringing Hank to a stop.

Quietly dismounting, Jessie gestured to his lips for Britney to remain quiet as he glassed the area with the 3-9x scope on his Marlin .30-30 rifle.

Turning to Britney, Jessie said softly, "It looks like the burned ruins of what once was a middle-class neighborhood. From before..." he explained, walking back toward her and Hank.

Looking around and thinking of their options, he said, "I don't like the idea of riding out into the open across those lots, but we're painted into a corner. If they track us, we need to be long gone. These woods aren't big enough to hide us. They're the remnants of the development from all of these cookie cutter suburban communities. They left just enough green to let people feel like they were out in the country, but that's about it."

Startled by an explosive boom in the distance, Britney flinched and asked, "What was that?"

"It sounds like Nate is giving them a hard time for us. C'mon. Let's not waste his efforts," Jessie urged as he boosted himself back into the saddle. Holding the reins in his left hand while keeping a grip on his rifle with his right, Jessie nudged Hank forward and into the clearing. Feeling exposed and vulnerable, Jessie nudged Hank once again, picking up the pace and bringing him to a slow trot.

Seeing a damaged portion of what was once a privacy fence to separate two several-acre lots, Jessie steered Hank to and through the opening, moving from one parcel to the next.

"There," he announced, pointing off in the distance. "There's the lake, and there's the bridge." Scanning the area, Jessie saw nothing but destroyed homes. It was as if Genghis Khan himself had rolled through the neighborhood, destroying and killing everything in his path.

As Jessie and Britney approached the bridge, Jessie reined back on Hank, bringing him to a stop. Looking around, he saw a man climb out from underneath the bridge while holding an AK pattern rifle in front of him.

"Trolls," Jessie mumbled.

"What?" Britney asked.

"Oh, nothing. I just hate bridges. They always come with surprises."

Nudging Hank forward, Jessie rode toward the man, looking him over as they approached. He could see the man was wearing well-worn denim jeans and a green wool button-up shirt. He appeared to be in his early fifties, and his face hadn't seen a razor in quite some time. *Well, at least he's not pointing it at us,* he thought.

"Hello, there!" Jessie said, laying his rifle across his lap and raising his right hand to wave.

"That's far enough," the man warned. "State your business."

"My daughter and I are just passing through is all," Jessie answered with a smile. "We'd be obliged if you let us pass."

"Where are you going?" the man asked.

"South of here," Jessie replied.

"A lot of stuff is south of here," the man replied while cocking his head to one side as if to study Jessie a little closer. "Where exactly are you traveling to?" he again probed.

"If you and a member of your family were traveling, would you want to give a total stranger specifics about where you were going?" Jessie responded. "Most folks these days have learned to keep certain details to themselves. I suspect you know what I'm saying."

Nodding, the man conceded, "Yes. Yes, I do." Leaning to look around Jessie, the man said, "She's your daughter, huh?"

"That's right. Now if you don't mind..."

"Now, hold on," the man insisted, interrupting Jessie. Tightening his grip on his rifle, the man walked closer, leaning to one side to get a better look at Britney.

"Are you okay?" he asked, looking directly at her.

Looking to Jessie as if she didn't understand, she saw Jessie nod. "Yes. I'm fine, thanks."

"Are you sure? You look kind of shook up. Don't be afraid of this man," the stranger explained. "What he doesn't know is the fact that there are quite a few rifles trained on him right now. He'll never bring that rifle off his lap to take a shot if he makes any sudden moves," he announced with a smile. "So, if you're in trouble, just climb on down, and we'll get you far away from this man."

"She's shaken up because..."

"Shut up!" the man barked, raising his rifle to the low ready position. "I'm talking to the young lady."

Looking the rifle over closely, Jessie identified it as an AK-74M, complete with the three-position selector. *Russian issue?*

"She lost her mother just a few hours ago. Of course, she's shaken up."

"Lost her mother, how? Did you kill her?"

"No, those bastards who hide behind the name of the UF did it. She was on a bus that was supposed to be traveling to a new camp. There was no camp, just a hole, and a dozer. She'd be in it right now, too, if a militiaman and his group hadn't come along and put a stop to it. Now, are you with the UF, or are you with us?" Jessie growled as he stealthily rotated the open bottom of his holster forward, cocking the old Colt pistol without drawing it. "If you do have buddies watching, they'll just be watching you die if you're one of them. Now, where did you get the '74? Did *they* issue it to you?"

"Damn it to hell," the man snarled. "I got it off one of them dead sons of bitches that came through last fall—them sons of bitches that burned out everyone around here. Now, don't you go accusing me of being one of them. You'll have to pull that trigger if you do!"

Seeing fire in the man's eyes, Jessie relaxed his grip, lowered the hammer gently, and rotated his holster back into place. "I guess we've got a few things in common, then," Jessie conceded.

"So much for the daughter story," the man chided. "That fell apart pretty damn quick. So, on to the truth: them militia boys that came through—where are they?"

"All but one is dead. He's running interference for us now so we can get some distance between us and those bastards in the Hind. So, if you would please call your friends off, if there really are any, and step aside, we need to get moving."

Hanging his head low, the man mumbled, "Damn it all to hell. Them was some nice boys. Damn shame it is."

"You knew them?" Jessie asked.

"No. Not really. But we gave them safe passage through the area. We knew where they were headed and wished the best to them. Such a shame, damn it. Such a shame."

Regaining his composure, the man turned and waved to another fellow that Jessie had yet to notice standing at the far side of the bridge. "Just get her somewhere safe," the man said. "You'll see mostly friendlies for the next mile or so. They'll spread the word to let you pass without harm. Once you get clear of the peninsula and south of the lake, make sure you don't find yourself on the south side of 411."

Tipping his hat to the man, Jessie nodded, "Thanks, but what's on the south side of 411?"

"I...we... don't really know for sure. But folks who've gone hunting in the hills down that way tend not to come back. It's best to just go east or west when you hit 411, for a ways at least, before turning south."

"I appreciate the intel. Thanks and best of luck, friend," Jessie said with a nod as he nudged Hank forward toward the bridge.

"You, too, mister. You, too." The man waved as he watched them ride away.

Them

As Hank carried Jessie and Britney across the bridge, Jessie could see bullet impact marks on virtually every inch of the green, metal bridge. Most of them seemed to follow a stream of fire as if fired by fully automatic weapons. He could only imagine what the man behind him had been through if he had been in the area the entire time.

Reaching the far side of the bridge, a younger man in his late twenties to early thirties nodded to Jessie as he and Britney rode by. "God bless," the man said with a smile.

Returning the smile and the kind words with a nod and a tip of his hat, it warmed Jessie's heart to run across what appeared, at least, to be good people with their fellow American's well-being at heart. People had lost so much. Many of the survivors had lost nearly everyone and everything they had. Some crumbled under the weight of it all, and some soldiered on, doing what they knew was right.

As they rode on past the Dandridge Municipal Park, they saw the remains of an old, wooden playground that lay in disarray. It was as if people had been harvesting its wood for their other needs, leaving behind the skeletal remains of what once was.

With one final bridge crossing ahead to get them clear of Douglas Lake, Jessie rode to within a hundred yards before gently reining Hank to a stop.

"What's wrong?" Britney murmured.

"Oh, I'm just waiting for the trolls to appear," he replied, looking back to her with a crooked smile.

Right on cue, a man appeared from beneath the bridge and waved them toward him. As they approached, Jessie could see that he, too, carried a well-worn AK-74M.

"Howdy," the man said with a smile. "You'd be the one they sent word about, I presume?"

"I guess that would be me," replied Jessie with a nod. "Word travels fast with you good folks."

"I reckon it does. I suppose they warned you not to go due south of 411, didn't they?"

"I heard such a thing," confirmed Jessie. "Might I ask why? The other gentlemen said you folks really don't know."

"Sadly, that's true. Most of us who are left around here have seen and heard enough to know how to stay alive. We know the area, and we know everyone who's left. We've lost a lot of people to those hills, and we've never been able to nail down exactly why. We've heard lots of stories, but most of it seems to be the rantings of those who've seen and done too much to think straight anymore."

"What sort of stories?" Jessie asked.

"Nonsense, I tell ya. Anyway, once you get beyond this bridge, you're on your own. Our little network of lookouts ends with me. Keep that in mind. Don't assume anyone else is friendly. They may be, but they also may not be. You may not find out until it's too late."

"I've come a long way and managed to stay alive for a few thousand miles by doing just that," Jessie said as he tipped his hat. "Best of luck to you good folks," he added as he urged Hank forward.

"Likewise, mister," the man replied as they rode away. "You take good care of that girl!" he shouted.

"They seem like good people," Jessie said to Britney.

Mumbling in reply, Britney responded, "So did the people at the camp who asked us to get on the bus. They also waved and smiled as we drove away."

Them

With a sigh, Jessie guided Hank until they were well clear of the bridge, then brought him to a stop and suggested, "Let's stretch our legs for a bit while I check the map."

Dismounting and then helping Britney down off the saddlebags, Jessie removed a laminated map from his pocket and looked around to get his bearings straight. "Just a little farther south and this road merges with 411. Since that was Nate's goal, I think we should set up camp in a position where we can keep an eye on 411 and wait to see a sign of him. I'm sure he'll have the same thing in mind."

"What if he doesn't show up?"

"He will," Jessie assured her.

"No offense, mister, but chances are he didn't make it."

"I dunno," Jessie replied. "You may be right, but I saw a fire in his belly that gives me a glimmer of hope that he did."

"Hope?" she chided. "Hope hasn't worked very well for me so far. My family and I had hope," she mourned, and tears welled up in her eyes.

Reaching out to wipe a tear from her cheek, she recoiled away from him. He looked down at the ground and explained, "I understand where you're coming from. I really do. You and I aren't so different. I've lost everything to this cruel, heartless world, the same as you. The only difference is, I've had a little more time to heal, whereas your wounds are fresh. I've seen a lot of suffering during my travels, but I've also made some amazing friends who stood up to those who took advantage of the situation to oppress others. Those people give me the hope I need to press on."

Attempting to smile while fighting back her tears, Britney asked, "But really, what if he doesn't show up? We can't live on hope forever."

"No, we can't. We've got to balance our hope with our surroundings and resources. That's a good question, though. Nate talked of a group where he planned on taking you, where you could be safe and begin a new life for yourself with people you can trust. He and I just happened to be heading in the same direction, although my exact destination is unknown. My plan was to tag along with him to help get you where you needed to be, and then be on my way from there.

"Without him, though," Jessie continued, "well, that muddies the waters a bit. Let's give him a day to get out of whatever bind he's gotten himself into on our behalf. If he doesn't show by tomorrow evening, we'll need to get on the move."

Once back on the road, the two kept their thoughts of what had been and what would be to themselves. Jessie kept a keen eye on their surroundings while watching for signs from Hank that he might sense something as well.

With 411 and the remains of the town of Chestnut Hill in the distance to the south, Jessie pointed and suggested, "Let's move off the road now and hug that overgrown fence line to the left. Then, we'll make camp on that wooded hill up ahead. We should be able to see our surroundings from there, and it will give us several ways to get away from a threat, as well."

Once they'd set up camp, Jessie used a brown canvas tarp and a length of paracord to build a shelter for Britney to sleep under. Her exhaustion was evident, and she quickly succumbed to the weight of her eyelids, falling fast asleep.

She desperately needs a good night's sleep, he thought as he gathered some forage for Hank to eat.

With everyone in camp settled in for the night, Jessie leaned back against a large oak tree overlooking 411 and got comfortable. Looking up at the stars that were appearing overhead as the last rays of the day's sun faded into memory, Jessie thought, *Nate, I hope you're enjoying this view as well. Hang in there, buddy.*

Chapter Four

Awakened by a loud roar and the screams of a young girl, Jessie leapt to his feet and grabbed his rifle. To his horror, Britney was no longer asleep under the shelter he had built for her. Running through the woods in the darkness, Jessie desperately shouted, "Britney!" as her screams seemed to get farther and farther away.

Barely able to see due to the canopy of the woods blocking the moonlight, Jessie crashed through brush and briars, ignoring the pain in order to keep up his frantic pace. Reaching the edge of the woods, Jessie ran into a clearing, only to find a large, black bear standing in front of him, baring its blood-covered teeth as the bear's powerful paw struck him in the side of the head.

Falling to the ground, Jessie struggled to his feet only to find that the sun was now cresting the eastern horizon, his rifle was still leaning against the tree where he had left it, and in the first rays of the morning's light, he could see that Britney was still safe and sound underneath her makeshift shelter.

As his heart rate started to slow, he reached for his rifle and began to wipe the dew from it with a cloth he pulled from his pocket. That simple act helped to convince him of the reality of his situation after such a vivid and horrifying nightmare.

Removing a small, cylindrical backpacker-sized rocket stove from his saddlebags, Jessie placed it on a small patch of dirt clear of anything combustible on the ground. He gathered a few dry twigs and small sticks, breaking them into the appropriate size for the small stove.

Once the stove was all set up and full of twigs, he heard Britney yawn and ask, "What's that?"

"It's a rocket stove," he replied.

"I thought you didn't think we should have fires?"

"Well, at night, a fire of any size could be seen from too far away, but this little guy here," he said, pointing to the small stove, "won't be seen in the daylight. It's what they call a rocket stove. You put your fuel in this little tube on the side, and when the air is drawn in and around the burning wood from underneath, it's preheated before reaching the combustion chamber, which makes it burn a lot cleaner. A small fire in one of these, using the right materials, will hardly produce any smoke at all. They're perfect for cooking in situations like this."

"Cooking?" she asked, perking up at the thought of a warm meal.

Smiling, he explained, "Yes, I figured you could use a good, hot meal. A few days before I bumped into you and Nate, I came across a trading post of sorts. It was a place where people in the local area could trade with those, like me, who were passing through. A few of the folks there were trading dehydrated food for whatever goods the travelers had."

"Did they have electricity there?"

"No. No, they were still without power like most everyone else, except for, well, government facilities. They had built themselves solar dehydrators. They're simple really. Back before the attacks, people thought you had to have electricity for everything, even something as natural as dehydrating food, but that's just not the case. Electricity should never have been seen as anything more than a luxury, not a way of life."

Chuckling at the thought of it all, Jessie pushed a bundle of twigs into the opening on the side of the stove and said, "People are starting to figure out now that we never needed to be as addicted to power as we were. Anyway, back to my point, I managed to trade a few things I had collected along the way for some dehydrated hamburger meat, mushrooms, and a few herbs and spices. With a little heat and water, it should make a nice breakfast for us."

Opening a small sackcloth drawstring bag, Jessie removed what looked like a pebble. "These hamburger chunks look like rocks until they rehydrate. I tried them the night I got them. They're better than they look," he commented with a smile.

Placing the chunks of dried meat into a small, stainless steel camping pot, Jessie poured in just enough water and placed it on the stove, stirring as the water began to warm.

After the meat had cooked for what he felt was an adequate amount of time, he tossed in a handful of the dehydrated mushrooms, and a pinch of mixed herbs.

Inhaling the savory aroma, Britney's stomach began to growl. "I guess it's been a while since I've had a hot meal," she admitted.

Considering her statement, Jessie was curious about how and what they had been fed at the camp, but he didn't want to stir up any lingering emotions by asking about times when her parents were still with her.

Pouring a helping of the concoction into a stainless mug, Jessie handed it to her, saying, "I know it's not much, but we need to conserve what I have to get us as far as we can."

Nodding as she began eating the delicious meal, she consumed it with enthusiasm, as if she hadn't eaten in days.

Once they had both finished their breakfast, Jessie cleaned up camp and put everything back in its place.

"Are we leaving?" she asked.

"No. Not yet. But we need to be ready, just in case. I don't want to leave anything of value behind, in the event we have to get moving in a hurry. It's hard enough to get what you need these days. There's no reason to have to replace things you already have."

"Can I help?" she offered.

"Hank could probably use a good brushing down. If we have to saddle him up in a hurry, we don't want burs or anything to be on his back between him and the saddle. That, and he could use some love. He's an ornery, but affectionate boy."

Handing her a small grooming brush from the saddlebags, he watched as she went to work, doing as he had asked.

Watching while she stroked the brush across the horse's back, Jessie saw a peace come over her that he hadn't seen since they had met. Her mental anguish was far from gone, but the act of being useful seemed to have a therapeutic effect on her. As a side benefit, Hank seemed to be enjoying his brush-down as well.

~~~~

When the sun reached its midday position high in the sky, Jessie saw a glint of light just south of their location on the hill on the far side of highway 411.

"What the..." he mumbled as he watched more closely, zooming in on the area in question. He then saw a series of flashes, and said, "Hey, that's... I believe that's Morse code. Yeah... it is. It says, dash dot, dot dash, dash, dot. N... A...T... E... It spells Nate!"

Fumbling around in his saddlebags, Jessie retrieved a signal mirror and flashed his reply, spelling, J.B. for Jessie and

Britney. He then saw a man appear from the woods, waving his right arm over his head. "It's Nate! He made it!" Jessie exclaimed with excitement. "C'mon. Let's get moving."

Quickly cinching the saddle and saddlebags onto Hank's back, Jessie mounted up, then reached down his hand and pulled Britney up as well, urging Hank forward and down the side of the gently sloping hill toward Nate's location.

Hearing the sounds of Hank working his way through the woods, Nate quickly crossed the road and met them just inside the tree line, keeping them out of plain sight.

"Nate!" Jessie exclaimed, dismounting with almost a leap, giving his newly found friend a hug. "What happened? Did they catch up with you? We heard an explosion."

"Yeah, they tracked us, but I always have a few Plan B's in my pack," Nate hinted, returning the embrace.

Turning to Britney, Nate smiled and said, "I'm glad to see you, too." Nate was surprised as she hugged him with a smile on her face.

"I'm tired of losing people," she said. "I... I didn't..."

"Well, we're all here now," he reassured, relieving her of the burden of continuing her dark thoughts.

"You just missed breakfast," Jessie offered. "Are you hungry?"

"No, I'm fine. I've got a few more MRE's in my pack."

"I was wondering how we'd find you. Didn't you think it was a bit dangerous broadcasting your position like that?"

Chuckling, Nate admitted, "Well, yeah. But if you were there, I knew you would be keeping an eye on the area and would only signal back if you deemed it safe. If anyone else homed in on me, I'd have just bolted or engaged them. I figured it would be better to broadcast from a position of relative cover like that than to just walk down the middle of the road yelling your name."

"So, what's the plan?" Jessie asked. "Do you have any new intel?"

Watching as the smile quickly extinguished from Nate's face, Jessie listened as Nate surmised, "Well, it's not gonna be as easy working our way to the east as I had hoped." Pulling out his wrinkled, well-worn map, Nate pointed and explained, "Some friendlies in the area informed me that they're..."

"They?" Jessie interrupted, seeking clarification.

"The UF, UN, whatever the hell you want to call them these days, are moving a mobile detachment from the Newport area to our east, and this way via 411. It seems they're searching homes and camps along the way. One can only assume they're trying to ruffle feathers, hoping someone will turn on our group and rat us out. Hits like the one we made yesterday really set them into motion. Sometimes I wonder if it's worth it. Putting other people in harm's way once the hornets' nest is shaken, that is. But the other side of me can't just lie down. If we live our lives trying not to ruffle the feathers of those who want to impose their wills on us, well, we'd just be submitting. I want these bastards to pay, and I want them to never get a good night's sleep. What they did yesterday happens all too often. If we don't fight back, well, what kind of Americans would we be if we didn't? No, I can't be a sheep. And if I can't effectively be a sheepdog, I'll be a wolf."

Looking at the map, seeing that they were effectively boxed in by mountains to the south, Jessie wondered, "So... what do you propose?"

"If we go west, well, we'll just be getting closer to the troops they have positioned in Knoxville. If we go east, we'll be walking right into their arms. North is obviously out of the question because they've installed more hunters in the area. That leaves south," he said, tapping on the map. "We need to move into the mountains behind us and lay low for a while. The only real drawback is that the terrain is too rough to get all the way through to the east in a straight shot. Those mountains get pretty steep. If we can get through this gap here," he suggested, tracing his finger on the map, "we can get over to Carson Springs Road and work our way south of this ridge to Carson Springs."

"That doesn't give us many outs," Jessie said, noting the terrain that would box them in on both sides.

"It's that or wait them out in the woods," Nate replied. "We simply don't have many good options."

"A few of the folks on the peninsula warned me not to go south of 411. Have you heard such things?" Jessie asked.

"Yeah, they told us that, too. I can't see how staying out where the UF hunters can find us is any worse than whatever the hell is in the mountains to the south. Maybe their guys just found something better and didn't return. Who knows? Or maybe the increasing black bear population in the area has something to do with it. With the human numbers being way down, the bear numbers are on the rise. Either way, it's not like we have a 'safe' option by the standard definition of safe. It's one threat or another. Pick your poison."

"Well, this is your area, so I'm good with whatever you feel is the best course of action," Jessie affirmed.

"That settles it, then," Nate asserted. "It's into the mountains we go."

Chapter Five

With Nate taking the point position, Britney riding Hank in the center, and Jessie covering them from the rear, the trio worked their way toward the gap in the hills where they intended to cross over to the other side of the mountain that lay before them. As they crossed through several parcels of land that had clearly once been highly productive hay fields and grazing pastures, Jessie couldn't help but observe that the grasses had lost the competition for survival without man's intervention. The fields were now overrun with weeds and brush that weren't at all suited for livestock consumption.

Even the grass has it rough these days, Jessie thought as he brushed up against some sort of prickly weed. Seeing Nate signal for them to stop up ahead, Jessie glassed the area through his rifle scope to see that Nate appeared to be investigating something on the ground near a large livestock pond.

Rushing ahead to join up with Hank and Britney, Jessie took Hank by the bridle and led him and Britney to Nate's location. "Damn," Jessie said, surveying the cattle skeletons that were strewn throughout the area.

"What do you make of it?" Nate asked.

"Hmmm, well, I don't see any signs of trauma, do you? No chunks of bone missing from projectiles or the like?"

"No, they look like they just dropped and died where they were."

Looking to the pond, Jessie cautioned, "Let's not water here. This could have been a way to run people out of the area—to destroy their ability to feed themselves by poisoning their livestock's water supplies."

"I've seen entire cattle herds wiped out by helicopter," Nate grumbled. "So, the poisoning of herds or the like wouldn't surprise me one bit."

Looking around, Jessie urged, "Let's get going. I hate being in the open like this."

Before Jessie took a step, they heard an ominous sound off in the distance.

"What the hell was that?" Nate wondered aloud.

Taking a moment to process it, Jessie said, "It sounded like a Viking war horn or something."

Looking around nervously, Nate pondered, "Where did it come from?" as they each surveyed the area around them.

"I dunno. But like I said, let's get a move on."

Continuing, the group reached the edge of a relatively level wooded area. Giving them the signal to hold their positions, Nate investigated the area ahead of them, then signaled them forward.

Joining the others, Jessie looked up to Britney sitting in Hank's saddle and bragged, "You're starting to look comfortable up there."

"I'm starting to feel comfortable," she replied.

"He's not guiding off me now, either," Jessie pointed out. "You've been doing it all since I've been bringing up the rear." Turning to Nate, he asked, "See anything?"

Pointing, Nate explained, "There's a trail up ahead. Let me go check it out before we all go."

"Sounds good," Jessie said, turning his attention back to Britney. "Are you sure you haven't ridden before?" he inquired.

"My parents and I went to one of those dude ranch places in Montana a few years ago for vacation. We rode horses there, but we really didn't control them. They followed the horse in front of them just like they had done day in and day out for years. We just had to sit there."

Chuckling, Jessie agreed, "Yeah, I'd imagine at a place like that, those horses have done that trail several times a day every day since the time they were saddle-broke. They learn the game. That's how people were getting to be before it all started falling apart. Just going through the motions, playing the game."

Looking back toward Nate, watching as he worked his way down the trail in the woods, Jessie noticed a glint of light on the hillside adjacent to the trail. "What the...?" he mumbled as a shot rang out, taking Nate's feet out from under him and spinning him around. A second shot erupted, striking Nate in the back and throwing him to the ground with great force.

Raising his Marlin .30-30, Jessie quickly fired several shots into the area from where the shots had come. Looking back to Britney, Jessie was horrified to see Hank rear up, nearly throwing her off his back.

Britney dropped the reins and instinctively gripped the saddle horn with both hands as Hank exploded into a full gallop across the field, then into the trees and out of sight.

Knowing he couldn't catch up with Britney, Jessie ran toward Nate as the bark of a tree exploded from the impact of a hard-hitting round next to his head, sending him ducking for cover behind a neighboring tree.

Getting as low as he could, Jessie hid in the weeds surrounding the base of the tree, expecting more shots to begin to rain down on him. After a few moments of silence and calm, Jessie again heard the sound of the horn they'd heard just moments before the shooting began; this time though, it was much farther away.

For the next several moments, Jessie remained hidden behind the tree, unsure of the whereabouts of the shooter who had fired on him, or if they still remained in the vicinity. Quickly taking a peek, he saw Nate lying still in the trail up ahead, face down in the dirt with his leg in a very unnatural position.

"Dammit!" Jessie grumbled. Leaving his position of cover, he rushed forward and then ducked behind another tree. Catching his breath, he peeked again and saw no change in Nate's position.

Making another advance, Jessie sprinted hard, ducking once again behind a cluster of trees. Now only fifteen or so yards away from Nate, he heard Nate grumble in a monotone voice as he attempted to not create any signs of movement, "Bait. I may be bait."

Feeling better knowing Nate was still alive, Jessie turned his attention back to the potential location of their threat. Scanning the area with his rifle scope, he could see no movement. Slipping out from behind the tree, Jessie worked his way through the woods and to the hill. Working his way up the hill with his rifle at the high ready, a round chambered and ready to fire, Jessie slowly cleared the area, unable to find the shooter. Reaching a dead and rotting fallen tree, Jessie knelt down and inspected a set of strange prints and two freshly fired twelve-gauge shotgun shells.

"I think they're gone!" he shouted down to Nate.

"I'll cover you! Come on down!" Nate yelled as he rolled over and sat up, raising his M4 and providing cover for Jessie's approach.

As Jessie reached his position, Nate reached out to him and said, "Help me up."

"What about your leg?" Jessie asked, concerned about Nate's injuries.

Reaching down and removing his prosthetic leg, Nate held it up and grinned, "This leg? It doesn't hurt at all."

Flinching, Jessie shuddered, "Damn, that just messed with my head."

"I'm lucky I lost this leg," Nate said. "I'd be bleeding to death right now if not for that," he asserted, pointing at the shotgun pattern that peppered its surface.

"Did you get hit anywhere else?" Jessie asked, looking him over expecting to find blood.

Wiping blood out of his collar, Nate looked relieved. "I think a few of the pellets got through, but I'm pretty sure my pack took the brunt of it," he concluded, sliding the straps to his pack off his shoulders.

Flipping the pack over and surveying the damage, Nate said, "Again, I'm lucky they hit my leg, throwing me off to allow the second shot to hit my pack. My guardian angel is working overtime today."

"I'd say so," Jessie agreed. "Can you walk? We need to find Britney before someone else does."

"Yeah," replied Nate, as he began putting his prosthetic leg back into place.

The two men worked their way through the woods, this time remaining clear of the trail, shadowing the field that Hank had used for his panic-stricken egress of the scene.

Seeing something lying just ahead in the overgrown field, Jessie said, "Look," as he pointed. "Is that...?"

After a slight hesitation, Nate replied, "I dunno."

Stuttering, Jessie mumbled, "I... I think it's... it's my saddle."

Carefully walking into the pasture while Nate provided cover with his M4, Jessie approached the saddle to find that the cinch had been cut. "Somebody wanted this off in a hurry," he muttered while noting the intentionally inflicted damage.

"Dammit, where the hell is she?" grumbled Nate.

Hearing a girl's scream in the distance, Jessie and Nate both erupted into a full sprint toward the sound. Catching a glimpse of what could only be described as a figure wearing animal fur for an outer garment while dragging Britney along behind, Jessie shouted, "There!" and he and Nate both changed course in pursuit of Britney and her captor.

Several shots rang out, slowing their advance and causing them to lose ground once again.

"Those shots didn't come from Britney's location!" shouted Nate as he took cover behind a tree with the realization that they were still completely unsure of the extent of the threat they faced.

"We need to leapfrog and cover each other until we know who, or what, we're up against," Jessie insisted, growing more impatient by the minute.

Nodding in agreement, Nate volunteered, "I'll go first." Running from his position of cover, Nate bounded ahead to a cluster of trees, taking cover once again.

Once Nate was back in a position of cover, Jessie quickly moved forward while Nate covered him. The two men continued this series of movements, but could not keep Britney and her captor in sight.

"What the hell is this?" Nate asked, urging Jessie to join up with him.

"It looks like a paw print, but it's the size of a human's foot."

"I saw the same thing back where you were ambushed," answered Jessie.

"You reckon this goes along with the get-up that guy, or thing, was wearing?"

Shaking his head, Jessie responded, "I'd imagine that's the only sane answer. Not that sanity has a place in this world."

Moving a little farther forward, Nate came across what could only be assumed to be the drag marks made by a kicking and screaming unwilling participant. "We're not gonna catch back up with them," he concluded. "We're gonna have to just stay on their trail and figure out where they're going."

"Why the hell would they have cut Hank's saddle off?" Jessie wondered aloud. "I mean, if you were going to take the horse and the saddlebags, why not the saddle?"

"A diversion maybe?" Nate pondered. "We did stop our pursuit to check it out."

"Ah, who the hell knows?" Jessie grumbled. "This whole thing is nuts. Let's just keep moving and worry about figuring it all out after we get her back."

Pressing on, Nate and Jessie worked their way through the woods, following the trail left behind by Britney and her captor, determined to return her to safety, a cause they would see through to the end, regardless of the cost.

Chapter Six

Awakening to a throbbing headache, Britney felt her body surge forward. Struggling to move, she quickly realized her hands and feet were bound and tied by two separate lengths of rope. Screaming in terror, she heard her voice echo in the darkness that surrounded her.

The figure dragging her through the dark, damp place grunted as if to show aggravation with her cries and struggles. For fear of reprisal, she suppressed her protest and just lay there, being dragged along in the darkness.

Attempting to survey her surroundings without the benefit of light, Britney could feel that she was being dragged along on some sort of animal hide or rug. Every sound seemed to echo as if she was in an enclosed space. There was a total absence of light—she was in total, utter darkness. She wondered for a moment if she had been blinded by the apparent blow to her head that had caused her unconsciousness.

Her surroundings felt damp and cool. The air was calm, with virtually no wind, merely the occasional cool draft. She was inside, but inside of what? The rough, uneven surface was certainly no floor. She could hear the echo of dripping water. There was something familiar about the strangeness of this place. But what was it?

She was startled to feel several hands grab her and heave her body several feet. She landed on a cold, metal surface, slamming her heard against a hard, rib-like structure. The surface moved side to side, and she could hear the sound of water lapping against it from its motion.

Them

A boat! she thought, still confused as to why she couldn't see.

Feeling one of the figures that had tossed her step into the boat alongside her, causing it to rock side to side, she recoiled and cowered the best she could, silently fighting against her restraints.

Hearing the sounds of a paddle or oar entering and exiting the water to propel the boat forward, she looked toward the sound and saw a faint green glow of light around what she could only assume was the face of one of her abductors. The sight both confused and horrified her.

Try as she must, Britney couldn't make out any details, just the faintest glow of light. *At least I'm not blind,* she assured herself.

After what she could only assume was traveling by boat for several minutes, she was grabbed once again and lifted up. No longer feeling the rocking motion of the boat, she presumed the figures holding her were now standing on dry land.

One of the figures heaved her up and onto his shoulder. The man, assuming it was a man, seemed very large and strong to her.

Feeling herself freefall, she impacted the ground once again. Her body ached and she struggled to regain her breath as she felt the sensation of being dragged along the floor on a rug or a fur once again. Rolling to her side, she reached out with her bound hands to feel the cool, damp sensation of rock and grit.

Allowing her hands to drag across the ground, she felt an object and took hold of it with her fingers, picking it up. *What is this?* she wondered as she felt the long, slender object. When the weight and feel of the object became apparent to her, her hands instantly released it, thinking, *bone!* as chills ran up her spine and shivers flowed through her body.

When the dragging sensation abruptly stopped, strong hands once again took hold of her, heaving her onto the figure's broad shoulders. She could feel the rhythmic motion of footsteps, with the occasional stumble. While she was carried through the darkness, she intermittently grazed against what felt like rocks above her as the overhead clearance of the space was low.

Bent over the large figure's shoulder, feeling the impact in her ribs with every step, Britney could smell a musky, animalistic, dirty scent, as if the figure carrying her was a beast and not a man at all.

Feeling the figure come to a sudden stop, Britney was tossed back onto the ground. Stunned by the impact, she could hear the sound of chains clanking together as she felt a hand pull her by the foot and fasten some sort of metal restraint around her leg.

Once the hand released her, everything went silent save for the sound of droplets of water splashing as they dripped from above.

Her mind raced, and she felt her senses, out of the sheer desperation of her unknown circumstances, becoming almost hypersensitive to her surroundings. Britney began to smell several foul odors. The smell of what she assumed was human waste began to waft through the confined space, as did the smell of urine, and what she could only assume was putrid, rotting meat.

Jerking her head in an attempt to shake a fly from her face, Britney heard a weak, raspy voice say, "I think they're gone."

Startled, she flinched, quickly turning her head toward the source of the sound. "Who... who's there?" she asked in a quivering, panic-stricken voice.

"Don't worry. I can't hurt you," the voice assured her. "I'm bound, like you," the young-sounding man's voice continued with the sound of rattling chains permeating the space. "See? I'm chained down the same as you."

"Where... where are we?"

"My guess is Hell," the voice lamented. "And those were the demons."

"Stop it!" she snapped, in no mood to have her emotions toyed with.

"You'll see," the mysterious person in the darkness sighed in defeat.

"Are there others here?"

"There were several. Now it's just him and me... well, and you."

"Was? Who's him?" she asked.

"There's a guy to my left. I hear his chains move every now and then, but he won't talk. A boy named Trent was here until yesterday. There were several others before that."

"Where... where did he go?" she asked, almost afraid of the potential answer.

"They took him."

"They? Where?"

"Wherever it is, it's not far from here. It's... down here, wherever here is. When I got here, there were other people in chains. Every other day, at least, from what my mind perceives as days, one of them was taken away. Not long after, the screams would start, and grow in intensity until they just stopped. You never even hear a whimper after they cease. Something bad happens. I don't know what, but they never come back.

"Based on how things work, I'm probably the next to go. To be honest, I'm ready. I can't take this anymore. It's hell. It's a maddening hell," he lamented as his voice began to crack.

Wanting to get as much information from the strange voice in the darkness as she could, Britney asked, "What's your name?"

Pausing, the voice replied, "Greg. Greg Toliver. Or at least I was, at one time."

"I'm Britney," she responded, in her best attempt at a friendly and calming voice.

"I'm sorry," Greg replied.

"Sorry?"

"Sorry that you're here," he sobbed.

Britney could only imagine why Greg was beginning to weep.

In an attempt to keep the exchange of information going, Britney asked, "So, where are you from, Greg?"

"Memphis," he replied. "My parents and I lived in a suburb on the southeast side of Memphis—not too far from the airport."

"I heard Memphis was hit pretty hard during the attacks," she blurted out, though quickly realizing her error.

Hearing a sniffle, she heard Greg shuffle a bit and then say, "Yeah, my dad never made it home from work that day. He was killed by one of the gunmen. I still can't believe the world got so evil so fast. Leading up to that, it seemed like the country was a powder keg, just waiting for a match. Neighbors were turned against neighbors by the powers-that-be. School shootings, protests turned to riots... it was obvious something was going to happen. So when a busload of gunmen were unleashed on downtown, well, I guess we really weren't all that surprised it happened. I was just surprised my dad got caught up in it. I'd always pictured him being there for us, no matter what.

"My mother and I joined up with my uncle and his wife. He was a marine before becoming a cop, so we knew we would be in good hands with him. Or at least, we thought we were. He was killed in the middle of the night in our camp when a group of strangers tried to rob our group. My aunt couldn't take it after all the losses and insanity. She took her own life a few days later.

"From there, my mother and I traveled east, heading for the hills, I guess. You know, that's what everyone always joked they'd do, when and if the shit hit the fan. Head for the hills and live off the land," he scoffed.

Hearing him try to regain his composure, Britney empathized, "I lost both of my parents recently."

"I guess we've got a lot more in common than just being here," he fretted.

"Yeah. I guess," she sheepishly replied. "The foreigners kept moving us from one refugee camp to another, with promises of having better resources. That was a lie, of course. They bussed us out into the middle of nowhere where there were no prying eyes, where they planned to murder everyone in cold blood. Women, children, the elderly, it didn't matter one bit to them. It was like we were merely cattle being brought to slaughter. Every single person on the bus...all, except for me."

Hearing her begin to sob in the darkness, Greg stammered, "That's... that's... I just can't begin to grasp how things could come to that. How did you escape? How were you the only one to get away?"

Clearing her throat, she explained, "A group of men, a militia, I believe, killed the UF soldiers and rescued me. It was only minutes later when a counterattack killed all but one of the militiamen. It was awful. Me and Nate—he's the militia guy—met up with a man on horseback who helped us to get away. It was like something straight out of a western. It didn't even seem real to me. Then again, none of this seems real. I was with both of them until we were ambushed and a big man covered in fur brought me here."

"I wish I could say something stupid like, 'don't worry,' we'll be fine,' but we won't. I've accepted that, and I just want to get it over with," he conceded.

"It!?" she exclaimed. "What's it? What do you want to get over with?"

"Like I explained, whatever happens when they scream. I look forward to the moment when I no longer scream. When I'm no longer hungry, suffering, or in pain. I look forward to the time when I'm finally at peace. Even if we somehow escaped from this hell hole and got away from here, something else bad would happen. I mean, look at your story. You were supposedly being taken care of, and..."

Hearing someone in chains moving around in the darkness, Greg said, "That's him. He spoke a few words the other day, but nothing since."

"Hello, over there," Britney called out, attempting to get the other stranger in the darkness to talk.

"It's no use," Greg grumbled. "I've tried. He doesn't even cry anymore. At first, he wouldn't stop. He cried for what seemed like a solid day. Now...now, nothing. Nothing but a few rattles of his chains here and there."

Laying her head back on the cold, dark rock behind her, Britney contemplated everything Greg had told her. Was this it? Was this where she would meet her fate? Why? Why would God bring her out of the hands of the UF only to leave her here, in this pit of utter darkness and despair, to die a miserable death? She couldn't accept that. She couldn't accept the fact that she would meet her end here, in this all too real version of Hell.

Chapter Seven

Following the trail, Jessie and Nate worked their way down the rocky hill toward what appeared to be a clearing ahead. "I've lost it," Jessie grumbled as he frantically scanned the ground for signs of Britney and her captor.

"Over here," Nate gestured, pushing his way through the overgrown brush toward the face of a cliff.

The clearing they could see through the trees was approximately fifty feet below their elevation. Between them and the clearing was a steep rock cliff that cut back and underneath, almost like a shelf or an overhang.

"We need to find our way down to the bottom," Jessie suggested, trying to spot an obvious path. "We may be able to pick up the trail again down there. It's all rock between here and there. That won't help at all."

"This way," Nate decided, working his way along the edge of the drop, hanging onto roots and trees as he went, until reaching a switchback that led them toward the clearing below.

Reaching the base of the cliff, they looked around for tracks or signs of Britney or her captor's presence, to no avail.

Nestled along the bottom of the rocky cliff was a seam of limestone that sloped downward toward the level area below. At the base of the rock face, where it met the limestone seam, was an opening. "Check this out," Nate said, pointing toward the opening. "And there are those crazy footprints," he declared, pointing at the fine, powdery dirt and rock debris surrounding the opening.

"Is that a cave?" Jessie asked.

"It appears to be," Nate replied while cautiously looking inside. "This area is riddled with cave systems. As a matter of fact, Tennessee has more caves than any other state, and that's saying something, considering the fact that it's not even close to being the largest state in terms of size.

"The mapped and documented caves number above eight-thousand, I believe. A cave on our homestead saved our bacon during an attack on us once. It served as the perfect place for folks to hide and live during the peak of the fighting.

"I'm not from here," Nate continued, "but someone explained to me that this part of the country was under a shallow sea millions of years ago. Sediment from that sea formed the limestone layer that lies so close to the surface throughout the area. When the tectonic plates shifted and pushed the mountains up, it formed the widened passages through the limestone, and the subterranean streams ate away at it until it formed the elaborate cave system beneath us. There are rivers and even lakes underground here. Several of them became big tourist attractions for the area, such as Forbidden Caverns, which isn't too far at all from here, and the Lost Sea down in Sweetwater."

"Hmmm," Jessie pondered. "Well, if I wanted a secure and secluded hideaway, a cave system would be on the list."

As Nate worked his way closer to the cave's entrance to get a better look inside, Jessie reminded him, "Be careful, we're sitting ducks out here, and there's a good chance someone in there is drawing a bead on you this very moment."

Thinking the situation over, Nate turned to Jessie, and declared, "You know what this means, don't you?"

"What?" Jessie asked. "That we have to go inside?"

"Yep, I'm afraid so," Nate concluded.

"Damn, I don't wanna go crawling in there, but..."

"Yeah. Trust me, I know," explained Nate. "But if those tunnel rats back in Vietnam could go crawling into a tunnel they knew was probably boobie-trapped or full of VC, we can do this."

With a sigh, Jessie agreed, "Yes. Yes, we can."

Looking around, Nate determined, "We're gonna need some light."

"Let's step away from the cave for a moment," urged Jessie while he pulled his pack off his shoulder. With his back against some large rocks for cover, Jessie knelt down, then looked up at Nate, saying, "Keep an eye out while I do this."

"Do what?"

"I'd prefer a flashlight, but usable batteries aren't readily available at the moment. I'm gonna unleash my inner Indiana Jones," Jessie quipped, with a sly grin while unzipping his bag.

Seeing that Jessie was beginning to work on some sort of small project, Nate said, "Don't you mean your inner MacGyver?"

With a chuckle, Jessie shook his head. Removing a small, brown bottle from the main compartment of the pack, Jessie placed it aside and then removed a roll of cloth bandages from a pocket on the side of his pack. Placing a lighter off to the side as well, he said, "Now, we just need a handle."

Looking around, he saw a young tree with a trunk at around two inches in diameter. Removing his hatchet from his pack, he quickly chopped through it and then fashioned a handle approximately two feet in length.

Placing the handle between his knees, Jesse took the cloth bandage and began wrapping it tightly around the handle. "You probably know this, but the trick here is to get the wrap really tight. If it's loose, it'll burn too fast."

Them

Once he had the bandage wrapped tightly and with sufficient thickness, Jessie placed it aside and opened the brown bottle.

"What's that?" Nate asked.

"Cooking oil," answered Jessie. Rotating the torch's handle with his left hand, he began pouring the oil on the cloth bandage with his right. After setting the oil bottle down, he began pushing the oil into the cloth with his finger. "The other trick to this is to make sure the cloth is saturated all the way through."

When he felt the cloth was thoroughly saturated, Jessie removed a small roll of metal wire from his pack, and continued, "Safety wire can fix damn near anything. If you've got this and duct tape, you're unstoppable."

"See? McGyver," Nate chided.

"No, that would be a paperclip and a nickel," Jessie joked in reply.

Rapidly bending the wire back and forth, Jessie broke off three pieces in lengths of approximately six inches. He then wrapped the sections of wire securely around the cloth, twisting them tightly with his multi-tool pliers.

"That ought to do it," he boasted, holding out his creation. "See? I meant my inner Indiana Jones. He always had one of those Hollywood torches that burned all day long. I'm sure mine won't live up to movie standards, but it's better than being blind."

"Are we gonna just go walking right in there?" Nate asked.

"I hadn't planned on that," explained Jessie. "I was planning on lighting it and tossing it inside. With the oil-soaked rags burning, it shouldn't go out.

"Hopefully, if there is a guard near the entrance of the cave, that'll elicit a response. If not, it'll illuminate things enough for us to make our initial entry. We need to move in bounds, covering each other as we go. It goes without saying that we're at a major disadvantage here and are taking on substantial risk."

"That we are," Nate agreed. "But my friends back there didn't die trying to free those people only to have me walk away from our only survivor now. They laid down their lives to get her out of there, and I'll lay down mine to get her out of here, if that's what it takes."

Looking Nate in the eye, Jessie paused, and asked, "What drives you? I still don't know what group or organization you're with, but you're obviously willing to give everything up for a person you just met, and you risked it all back when you didn't even know her. For all we know, stepping into this cave will be the equivalent of stepping out of a landing craft on D-Day, yet you're willing to charge right into it?"

"It seems I could ask the same of you," Nate retorted. "Hell, you weren't even in our group and had no clue who we were, yet you jumped right in to help. At least I had a cause to die for."

"You have a cause to die for, and I very likely don't have anything to live for," Jessie replied. "I lost everything. My wife and children were murdered. They lost their lives because I couldn't protect them well enough on my own. The pain from that nearly ended me. Quite frankly, I wanted to die.

"Then, when I was at the very bottom, a father and his young daughter stumbled across my place high up in the Rocky Mountains. I saw a spark of hope in them. I saw a reason to keep going, for others, even if not for myself.

"Setting out across the country to find my sister may simply be another sad tragedy for me to find, more pain for my heart to bear, but at the very least, I have to try.

"Along the way, though, I've met a lot of folks, like you, who give me hope that we'll claw our way out of this hole we're in and be stronger for it in the long run. I'm hoping the next generation of leadership in this country, and around the world, will be those who were forged in the fire of all this hell we're going through now.

"Several months back, I met up with a group in Arkansas. One gentlemen, Isaac, became a very dear friend of mine. He explained to me the concept of clay forging, and how it was used to make swords back in the days of the Samurai. Have you heard of clay forging?"

"No. I can't say that I have," Nate shrugged, curious to where Jessie may be going with this.

Jessie explained, "If you look closely at a Katana, there is a line that runs through the center of the blade for the entire length of the sword. That line is caused by the process of clay tempering. When the blade is forged, the metal is soft. This is, of course, required so the swordsmith can shape the blade into its desired form. Tempering the blade hardens it, much like this world has hardened the soul of many a man. Achieving balance, however, is important to the soul, same as it is to the sword.

"Isaac explained to me that a blade that is too hard will break, but a blade that is too soft will bend. To achieve balance, the swordsmith applies clay to the freshly formed blade. He applies a thin layer of clay over the edge and a thicker layer of clay over the spine. This allows the blade to cool at different rates when tempering, giving it the hardness it needs to hold its edge, with the softness and flexibility it needs to survive a very hard hit.

"As with the blade, if a person is hardened too quickly, they tend to break. Yet if they remain soft, they bend far too easily.

Both the soft man and the hard man will eventually succumb to the challenges they face. But if the right amount of clay was placed into your heart before you were tossed into the fires, you'll find that you emerged with both the hardness you need to do what must be done and the softness you need to retain your humanity.

"This world is going to need more people like you, who have been forged by the fire of this hell we've found ourselves in, yet retain their hearts, in order to rebuild our nation and our world."

"That's pretty deep for Arkansas," Nate chuckled. "I'm just kidding. I know exactly what you mean. That Isaac fellow seems like a wise man."

"He was something else," Jessie said, thinking about his friend for the first time in a while. "Like you, though, he was willing to put it all on the line when the time came."

Seeing Nate fiddling with his prosthesis, Jessie asked, "Did you lose your leg before or after the collapse?"

"After," Nate quickly replied. "I had to make my way from the west coast to try to find my parents, much like what you're doing now. I ran into a little trouble along the way, but like you, I met just the right kind of people to keep me going."

Placing his hand on Nate's shoulder, Jessie said, "I rest my case. Now, let's get on to what's important in this very moment, and that's Britney."

"Right on," Nate affirmed, with enthusiasm in his voice. "By the way, I've got an idea. I've got a few flares in my pack that my team would carry to assist during an exfil. They wouldn't make good walking around lights, but they could help out. I can toss one in, and we'll see from its light if the coast is clear. Once we move forward to that position, I'll toss the flare deeper into the cave. When we advance to that position, I'll toss it again.

"We can use the flares to light up the spaces ahead of us while using the torch for our personal light. The sparks and intense light from the flares may also obscure the view for anyone trying to observe us from deeper within the cave, because they would be much brighter than your torch."

Shaking his head, Jessie grumbled, "I sure wish I'd known you had flares before I spent all this time making a torch."

"You didn't exactly share your plan with me before you started," Nate countered.

"Touché," Jessie conceded. "Well, I don't see any other way to do this. I'm not in favor of just walking into the darkness with the light of the entrance at our backs, so I guess this is the only way. They'll definitely know we're in there, though."

"There's no avoiding that."

"I reckon so," Jessie confirmed as he looked at the entrance to the cave. "Well, like you said, this can't be as bad as what those tunnel rats had to do in Vietnam. If they could suck it up and crawl into those little holes, and often times for a mission that to them, at least, was hard to see as worthy of giving up their own lives, then we can do this for her."

"This is nuts, but I agree," Nate conceded as he patted Jessie on the shoulder.

"I'll cover you from here," Jessie said as he raised his Marlin to the ready position. "Work your way around to the side, hugging up against those rocks. That way, you at least can't be shot from the inside when you toss the flare inside. If the entrance is clear, I'll move up to your position, and we'll take it from there. If it's not, I'll cover you while you make your way back to safety."

"I sure wish I was smart enough to come up with another plan, but... well... here goes," Nate added as he turned and began working his way toward the cave.

Once alongside the face of the cliff, Nate hugged it tightly, inching toward the opening of the cave. Pausing occasionally during his advance to read Jessie's face and hand signals to ensure the coast was still clear, Nate drew nearer and nearer to the opening.

Stopping just a few feet from the cave entrance, he saw Jessie giving him the thumbs up. Nodding, Nate drew the flare from his pack, removed the cap, and using the striker in the cap, ignited the flare and immediately tossed it into the mouth of the cave, then quickly pulled back.

Looking through the scope of his rifle, Jessie watched intently for any signs of movement within the cave that might be illuminated by the flickering light of the flare.

Signaling to Nate to cover his advance, Jessie left his position of cover, and quickly joined Nate along the cliff, adjacent to the cave opening.

"I couldn't see anything," Jessie whispered. Reaching into his pocket, Jessie retrieved simple plastic Bic lighter. Flicking the lighter several times to get it to light, he held it to the oil-soaked cloth.

Once the torch was burning adequately, he put the lighter back in his pocket and said, "I'll toss this inside just short of the flare. Once you make your advance, you can pick it up and get a good look around while I move up behind you. We can then start our game of 'flare leapfrog'. If we make contact, well, we'll just go with the flow."

And with a nod in the affirmative, Nate crept silently around the corner and into the mouth of the cave.

Them

Covering Nate as he bounded forward, Jessie watched as Nate took a position of cover behind a pile of rocks that at one time had been part of the cave's ceiling. With Nate now covering for him, he tossed the torch to Nate and advanced, joining up alongside him.

Slipping over to the flare, Nate picked it up and tossed it deeper into the cave. Bounding forward again while Jessie covered him, Nate took cover yet again and signaled for him to follow.

Picking up the torch as he moved forward, Jessie illuminated the floor of the cave to reveal several sets of the odd tracks they had followed to the cave, as well as the tell-tale signs of someone, or something, being dragged along behind, obscuring some of the tracks as they went.

Joining up with Nate again, Jessie said, "They're definitely in here. Their freshest tracks, the ones that disturb the others, are all going in, not out."

"How far do you think this cave goes?" Nate asked.

Picking up and tossing a rock into the darkness ahead, Jessie listened to the echoes caused by its impact, and said, "I'd venture to guess it goes a good distance back in there. There's a reason they're using it. They wouldn't have run into a dead end knowing we were behind them. They'd have no options if this were all there was to it."

"Well, let's keep moving," Nate urged as he left his cover and moved toward the flare. Just as he reached out to pick up the flare, he and Jessie heard the bone-chilling sound of the horn they had heard out in the woods, only this time it was coming from deep within the cave.

Quickly picking up the flare and tossing it farther into the cave, Nate scurried back to Jessie's location. "Holy hell!" he exclaimed. "That came from within, and it wasn't close. This cave must be huge. This may be an entire cave system and not just a simple cave.

"Do you reckon that horn is to warn us and scare us off, or to warn others of our presence—you know, like an alarm system."

"Based on what we heard before, I'd imagine they use it to signal each other to advance or retreat," Jessie posited. "Maybe like a bugler would do back in the day before field radios?"

"Either way, they've gotten word we're here," Nate replied.

"Hooray for us," Jessie whispered sarcastically. "Well, tunnel rat, let's keep moving."

Moving forward toward the light of the flare, Nate got a glimpse of what was up ahead and signaled for Jessie to move up to his position.

"What's up?" Jessie asked as his eyes struggled to focus in the darkness after having accidentally looked directly into the bright light of the flare.

"The cave slopes downhill ahead. It looks pretty rough and rocky, too. Damn, I wish I had night vision."

"Amen to that," Jessie concurred. "I'm not sure the flare is helping at all. If anything, it's signaling our arrival as much as anything else. And that smoke," he added, waving his hand in front of his face. "I'm no geologist or spelunker or any such thing, but I'm also a little paranoid about explosive gasses being down here and us tossing a torch right into it."

"I had the same thought. But, we wouldn't be able to see crap without it. Besides, I think most of those scenarios occur during mining operations when they're releasing trapped gasses. Surely any such thing would have flowed out of here by now after having been vented long ago. But then again, I'm no expert either."

"Maybe our paranoia is just getting the best of us," Jessie conceded. "Let's keep moving."

Working their way toward the flare, Nate picked it up and tossed it again. This time, he was able to get it approximately twenty yards or so farther into the cave, and down onto the jagged, rocky downward slope.

Jessie and Nate continued this pattern of leapfrogging with the light until they reached the bottom of the descent, and to what was a broadening in the cave's opening. They could now see that the floor of the cave was smooth, sloping from the edges of the cave down, with the lowest point being in the middle. The smoothness of the limestone chamber was interrupted only by the formations of stalactites and stalagmites extending from both the ceiling and the floor, creating a fantastic array of shapes and forms that rivaled the set of a Hollywood fantasy film.

"It's getting damp in here," Nate whispered once Jessie had joined up alongside him.

Holding the torch as far out to his left as he could, both to reduce his being a target, as well as attempting to allow his eyes to adjust to the darkness of the cave, Jessie watched as droplets of water traced the forms of a stalactite. When the water reached the sharp point at the end, it formed a droplet of water that blipped onto the stalagmite below.

"How many years do you think that took?" Jessie whispered, gesturing to the rock formations.

"Huh?" shrugged Nate, confused by Jessie's statement.

"For these drops of water, carrying tiny particles of limestone, to form these shapes and structures?"

"Oh," Nate responded with a chuckle. "A damn long time, I guess." Thinking through the situation, he noted, "It looks like that flare is just about spent. What do you think? Light another?"

Looking around, Jessie said, "Well, it's been working so far. Besides, I can't imagine not being able to see what's up ahead."

"Alright, then," Nate said as he slipped his pack off his shoulder and fished around inside for another flare. Once the new flare was lit, he tossed it farther into the cave, only to have it splash and extinguish upon landing.

"What the...?" Jessie mumbled, confused by the sound as he began working his way forward with the torch lighting the way.

After moving forward approximately fifty feet, the light of Jessie's torch revealed a flooded chamber of the cave. "That's a lot of water," he said, unable to see beyond the water to the other side with his faint, flickering torchlight.

As Nate joined him, the two looked around, then down at the ground to reveal scuff marks and more of the strange looking prints they had seen all throughout their pursuit.

Studying the scuff marks on the limestone floor surrounding the edge of the water, Nate proclaimed, "This water must go a lot farther than we think. They've got a damn boat down here."

"Well, I'll be damned," Jessie said with the origin of the scuff marks becoming evident to him as he processed Nate's observation.

"What do you think? Flat bottomed Jon boat?" Nate asked.

"That's what I'm thinking," Jessie agreed.

"That means one of two things," Nate decided. "We're either a lot closer to them than we think, or like I said, this water goes a long way."

"Didn't you say there were underground lakes in the area?"

"Yeah," Nate replied. "Down in Sweetwater, there's a tourist attraction called The Lost Sea. It's an underground lake in a cave down that way, turned into an underground boat tour. It's pretty big."

"This place is perfect," Jessie marveled. "Not only is it well hidden, and would be easy to defend, but it's got a damned moat. I'd imagine there are other access points, too."

"Why do you say that?" Nate asked.

"Well, tactically speaking, it makes a great hideout, so long as you have an alternate point of egress. If a hostile threat camped out at the mouth of the cave and you had no other way to escape, they could easily starve you out. Surely, whoever is down here would have thought of that."

"That's possible," Nate admitted. "Or maybe they've just been lucky so far and not been followed home?"

"Either way, I guess we're about to get wet," Jessie said as he removed his pack. "Damn. Do you think there are snakes in this water?"

"Ah, hell, why did you have to go and say a thing like that?" Nate grumbled. "Now that's all I'm gonna think about."

"We've gone from tunnel rats to river rats," Jessie joked as he mentally prepared himself for what lay ahead.

"What about the torch?" Nate asked.

"I'll extinguish it for now, and we can try to keep it dry and relight it on the other side. We'll just have to feel our way through for now." Looking around, he handed the torch to Nate and requested, "Here, hold this for a minute."

Removing the cloth containing his jerky from his pack, Jessie handed Nate a piece and said, "Eat up. We don't know when we're gonna get a chance to refuel again." He then placed the rest of the jerky in a side pocket on his pack and removed two small dry bags and a box of ammunition for his rifle.

Jessie placed the box of ammunition in one of the dry bags and wrapped it up tight. He then placed the pack off to the side behind several of the exotic cave formations, attempting to hide it the best he could.

"Are you ready to go dark?" he asked.

"No, but I don't really have a choice, do I?" Nate sarcastically replied.

"No, sir, at least not one that I can see." Reaching out and taking the torch, Jessie whispered, "Well, here goes," as he smothered the small flames of the torch with the cloth and the two men quickly found themselves surrounded by a total and absolute darkness.

"Damn it!" Jessie exclaimed quietly.

"What?"

"Just burned my hand, that's all," he replied.

Fumbling around in the darkness, Jessie grumbled, "I sure wish I would have gotten my lighter out of the pack before turning out the lights."

Hearing Nate chuckle, Jessie fumbled around in the darkness for his pack and dug around by feel until he found his lighter. After placing the lighter in the dry bag containing the ammunition, Jessie touched the torch to see if it had sufficiently cooled. "Just a few more minutes," he said.

"A few more minutes for what?" Nate asked.

"It's still a little hot. I'm going to wrap the torch with the other dry bag, then stuff it down the back of my shirt, keeping it up above my head and hopefully out of the water the best I can. With the handle sticking out, the drybag won't seal, but it should protect it from splashes and such. I'm gonna give it a minute to cool, though. I don't want the dry bag to melt from the heat."

After a few more minutes, Jessie touched the torch, and now being happy with its temperature, he wrapped the end of it tightly with the dry bag and slipped it into the collar of his shirt behind him. "Can you swim with your prosthetic?" he asked.

"While you were fidgeting around in the dark with the torch, I took a piece of paracord from my cargo pocket and made a tether for it, running up to my belt. I don't want to take any chances with it in the water and being unable to see. I'm hoping we can wade through this. I'd really rather not be swimming. Just imagine swimming overtop of a sharp stalagmite, then sinking down on top of it."

"Damn!" Jessie swore. "Let's stop talking about snakes and possible impalements and get on with things before we talk ourselves out of it. Are you ready?"

With his rifle slung around his neck, preparing to step into the unknown, Nate grunted, "No, but let's get on with it."

Chapter Eight

"Are you still there?" Britney asked, attempting to break through the feeling of utter loneliness in which her world of darkness surrounded her.

"That's a stupid thing to ask," grumbled Greg.

Taken aback by his hostility, she relaxed, took a deep breath, then asked, "So... what kind of music do you listen to?" She almost immediately felt embarrassed by the silliness of her question.

Hearing only a shuffle against the floor along with the jingle of Greg's chains as he moved, Britney sighed and wished for sleep. Fatigue was setting in from the accumulated stress of the past few very long days. The bus she and her parents traveled on the previous day had departed very early, around 4:00 AM, and the stress of it all had taken a lot out of her already malnourished and weakened state. Time was already becoming a foreign concept to her. She had no idea how long she had been unconscious earlier, or what time it may be now. It was all a blur. A horrible, painful blur.

"Can I ask you a simple question?" she queried.

"Go ahead," he mumbled.

"How do you drink? If you're here for several days, they obviously give you water, right?"

Exhaling, as if fatigued by her interest in talking, Greg explained, "Do you hear all that water dripping around you?"

"Yes."

"Well, it's all around you. The water that drips from above collects in little pockets on the floor. You just have to find them. You'll get as much grime in your mouth as water, but it works."

Them

"Thanks," she replied softly. She could hear Greg shift around as if turning away from her.

As she laid there in the total darkness with nothing but the sounds of dripping water to remind her she was even still alive, the sound of a horn, the same primitive sounding horn they had heard in the forest before their encounter, echoed through her surroundings, bouncing off the cave walls and creating a confusing and scary sound.

Hearing the chains of both Greg and the other captive begin to rustle, Britney could hear a voice quivering beyond Greg. "No... no... no, no, no, no!" the voice began shrieking with fear.

Britney could hear several heavy-sounding figures enter the room. Communicating with only a few grunts, the captors made their way through the darkness. Britney shook in fear when the voice on the far side of the room began to scream as sounds of a struggle were now evident. "No! No! Let me go! Let me goooo! Please! Please, let me go!" the voice cried, eventually being overcome by uncontrollable sobbing.

Hearing the chains that had once been secured firmly to the panic-stricken young man on the other side of the room drop to the floor, she realized that the sounds had begun to fade and she could tell they were walking away, carrying their victim along with them just as she had been carried into this chamber of the cave.

Noticing sobbing in the darkness, still in the chamber alongside her, Britney's voice trembled as she called out, "Greg... are you still there?"

"Shhhh..." Greg responded. "Try not to listen."

"Listen to what?" she asked.

Before Greg could answer, blood-curdling screams of agony could be heard echoing all throughout the chambers of the cave.

These weren't merely sounds of a frightened individual; these were truly sounds of agonizing torment. The screams soon began to gurgle, and then, there was only silence.

Afraid to ask what had just occurred, not wanting to know the answer, Britney closed her eyes and prayed quietly, "Dear Lord. Dear Lord, please rescue us from this place. I've prayed to you so many times before, asking for help, asking for mercy on me and my parents, but it never came. Dear God, please hear me now. Please rescue us from this living hell. Don't let our lives end like this."

Sniffling, Greg said, "Praying doesn't work. I've tried. Others have tried. I'm next. You'll hear my screams next. There's nothing your empty words can do to stop that."

She tried to think of something comforting or positive to say, but she knew Greg had been through much more than herself down in this hellish dungeon. She knew her words would fall on deaf ears and he would likely just say something to dash her fading hopes. Greg's spirit had been completely broken, and there was nothing Britney could say to ease his pain.

Putting herself into Greg's shoes, Britney not only dreaded what would come next, but she also dreaded the thought of her own resignation of death. The only thing she'd had to keep her going through so many of the hard times she and her family had gone through was a hope that one day the hell that befell her nation would begin to heal, and they could begin to rebuild their lives.

But now... now her parents were gone, and her hope that had once shone brightly to everyone around her, was beginning to fade. That horrible, helpless feeling of resignation that had already consumed Greg was creeping into her soul. She could feel its darkness washing over her.

~~~~

Slipping into the cold, dark water, Jessie took several steps and found himself standing waist deep. "It gets deep pretty quick," he whispered.

"Is it slick?" Nate asked, concerned about the footing he would have with his prosthetic leg.

"The limestone is pretty gritty. I don't think you'll have a problem.

"If you say so," Nate replied as he, too, entered the water. "Whew, that's cold."

"You ain't kiddin'," Jessie agreed, continuing his way forward with one hand on his rifle and the other reaching out into the darkness in front of him.

With the water now reaching his neck, Jessie said, "I sure hope it doesn't get any deeper. I'm not a frogman. I'm not sure how well I'd do swimming with boots and a rifle."

"Try doing it with only one good leg," Nate mused.

"Right," Jessie chuckled as his fingers grazed the side of the cave. "If I move any more to the right, it seems like it would get really deep, really fast. The left side slants upward. Let's try to keep to the left for now."

"Right behind you," Nate said, following the sound of Jessie's voice. Barely holding his face above the water with his head tilted all the way back, he added, "You're what, an inch, maybe an inch and a half taller than me?"

"Something like that," Jessie replied.

"Lucky bastard. I'd give anything for that inch right now," Nate said as water entered his ears.

Feeling a dip in the floor beneath them, Jessie paused and whispered, "Hold up."

Doing as Jessie instructed, Nate patiently awaited Jessie's next move as the two men heard the sound of a metallic thud and the sloshing of water up ahead. The sound was faint, and both men instantly ceased all movements. Listening intently, they could hear the familiar sounds of water swirling around an oar.

Hearing what they assumed was a boat gliding through the water ahead of them, both Jessie and Nate lowered themselves into the water as far as they could to reduce the chance of being spotted.

How wide is it right here? Jessie began to wonder. *Will there be room for a boat to go past us? How are they guiding that thing? How can they see?*

As the sounds drew nearer, Jessie wanted to bring his rifle to bear, but he knew the sounds of moving it in the water would give away the fact that he and Nate were there. Resisting the urge to act, Jessie hoped Nate would do the same, but mentally prepared himself for that not to be the case.

When the boat reached their position, Jessie felt the water from the oar wash over his face and into his eyes. Nearly choking on the water as it entered his nose mid-inhale, Jessie struggled to contain his reaction as the boat continued to slip on by.

Reaching the point where they had entered the water, Jessie could hear the metal-hulled boat dragging against the limestone as he heard what sounded like at least two occupants exiting the boat, and stepping out onto the floor of the cave.

Raising his mouth above the waterline after hearing the boat's occupants work their way toward the entrance of the cave,

Them

Jessie whispered, "C'mon," as he continued working his way forward. "They're gonna see our tracks and find our gear. Be careful, there is a hole or dip right here," he warned as he felt his way along the cave wall, wading as fast as he could while trying to reduce the sounds he made while moving hastily through the water.

Having traveled a considerable distance, Jessie realized the water had begun to shallow out. Believing he was reaching the end of the underground waterway, Jessie had started to communicate his findings with Nate when they heard the horn sound yet again. This time, it was behind them, toward the entrance of the cave.

"They found our stuff!" Nate whispered with panic in his voice.

Hearing trickling water and feeling a cold current flowing from his immediate left, Jessie felt around and determined it to be a downward flow through an irregularly shaped tunnel. He imagined it would be the source of a strong water flow following a storm on the surface, but with the dry conditions as of late, it was merely a trickle.

"C'mon! In here," he whispered, urging Nate to follow.

Feeling around with his hands, Nate found the passage and began to climb inside, following along behind Jessie who was now scurrying through the upward slanting tube, approximately ten feet inside.

Hearing heavy metallic thuds coming from the direction of the boat, they knew whoever it was who had been moving around so efficiently in the cave was returning, probably to deliver the news of signs of their presence.

"Take my hand," whispered Jessie as he wedged himself tightly in the water passage, reaching into the darkness and hoping to feel Nate take hold.

With the boat rapidly approaching their position, Nate's boot slipped, sending him splashing into the water below.

As the boat drew closer, Jessie heard a grunt as one of the boat's occupants dove from the boat and into the water after Nate.

Still below the surface of the water from his fall, Nate heard the splash and felt the turbulence of the boat's occupant aggressively entering the water. Attempting to swim away, he felt a sting on his thigh, followed by severe, searing pain.

Drawing his knife, he swung it blindly beneath the water, making contact with a fleshy material as a hand grabbed him by the wrist.

Hearing the other figure stumble around in the boat as if he was following the struggle from above the surface, Jessie blindly launched himself from his position of visual cover toward the sounds of the boat.

Feeling his chin contact something hard and angular, followed by the soft fury feel of a large body, Jessie felt as if the entire cave was tumbling as the boat leaned over, spilling him and his target into the water.

Feeling a sudden impact as his target's head smashed against the side of the cave underneath the water, Jessie drew his knife and began slashing and stabbing wildly until his victim's struggles ceased.

Taking hold of what he had impacted with his chin, Jessie immediately recognized it to be goggles of some sort. Hearing a gasp for air, Jessie struggled to don the goggles, just in time to see a blurry image of Nate breaking through the surface, gasping for air.

"It's me!" he shouted as he reached out for Nate, grabbing him by the sleeve and dragging him to the edge of the water. "This way," he said, pulling Nate toward the nearby rocks and deeper in the cave.

Struggling to their feet, Jessie asked, "Are you okay?"

"My leg. It burns," Nate replied.

"C'mon. I can see. Those bastards had night vision. Let's get moving before more of their comrades show up. They didn't blow that horn because they were alone. That was a signal."

Removing the monocular and attempting to wipe it dry to no avail, Jessie looked around to see the distorted image of Nate's rifle being dragged along behind him.

"Good call with the paracord," Jessie said as he picked it up and placed it in Nate's arms.

Confirming that he, too, still had his rifle slung securely over his back, Jessie led Nate to a fork in the cavern. To his right was a well-traveled corridor in the shape of an ellipse. To his left was a narrow passage made up of many irregular rock forms and outcrops, as if carved by years of turbulent water flow.

Seeing something strange lying between the two passageways, Jessie wiped the lens of the night vision once again to see what appeared to be a pile of human bones and skulls. "Holy hell," he mumbled, taking in the macabre sight.

"What?" Nate asked.

"Sick bastards left a warning of sorts. C'mon, this way," he said, pulling Nate along behind him and into the passage to the left.

"Watch your head," he said, leading Nate beneath a stalactite and several other overhead formations.

Trying to get some distance between themselves and the location of their encounter, Jessie pushed Nate hard, although he could feel his efforts begin to fade.

"My tourniquet," Nate muttered through gritted teeth. "Here," he said as he fished around in his cargo pocket. "Put this on my leg. Above here," he, groaned, pointing to his wound.

Looking at Nate's leg with the night vision he had placed over his head with attached headband, Jessie said, "Oh, yeah, that's pretty bad. That went deep."

Working the tourniquet around Nate's leg, Jessie drew it tight and tied it off. "C'mon. We'll check it again once we get some more distance between them and us."

On the move once again, Jessie began leading Nate up a slippery incline covered with what appeared to be fresh soil and sediment.

Around a large pile of rocks that were present from an apparent partial ceiling collapse, Nate said, "I see light."

Seeing a bright spot through the monocular, Jessie raised it off his eye to see sunlight shining in from the outside.

"C'mon!" he said, leading Nate up the steepening incline toward the opening above and ahead.

Reaching the opening, Jessie desperately dug with his hands, quickly transferring to his Marlin rifle, smashing at the rocks and roots above them, exposing more of the cave's passage to the final rays of the day's light above.

Partially climbing out of the hole, Jessie found that they were between two large rocks that reached out from the side of a steep hill in a heavily wooded area.

Climbing up and out of the hole, Jessie reached inside, taking Nate by the hand and heaving him upward and out of the hole.

Them

"Fresh air at last," Nate said jokingly to mask his pain. Taking Nate by the hand, Jessie pulled him over his back and into the fireman's carry position.

"What the hell are you doing?" Nate asked.

"I'm getting you far from here so we can get you fixed up."

"We can't leave her behind!" protested Nate. "We know where she must be now!"

"We won't," Jessie assured him. "Trust me."

Chapter Nine

"Damn, that hurts," Nate cursed as Jessie administered a more proper level of first aid to his leg.

"Yeah, well, so will gangrene," Jessie countered. "Just how many legs do you want to lose? You've not got many options left."

"That's not funny," Nate grumbled. "But you're right. I've got to hang on to that one. It carries the lion's share of the load."

"It's gonna be dark, soon," Jessie observed, taking a moment to notice the fact that the sun was almost lost through the trees. "I need to go get help. You're in no condition to press on, and we know for a fact this isn't something I can handle on my own. You need help, too. I can't do both. Maybe those folks on the other side of the bridge?" he wondered aloud.

"No. Not them," Nate rebutted. "There's a reason they knew something was going on here and merely chose to avoid it. I mean... don't get me wrong. Clearly, they're good people, but not all good people are willing to trade their own lives for strangers. They'd eventually run out of lives to spare. No, I'd say they've seen and done enough of that over the past few years to want to hold their position and hold their own, and not much more."

"Then.... Who? Any suggestions?" Jessie asked as he watched Nate pondering their options.

"Okay, well, I guess you've proven you can be trusted," Nate said with a chuckle. "We, my group, that is, have seen enough people turn on each other in recent times to have good reason to keep things to ourselves. We took on new recruits that seemed as motivated and dedicated as the rest, only to have them turn out to be double agents for the powers-that-be, or to simply give in to the pressure applied to their families in order to save them, at the expense of us, our families, and our cause."

"I've seen the same," Jessie conceded. "So has every rebellion or insurgency in history. It's easy to join; it's hard to stay the course."

"Still, I think the standard of trust I've held you to is far beyond reason," Nate admitted, wincing in pain when Jessie pulled tight on a suture. "After that, though, maybe I should reconsider," chuckled Nate. "But seriously, I apologize for treating you like you couldn't be trusted. Clearly, you can."

"No need to apologize," Jessie replied. "You've been very prudent, and loyal to your cause."

"Anyway," Nate continued, getting back on track. "Here's what I want you to do. Travel east to the town of Del Rio. Once you arrive, you'll encounter armed men guarding every entrance to the town. Unless things have gone awry since I left, they're good people, and they have the local population's best interest at heart, even though they may seem rather unwelcoming and threatening to you as a stranger. An armed stranger, at that.

"They aren't gonna let you just waltz right into town. Tell them you need to get to the Del Rio Baptist Church to find Pastor Wallace. Tell those guys Nathan Hoskins sent you.

"Once you get to Pastor Wallace, tell him everything. Tell him to relay to my wife, Peggy, and our little boy, Zack, that I love them more than anything, and I will be home when this is all over."

"Will he believe me? That you sent me, that is?" Jessie asked.

With a sly grin, Nate replied, "They know I'd never give my family's names and whereabouts away under duress. That'll be all he needs to hear to know your story is legit.

"He'll contact our group, the Blue Ridge Militia, through all of the proper channels. He'll get you the help we need. There's no question about that.

"Del Rio is probably thirty miles or so from here. My map is in my pack back in the cave, so I can't be sure, but that's a good guesstimate. That's a long way by foot, especially given the terrain between here and there."

"I'll do whatever I can to get there as fast as humanly possible," Jessie replied, patting Nate on the shoulder. "By the way, it's good to finally receive a proper introduction, Nate Hoskins," he said, holding out his hand.

Smiling, Nate reached out and shook Jessie's hand firmly, and insisted, "Now get the hell out of here."

"Wait," Jessie said. Reaching to his side, he picked up the night vision taken from one of the hostiles in the cave. "This is the good stuff. It's a PVS-14. I'm not sure how much longer the batteries will last, but this will let you keep an eye on things tonight. Even if those bastards don't track you here, there may be other critters, like coyotes, feral dogs, or black bear that smell your wound and come looking. How many rounds of ammo do you have left?"

"I've got a few mags," Nate replied.

"Don't give away your position by shooting at a coyote if you don't have to," Jessie said, "but, you know that already."

Pushing the goggles away, Nate said, "You keep these, you may need them to travel at night."

"Nonsense," Jessie replied. "I've got freedom of movement on my side. You don't. You need everything you can get to level the playing field with whatever may come along, sniffing you out. I've still got my torch in the dry bag. I'll use that if I absolutely have to have light, but once my eyes adjust, the moon may be enough. Like you, I've traveled a long way for a long time, mostly in the dark. I feel right at home in the dark now."

Standing up and looking around, Jessie looked up at the stars, gathered his bearings, and said, "Well, I'd better get going. Take care of yourself out here until I get back."

"I will," Nate assured him with a nod.

And with that, Jessie turned and ran off into thick trees and underbrush of the forest, disappearing almost instantly, like a ghost.

Leaning back against the log Jessie had hidden him behind, Nate picked up his M4 and placed it in his lap, easily within reach, and donned the night vision monocular. Doing a quick function check, and fitting the headband snugly and securely, he powered it down and then flipped it up and out of the way. *I'll save the batteries and use my eyes as much as I can. There's no telling how long it'll take him to get back.*

~~~~

Jogging through the woods with his Marlin slung across his back, Jessie thought of the miles he'd traveled during his journey and reasoned *thirty or so miles? That's nothing. It's barely more than a marathon. Time is the only thing that makes it a big deal. Neither Nate nor Britney have time to spare.*

Running in a steady, rhythmic cadence, Jessie leapt over obstacles that lay in his path like a hurdler at a track meet. He'd always been a naturally fit man, and even at his age, he found prolonged cardiovascular workouts to be soothing and rejuvenating, rather than exhausting. Still, thirty miles is two or more days, even at a steady pace. That was two days too long in his book.

Just get to a town, he thought. *Maybe I can find a bicycle or something, but then I'd have to stick to paved roads to make any time. I'm not sure that would work. Something... some opportunity will present itself. I just have to keep my eyes open to see it and take advantage of it. But for now, I run.*

Tripping on a root that lay across his path, Jessie hit the ground hard with a thud, sliding to a stop on his face. "Dammit!" Picking up his hat and dusting himself off, he said aloud, "Keep that up, and you'll hurt your damn fool self. Then where will that leave Nate and Britney? Focus!"

Picking up the pace once again, Jessie heard the spine-chilling sound of the horn that had been haunting them since entering these woods.

Was that for me, or for Nate? he wondered. *Focus! You'll find out one way or another soon enough. Just keep moving.*

~~~~

Nearly dozing off to sleep from fatigue, Nate's eyes immediately opened wide when he heard the sound of the horn echoing through the woods.

Ah, hell! he thought as he picked his rifle up from his lap. Attempting to focus his eyes in the darkness of the night, Nate quickly gave up such a futile effort and pulled the night vision monocular down over his right eye. *I wish I had an IR laser on my gun now,* he mused. *That's what I get for not wanting to deal with the extra weight of all the tacti-cool stuff.*

Hearing the crack of a branch behind him, Nate slowly turned around and surveyed his surroundings for threats.

Quickly conditioning himself to the detail provided by the PVS-14 monocular, he searched for movement.

Whatever that was, it was big and heavy. That wasn't any squirrel or bird.

Hearing what sounded like a large animal pushing through the weeds, he caught a glimpse of something off in the distance. *It's a horse!* he thought as the picture became perfectly clear to him in the green image of the monocular. *There's a rider, too. Damn it.*

With no IR laser, I can't aim with this thing. What the hell do I do? I guess I can only fire when the target is close enough to point aim without the use of my sights.

As Nate watched the horseman closely, the rider appeared from behind a tree to clearly reveal himself through the night vision. It was one of them. A large figure sitting atop the horse, wearing what appeared to be animal fur, along with a hat or headdress made of animal hide as well. The figure held a rifle in one hand and the horse's reins in the other. Around the figure's neck was a horn.

They must use those for communications somehow, he proffered. Seeing the figure turn toward him, it was clear the horseman wore night vision as well.

Crap! Nate thought, ducking down behind the log and out of sight. *If I can see him, he stands a good chance of seeing me as well.*

Remaining below the log, Nate nervously listened as the horse and rider worked their way through the woods. Nate gripped his rifle tightly, playing through his head how he may react if it came down to it, which was something he'd prefer to avoid if at all possible.

If I engage this guy, the others will know where I am. I can't run. I'm a sitting duck. I guess it's best if I just lay low and hope he passes on by.

With the horse and rider now within what seemed to be only twenty yards from his location behind the log, Nate prepared for the worst-case scenario. Just as he began to make his move to pop up above the log to fire, he heard the distant sound of a horn. The horse and rider quickly turned, and in almost an instant, darted off through the woods toward the direction of the horn's blast.

Still holding his rifle tightly, Nate waited and listened, afraid to make a move.

~~~~

Dodging brush and branches as best he could, using only the moonlight to navigate while he ran along the ridgeline of a hill, Jessie heard the familiar sound of hoof beats bearing down on his position.

Turning sharply to his left, Jessie took a leap of faith and began working his way down the steep hillside, one leap and bound at a time. Knowing the rider on horseback couldn't follow him straight down the side of the steep hill, he hoped the move would buy him some time or present him with an opportunity on which to capitalize.

Leaping into the darkness below, Jessie's boots sank down into some soft, muddy soil along the side of the hill where a spring trickled from a small rock slide.

Losing his balance from the unexpected stop, Jessie fell headfirst down the hill, tumbling end over end several times before coming to rest in a large, briar-filled bush.

Them

With his head reeling from the impact, Jessie struggled to regain his bearings, and to his horror, he realized his rifle now lay somewhere behind him on the hillside. Feeling for his Colt, Jessie was relieved to find his faithful old friend still in its well-worn leather holster.

As he slowly and quietly drew the pistol, Jessie found it difficult to move without disturbing the bush with the surrounding thorns having embedded themselves into his clothing, causing the brush to move along with him.

There he comes, he thought as he heard the hoof beats draw near.

Looking around, Jessie realized his tumble had ended on the side of an old, overgrown logging road, giving the horseman easy access to his location.

With the horse closing in on his position, Jessie hoped the horseman's view of him would be obscured by the bush. *Don't move a muscle,* he reminded himself.

As the rider brought the horse to a stop alongside the bush, Jessie knew the rider was searching the hillside in an attempt to locate him. As a cloud drifted by, allowing the moonlight to highlight the silhouette of the rider and horse, Jessie saw a large figure wearing fur, just like the one he'd caught a glimpse of during their pursuit after Britney was taken.

As he stared at the figure, he thought back to his encounter with the boat in the darkness of the cave. *I guess that's what I felt when I tackled the other one. Do they all wear that crap?*

When the figure turned his head, the moonlight exposed the outline of a night-vision monocular of a similar make and model to the one he left behind with Nate.

Do all those bastards have those? Well, that explains their ease of movement through the darkness of the caves.

After he studied the man, he looked down at the horse and realized, *Hank! He's riding Hank!* Excited to see his equine friend, Jessie nearly yelped in excitement, which would have surely given away his position.

Seeing that Hank was getting anxious, Jessie wondered if the horse was beginning to pick up his scent. Just then, the rider began turning Hank, and nudged him away, back in the direction from which they had come. Sliding his Colt carefully back into its holster, Jessie drew his knife from its sheath, and yelled, "Hanky boy!" as he erupted from the bush.

Hank immediately reared up, throwing the rider from his back. Grabbing hold of the man as he fell off Hank's back, Jessie stabbed him repeatedly in the chest until the man's struggles ceased.

Removing the night vision monocular from the man's head, Jessie donned it and looked him over carefully. The man had a thick, black beard, and wore a coat made of what appeared to be the fur of a black bear. The man had also worn a hat that was sourced from a bear. Looking at the hat more closely, he could see that the front of the hat was adorned with a small black bear's muzzle, whiskers and all.

Even the man's boots were wrapped with the fur, claws and all. *That explains the tracks,* he thought. Taking the man's weapon, a sawed-off double-barreled shotgun, Jessie cracked it open to reveal one slug and one load of buckshot. Being fitted with double-triggers, the gun was perfectly suited for a choice between close up shots with the buck, and longer range or penetrating shots with the slug.

Opening the man's fur coat, Jessie found that he was wearing a bandoleer of shotgun shells, which he quickly removed and tossed across his shoulder.

Them

Turning to Hank, who had circled back around, attracted by his owner's familiar voice, Jessie walked up to him and began to scratch him on top of the head, followed by giving him a warm hug, and saying, "That's my boy."

Looking back to the hillside where his rifle lay somewhere in the darkness, and then hearing more hoof beats off in the distance, possibly headed his way, Jessie knew he needed to cut his losses and get moving with his old friend, Hank.

Moving back alongside Hank, Jessie looked at the horse's tack with confusion. "What the hell is this?" he whispered allowed. "A bear skin saddle. Well, it's sort of a saddle. Oh, well," he said as he climbed aboard, nudging Hank into action. The two then galloped off in the opposite direction, away from the approaching threat.

Chapter Ten

Running through the darkness of the caves, chills shot up Britney's spine as she could feel her pursuer gaining ground. Seeing light from the cave's entrance up ahead, she dug down deep and ran with every ounce of effort in her tired, shaky legs.

Just as the light of the outside world seemed to be within reach, her legs felt as if they were beginning to slow. No matter how hard she tried to push ahead, the muscles in her legs seemed as if they had turned to mush. She began to falter and felt the firm grip of her pursuer on her shoulder.

Jerking away, Britney was awakened by her chains when they abruptly stopped her spastic movements and rattled in the darkness from her sudden moves. Screaming with rage as she realized she had merely fallen asleep from exhaustion and was still confined in her own personal hell, Britney gritted her teeth as her heart pounded in her chest.

Her tears were burned as fuel in the fires of rage that now flowed through her veins. She had lost everything. Her family had lost everything that was dear to them. She had lost them, and now these... whoever or whatever they were, had taken her freedom and threatened her very right to live.

Instead of cowering and crying in the darkness, she wanted to wrap the chains that bound her to the floor around the throat of one of her captors and squeeze the wretched life right out of him. She wanted to rip the chains from the floor and lash out at them, whipping them with the very instruments they used to keep her captive.

Them

She'd simply had enough. She had nothing else in this godforsaken world to lose, and she refused to waste her last breath with a whimper; no, it would be a vicious roar.

Startled by her cries of anger, Greg's chains rattled as he stammered the words, "St... stop it. You'll just make them come in here. Please, stop screaming."

With her heart pounding and her chest heaving, she closed her eyes and began to calm herself. Turning toward the sound of Greg's voice in the darkness, she said, "If they come, don't go easy. Don't give them the pleasure of your tears. Don't give them the power they crave by cowering to them. Fight! Fight with everything you have!"

"We're in chains. We can't fight. We can't get away. What are we supposed to do?" he retorted.

"Anything and everything," she contended. "What do you think is going to happen to you when they come that final time?"

"I don't even want to think about it," he whimpered.

"You can surrender your life to them if you want, but I'm going to make them earn whatever it is they plan to do."

"They'll kill you either way," he argued. "They'll just make things worse on you if you struggle and fight."

"So be it. I'd rather die a painful death knowing I made them earn it than to simply have my life end in submission and tears. Submission is why I'm here. It's why my family died. We submitted to those who wielded power over us. Never. Never again. If I never see the sunlight outside of this hell again, at least I'll die knowing I didn't just give up."

"Just wait..." Greg said. "Just wait until you've been down here as long as I have. We'll see how tough and brave you are then. Just wait until you hear my screams. Just wait until they drag me out of here and you're the only one left, knowing you're next. I know I'm next, and it's killing me inside. I just want it to be over. I just want to stop being afraid. I want to stop being hungry. I just want it all to stop."

Laying her head down on the cold, damp rocks beneath her, staring into the dark, empty abyss above, confusion and emotion swept through Britney's body. Was he right? Would she still be so tough when it was her turn? Would she still be able to fuel her anger and rage once she knew they would soon be coming for her?

Shaking the negative thoughts from her head, Britney said a silent prayer that God would allow her to drift off to sleep once again. *But this time, Lord, please, let me dream of my mom and dad. Let me feel like we're together, once again, at least one more time.*

Chapter Eleven

After a long, sleepless night, Nate awoke and stared at the sky. He was just beginning to be able to make out the silhouette of the treetops with his naked eyes. *Hello, morning,* he thought, as a smile came across his face. *I wasn't sure I'd see you again.*

Looking at his wound, Nate could see his leg had become very swollen. *Damn, I'm cold,* he muttered with a shiver as he pulled his coat collar tight around his neck.

Hearing a twig snap out in front of him, Nate's attention was piqued. He focused his eyes with laser-like precision in the direction of the sound. With the sun now cresting the horizon and providing ample light to see his surroundings, Nate slowly and carefully lifted his rifle and held in the direction of the potential threat.

Hearing the rustle of the underbrush, along with another sound of a snapping twig, he clinched his rifle tightly and slowly brought it to bear. Catching movement in his peripheral vision, Nate homed in on it and focused. *Those bastards just aren't gonna leave me alone,* he thought as he mentally readied himself for a fight. *You bastards may get me, but I'm going down swinging.*

With the threat now behind a dense patch of briars and brush, Nate couldn't get a good look, but he could hear it working its way toward his position.

C'mon, you bastards. Get on with it.

There! he thought, and his heart raced with his finger grazing the trigger of his M4. Chuckling and feeling a sense of relief sweep through his body, Nate smiled and lowered his rifle as a large whitetail buck rounded the brush, sifting through the leaves for acorns on the ground.

Hearing him chuckle, the buck froze in its tracks, looking in his direction. Whispering as if he was speaking to the deer, Nate said, "How the heck have you survived this long, boy? I guess those creepy bastards in the cave have kept people from hunting the local area. Hell, maybe that's their plan? Scaring people off to keep the local game and wildlife for themselves, that is. I dunno, but either way, godspeed, ol' boy."

Watching as the buck turned and quickly disappeared into the woods, Nate lay his head back against the tree and looked to the sky, thinking, *with all the ugliness that surrounds us, there is still beauty in the world. Thanks for the subtle reminders of that from time to time. We need that. And I pray I always see them when You show me.*

~~~~

Feeling something brush across his face, Nate awoke in a panic. Swatting at his face and reaching for his rifle, Nate realized it was merely one of the many autumn leaves falling from the trees surrounding him and drifting on the wind. Relaxing at this simple revelation, Nate began to visually search through the treetops for the position of the sun.

I must have dozed off for a while, he thought, noting that the sun was now directly overhead. Feeling his forehead once again, he realized he had been sweating. *It's way too cool out for that.* Looking down at his wound, Nate began to fear his body must be fighting off an infection. He felt shaky and feverish, and his wound also appeared to be a little more swollen than he'd hoped.

Them

Damn, that must have gone deeper than we thought. I've been cut before, but this... this feels different. It feels bad. Really bad.

Looking around, Nate began to think about all the 'what ifs'. *What if Jessie doesn't make it back? The odds aren't in his favor. With the UF pushing this way, and with... 'them' out here in the woods, no doubt looking for us and, well, the cards are stacked against him. I know I'd rather face the UF hunters than these fur-covered bastards any day*, he lamented.

But the worst part is... I'm not in any shape to take on anyone. Laying his head back while looking up through the sway of the trees while they moved with the breeze, Nate couldn't help but think of Peggy and Zack, along with his mother, Judith, and all of the other friends and family he had left behind to go on this mission.

He thought it would just be another hit and run. Another small victory for the Blue Ridge Militia. Another hit and run that would keep the UF busy and out of their hair back home. The more of a ruckus they could cause the UF, drawing them away, and keeping their attention focused elsewhere, the less likely they would be back in their neck of the woods. Take the fight to the enemy, as one would say. Never let them rest. Never let them relax, and all of those other textbook methods of guerilla warfare.

No, ever since the devastation and heartache the UN troops had brought to their quaint little mountain world back in Del Rio and Hot Springs, the last thing the militia wanted was to see a replay of those events. The days of just sitting at home and hoping they'd pass you by were over. Nate and the others in the Blue Ridge Militia were determined to keep the UF on the move elsewhere around the region, all while helping out their fellow citizens as best they could.

And when this mission came up, Nate just couldn't turn it down. He'd imagined what life would be like for Peggy and Zack if they were to be run out of their mountain home and ended up in one of the camps. He couldn't bear the thought. And when he heard of what the UF was doing with the "excess," well, to say his blood boiled was an understatement.

Thinking it all over and looking back through his life, Nate had no regrets. He'd have done it all over again. Every move, every decision. If Peggy and Zack had ended up in the position of Britney and her parents, he'd hope someone, like him, would be willing to risk it all to save them from the horrors of the UF's mass graves.

Lord, if it is Your will to take me here... if it is Your will to end my struggles in these woods, please take care of my family and friends back home. And Lord, please... please take care of Britney. She's gone through enough in this awful world. I'll gladly trade you my soul for hers. Take me, and spare her. Help Jessie on his journey, so that he can bring the help she needs. In Your name I pray, Lord. Amen.

Opening his eyes, Nate looked to the sky as he heard the gut-wrenching sounds of a Mi-24 Hind when it passed overhead at near treetop level. The massive Russian-made helicopter was traveling in an easterly direction. *I wonder where those bastards are going?* he thought. As he contemplated the ramifications of the ominous sight, his worries for Jessie were immediately intensified.

Soon after the helicopter had flown overhead, Nate heard gunshots begin to echo through the woods from a distance. "That's an AK. That's a '74," he whispered, referring to the

Them

venerable AK-74M that had been standard issue for most of the UF troops in the area. He, too, had fought with them on many occasions as supplies or tactics dictated. He was a big fan of the 5.45x39 Russian cartridge they fired, but he didn't want to be on the receiving end of one. The Mujahedeen called it the poison bullet for a reason. It tended to leave wounds that were not easy to deal with.

He could tell from the rhythm of sustained fire, and by the crack and note of each round's report, that it was certainly a '74. "That's not Jessie," he mumbled to himself as he struggled to roll to his side, so he could keep an eye on the direction of the rifle reports. "His .30-30 is distinctive."

He soon began to hear other intermittent shots, not at all similar to the sound of an AK-74. *Who the hell is that?* he thought, and the realization set in that it might very well be the ones from the cave. "Maybe it's them," he mumbled, wondering aloud.

Thinking to himself, trying to make sense of the situation, he pondered, *if they inserted a hunter group nearby to look for Jessie and me, they might be getting more than they bargained for. Those furry bastards don't seem to take to strangers very well.*

Feeling conflicted, Nate wasn't sure exactly who he preferred to win this particular altercation. *If those damn foreign occupiers with the UF take out the... whoever the hell they are, where does that leave me? They'll eventually find me. I guess that's better than dying out here from a fever or dying at the hands of those beasts. At least I'd stand a chance of receiving first aid as a prisoner. What the hell am I thinking? Kill those bastards!*

~~~~

Picking their way along a mountain ridge, Jessie drew back on Hank's reins, saying in a soft, gentle voice, "Whoa, boy." Patting the horse on the neck, Jessie looked through a gap in the trees he'd seen from a distance as a good vantage point.

Seeing a few houses in the valley below, Jessie noted no smoke coming from their chimneys, nor did he see any other immediate signs of habitation.

"Ah, hell. It's probably no use, boy. Even if they're empty, everything has been picked clean by now. Pickin's are gettin' slim for a vagabond and a drifter these days."

Hearing a rotor beat, Jessie looked back as Hank began to shift his feet with anxiety. To Jessie's horror, a Mi-24 Hind was flying up the valley between the two ridges. The helicopter flew right by him at nearly eye level. His heart sank when he realized he and Hank were in a visually exposed position.

Kicking Hank into action, Jessie ran his horse into the cover of the trees and had to make a quick decision as to which side of the ridge they would descend, in an attempt to become lost in the thick forest below.

Although the helicopter had passed him to his right, which was south, he knew that Highway 411 lay to the north. If he opted to descend from the ridge to the north, he'd end up on the UF's main route of travel. Additionally, he'd end up faced with either passing directly through the town of Newport or ascending the very same ridge to pass back to the south to get safely around Newport and in a position to continue toward Highway 25 and eventually, Del Rio.

"C'mon, boy," he said, urging Hank to his right to descend the mountain to the south. "Hopefully, we can get lost in the thick of it."

While they worked their way through the thick Appalachian forest, Jessie could hear the large, twin turbine powered helicopter off in the distance. Concerned as to why they had yet to leave the area, Jessie brushed his feelings aside and pressed on. The clock was ticking for both Nate and Britney, and he knew it. Caution had to take a backseat to timeliness for the next few days of his journey.

Reaching the floor of the valley between the two mountain ridges, Jessie oriented himself, and pondered, "I believe that's Carson Springs, there. I remember it from before the madness in the mountains south of 411 began. Nate and I discussed our possible routes east. I believe if we can skirt around Carson Springs, we'll cross Highway 32, Interstate 40, and then Highway 73. All three of those run north and south, giving us a clear shot to Highway 25 and Del Rio once we're beyond them."

Patting Hank on the neck, Jessie chuckled, saying, "Just talking to you about our plans makes me feel better, even if all you hear is a series of grunts and moans. C'mon, now. Let's get moving," he said as he urged Hank forward.

Arriving at an area that had been extensively logged in previous years before the collapse, on the western side of the valley, Jessie scanned the skies above for threats and then began quickly working Hank through the young trees that were beginning to take hold again in the once thick forest. Feeling visually exposed, he kept Hank's head up and moving, not wanting to let his tired companion slow, potentially allowing them to be spotted.

"C'mon, boy. Being a little tired is better than catching a bullet."

Hearing the helicopter circle back around from the north, Jessie grumbled, "Now what is that bastard doing?"

Reaching a cluster of unharvested trees alongside the dirt logging road left behind by the logging company, Jessie took visual cover in the trees while he watched with horror as the helicopter looked as if it were descending into Carson Springs on the other side of the next ridge.

"Damn it to hell," Jessie grumbled. "C'mon boy. Nate can't afford for us to wait them out. We've gotta get moving and stay moving."

Knowing that once they got underway, he couldn't guarantee the next time he would have the luxury of stopping to water his horse, Jessie dismounted and led Hank over to a small trickling stream that followed the logging road in the bottom of the valley.

Once he and his horse had their fill, Jessie wiped his mouth with his sleeve and walked over to Hank, saying, "We can do this, boy. I know we can," as he put his foot in the stirrup and boosted himself up and over, settling into the saddle for what he knew was an uncertain ride.

Nudging Hank forward, Jessie worked him toward the southern side of Carson Springs. He knew if he had to turn and run, he'd be ultimately blocked by Newport to the north, where the helicopter's allies likely had freedom of movement. To the south, other than a few roads that took people through the area, there wouldn't be anywhere near as many assets for the UF to utilize in his pursuit.

Chapter Twelve

The silence of the hellish cave was broken only by drips of water tracing their way down the cave's ceiling formations, finally breaking free and falling to the floor. Not another sound could be heard. Not even a whimper from Greg beside her.

Britney's mind seemed to wander aimlessly and her concept of time now seemed like a distant memory. With no sunrise, no sunset, and no sounds from the outside world at all, she found the silence of it all disorienting and maddening.

They should have found me by now... if they were coming, that is, she thought as her mind sifted through all the possible scenarios. Even though she had just recently met both Nate and Jessie, and even though their time together was tense and fast-paced, to say the least, she felt as if there was anyone on Earth she could trust to be there for her—to come for her—it was those two men.

As doubt from the hopelessness of her situation began to create conflict in her heart, she thought, *I guess I was just fooling myself. They didn't even know me. Heck, they didn't even know each other. It was just a matter of chance that we were together, nothing more.*

Her thoughts were suddenly interrupted by the ominous echoes of a horn reverberating through the cave.

Hearing Greg begin to cry, she whispered, "Be strong. They may be coming for me. You don't know for sure they're coming for you. It may mean something else."

"No..." he sobbed. "It's time. It's the only rhythm they have. They always go in order. They've never deviated from that. It's time," he cried as panic and fear began to set in.

"Please, no!" he cried out in the darkness. "Not yet! I'm not ready! Please, no! Please, no! No! No! No!"

Hearing movement in the darkness, Britney listened as Greg's chains began to jingle from his uncontrollable shakes. Heavy footsteps could be heard drawing near, making Greg sob uncontrollably from fear, allowing his bowels to evacuate their contents as he began to lose control.

The hair on the back of Britney's neck stood on end as she sensed someone, or something, very close to her. She couldn't see at all in the total darkness, but she knew as certain as anything if she reached out her hand, she would touch one of them in the darkness.

Trying to maintain her composure the best she could, Britney painted a mental image from the sounds around her. She could almost see in her mind how Greg was being taken hold of while he flailed around in sheer panic. Hearing the chains drop to the floor and feet begin to shuffle, she could tell they were carrying him away, and his cries soon faded to echoes in the distance.

How many were there? she thought. *Two, maybe three? They didn't say a word. They didn't make a sound other than the sounds of their feet shuffling on the floor. Why? Why don't they talk? Why don't they seem to communicate at all, yet seem to work in perfect unison?*

Feeling fingers run through her hair in the darkness, Britney flinched and pulled away as chills ran up her spine. Her heart began to race as she realized she wasn't alone. They hadn't all left with Greg like she'd thought.

Curling up into a fetal position, Britney held her eyes shut tightly as she just wanted the moment to pass. Unable to help herself, she stuttered, "Who... who's there?"

Them

Hearing a figure shift around in the darkness, Britney knew she hadn't imagined it. She wasn't alone. But was she ever? Was there always someone, or *something* sitting there in the darkness, watching and listening? Waiting? Britney's mental hell intensified tenfold with that revelation, and with the new unknowns it brought with it.

And now, she was the only one to remain. Greg, based on the accounts he'd given her, would not be returning, and she knew it. The unknown horrors he was about to experience would soon befall her. Try as she might, she attempted to block his screams from her mind to no avail.

~~~~

Being carried through the network of caves by several of their captors, Greg's will to survive intensified with each step they took. Every step was one step closer to his fate, and that was something he was not as ready and willing to accept as he had tried to convince himself.

With his hands and feet still bound, there wasn't much he could do, and add to that his captor's physical strength was far greater than his, especially given his weakened, malnourished state. He wondered what he could do to fight back, hoping an opportunity would present itself.

He flashed back to Britney's previous comments about this very moment, *"You can surrender your life to them if you want, but I'm going to make them earn whatever it is they plan to do. I'd rather die a painful death knowing I made them earn it than to simply have my life end in submission and tears. Submission is why I'm here. It's why my family died. We submitted to those who wielded power over us. Never. Never again. If I never see the sunlight outside of this hell again, at least I'll die knowing I didn't just give up."*

Seeing a glow of light from a chamber up ahead, Greg squinted because it was the first image or light of any kind his eyes had seen since his abduction. He could now see the ominous outline of his captors, two of whom carried him, and two who stood just ahead at the entrance to the chamber that emanated with light.

The only details he could make out were that the two large individuals who were carrying him were covered in fur. As they neared the entrance to the chamber, they both used one of their arms to remove something from their heads.

The two who stood by the entrance of the chamber stepped aside, allowing Greg and those who had retrieved him to enter the room. Once inside, the light was much brighter, giving him his first detailed image inside the cave system.

If not for the situation, he would have found the space to be beautiful and awe-inspiring. An oval fire of red-hot embers glowed in the center of the room, which was oblong shaped and appeared to have been carved by water and time over the millennia. Amazing mineral formations adorned the room. Reflections of the red-hot embers flickered off the walls and formations of the chamber, making it appear to sparkle with a brilliant radiance. It reminded him of a cathedral or something he would have seen in a fantasy movie.

His wonder soon reverted to horror and fear as the two who had carried him lowered him to the floor, and all four of the captors moved close and stood around him. Seeing two more figures join them, he realized that six now stood there, staring down at him.

"Who... who are you?" he stammered. "What do you want?"

Them

Hearing no answer, he noticed one of the figures, who appeared in the faint, flickering light to have the curled horns of a goat or ram coming out of his head, give a signal. A seventh figure Greg had not previously seen appeared from the shadows, and his captors began to release his leg restraints. Attempting to kick, his struggles were quickly overpowered by the figures holding onto his ankles tightly.

Two of them stepped aside to reveal the horrifying sight of the seventh individual, who Greg could now see was carrying a large, two-sided axe.

"Nooooo!" he screamed as he was stripped of his pants and soiled underwear. The two figures holding his ankles spread his legs open, holding him tightly while the seventh figure raised the axe high above his head.

As Greg gazed up at the axe, he saw a glow of light off to his left. Turning his head, he could see that one of the figures carried some sort of metal, scissor-like objects that functioned as grasping mechanisms in each hand. At the end of each device was a glowing, red-hot coal.

While one of the figures held on to his forehead tightly, bearing down on him with great force, the other placed the hot coals onto Greg's eyes, blinding him instantly as the fluid in his eyes flashed to a boil. The intensity of his screams nearly damaged his vocal cords.

The pain was unbearable; at that moment, all of his fight was gone. Greg simply wished to die. He simply wanted to be released from this hell.

With a nod from the one adorned with ram's horns, the seventh figured swung the axe down hard onto Greg's right leg, nearly severing it just below the hip.

Screaming in agony and covered with a splatter of his own blood, Greg felt a level of pain and sensation he had never before felt as nerves fired throughout his body.

Realizing that the blow had failed to sever the leg as intended, the seventh figure raised the axe once again, swinging it hard and missing the original wound by several inches.

Tossing the axe aside, the seventh figure took hold of the leg and began twisting and wrenching on it, attempting to tear it off at the shattered bone.

Feeling the crunching and splitting of the bone, along with the tearing of tissue and tendons as the leg came free from his body, Greg let out one final, blood-curdling scream when they tossed his leg onto the hot coals.

Hearing the sizzle and smelling the aroma of his own cooking flesh, Greg felt a metal object thrust into his mouth, prying open his jaw while breaking several of his lower teeth. A hot coal was then placed into his mouth, silencing his screams as he faded into darkness, expiring from the massive loss of blood and the extreme shock to his system.

Laying on the cave floor, partially dismembered and in a puddle of his own blood, Greg's struggles were finally over.

~~~~

Lying in the darkness of the cave, Britney heard Greg's final, agonizing scream fade away, the echoes of which seemed to live on throughout the vast network of underground tunnels and chambers for several minutes.

She conceded in her mind that he'd been right about what would come next. She was unaware of the hellish events that had taken place in Greg's last few moments of life, but the one thing she did know for a fact, the only thing she was certain about—was that she was next.

Chapter Thirteen

As Nate lay listening to the fierce gun battle in the distance, he noticed the shots beginning to subside. Once the guns fell silent, the woods became eerily quiet. No birds could be heard singing. No squirrels could be heard barking. There were no sounds at all, save for the gentle breeze swaying the trees, setting free a few more of fall's dying leaves.

After a few minutes of total silence, Nate could hear a disturbance to his left. It sounded as if a large animal was crashing through the woods with reckless abandon.

Listening carefully, he could make out the rhythm of the movement to be human. His heart began to race, and his muscles tightened with anxiety. He could feel the throb of each beat of his heart in the pain of his wound as his blood pressure increased.

Slowly reaching for his rifle in an attempt to not move too quickly, thus giving away his position, Nate began to raise the weapon when a UF soldier crashed through the brush, nearly tripping and falling directly in front of him.

Nate aimed his rifle at the soldier, flipped off the safety, and prepared to fire. The UF soldier caught a glimpse of Nate out of the corner of his eye and swung his rifle to meet the threat Nate imposed.

Squeezing the trigger, Nate's M4 gave the horrifying 'click' of the hammer falling on the firing pin, without the accompanying crack of the rifle's report. When Nate reached for the charging handle with his left hand to rack the rifle in a desperate attempt to clear the malfunction, the soldier aimed his rifle directly at him and gestured for him to lower his weapon.

Them

Reluctantly, Nate lowered his M4 and laid it across his lap with the barrel pointing away from the soldier. The soldier looked back toward the direction from which he'd come, looked down at Nate's leg, and then lowered his own rifle. With a nod to Nate, showing his respect, the man disappeared into the woods as quickly as he had arrived.

Laying his head back against the log, Nate breathed deeply and his heart rate began to slow. His moment to relax was soon over, however, when another figure burst out of the woods. This time, it was one of them—one of the mysterious people from the cave who had taken Britney.

Nate's heart sank in his chest when he realized he had yet to clear his malfunction. *Shit!* he thought to himself as the figure bounded past him, in obvious pursuit of the UF soldier.

Nate's heart skipped a beat at the sight of the individual. It was a large man, wearing what appeared to be animal hides from head to toe, including his boots. The man ran like a beast, stealthily leaping over downed branches and foliage with precision. He created only half the sound making his way through the woods as the UF soldier. He moved with the stealth of an animal.

Although he got a good look at the figure's attire, Nate was unable to see his face because his head was also adorned with some sort of animal-hide hat that covered around the sides, leaving only the front open.

As the beastly man disappeared into the woods, Nate lay silent. He desperately wanted to clear his weapon of its malfunction, but didn't want to give away his position with any unnecessary movement or the sounds of working the rifle's bolt in the event there were other pursuers nearby.

After waiting what seemed like an eternity, Nate was finally confident no other pursuers were behind the solder, at least not from his direction. He gently picked the rifle up and eased the charging handle back, ejecting a round.

He slowly released the bolt, watching as it picked up another brass-cased 5.56 NATO round from the magazine and pushed it into the chamber. He tapped the forward assist to ensure that the bolt was fully in battery, then reached to his side to pick up the ejected round.

Rolling the cartridge around in his fingers, Nate inspected it to see the dent of a good, solid firing-pin strike on the primer. *A dud,* he noted.

Smiling, he looked up through the treetops to the sky above and whispered, "Thanks. If this had gone off, they'd have found me for sure."

~~~~

After having worked his way through the lowest lying areas of the surrounding terrain, Jessie reined back on Hank and said to himself, "It's uphill for a bit, but at least it's into some evergreens where we'll get some visual cover from above."

Nudging Hank forward, Jessie picked his way through the increasingly tighter squeeze between the trees. "At least the fallen pine needles keep the underbrush down."

Realizing he couldn't continue to stay in the saddle since the low hanging branches were getting too tight, Jessie swung his leg over Hank's back and dismounted. "I'm guessing you needed a break, anyway. Huh, boy?" Jessie said as he began leading Hank by his reins.

Catching movement up ahead in his peripheral vision, Jessie focused on the area, only to see a glint of light from between the trees. Jessie tossed Hank's roper-style reins over the saddle horn, smacked him on the rump, and yelled, "Git!" sending Hank darting off into the woods just as a round from a high-powered rifle came smashing into the trunk of a tree next to Jessie's head.

Feeling the bits of wood and bark debris slam against the side of his face from the impact, Jessie winced and turned to run into the thickest area of trees in his vicinity. Several more shots were fired in rapid succession as he dodged and weaved, before leaping into a dry rainwater washout for cover.

Being approximately three-feet deep, the washed-out ravine provided Jessie with adequate cover while he surveyed the scene, trying to determine just how many threats there might be lurking in the woods ahead and around him.

Several more shots rang out, and Jessie had an eerie feeling they were intended to keep his attention focused and his head down while other threats moved in closer to him.

If those are the UF hunters, those bastards are probably working as a pack, moving in on my flanks and six, while their buddy there keeps me pinned down.

Well, I know where he is, and I know he can't hit me for now, Jessie thought, turning his attention to his other vulnerabilities. Looking down the ravine in the direction where the water that had carved it would be flowing if it were raining, Jessie thought, *That's my only way out of here using cover, but they probably realize that, too.*

Catching him completely off guard, Jessie heard the heavy pounding of boots from a man running toward him on his right flank. Raising the shotgun in the direction of the threat, Jessie saw a soldier enter his view through the thickly-wooded evergreen forest. The man was drawing his arm back as if preparing to throw something Jessie's way.

Grenade! Jessie thought as he let the barrel containing the buckshot load fly, striking the man directly in the chest, taking him completely off his feet and knocking him backward as a red mist of blood appeared around him on impact.

Jessie then ducked down in the ravine as the concussion grenade erupted where the man he'd shot had fallen.

Hearing more footfalls now from directly behind him, Jessie raised up and swung around, firing the remaining barrel containing the slug. Missing his target, Jessie released his grip on the shotgun, letting it fall to the ground while he drew his trusty Colt revolver. Just as he aligned the barrel of the pistol with the man, he could see the man was aiming squarely at him with an AK-74.

Upon realization that the man's rifle was bearing down on him, Jessie prepared for a flash from the man's muzzle as his brain transmitted the signal to his finger to pull the trigger on the Colt. This split second felt to Jessie as if it was all moving in slow motion. The entire world around him had slowed down to a crawl.

Just as the man's rifle discharged and a flash of light emanated from the man's muzzle break, Jessie's Colt discharged mere fractions of a second later, sending a recoil impulse into his wrist as he waited for the bullet to strike.

Seeing the man twist to his side and begin to fall to the ground, Jessie felt a searing burn on the side of his face as he, too, fell backward. As he impacted the ground, now lying flat on his back, Jessie realized more gunfire was erupting around him. This wasn't the continuation of an attack on his position, however. The men attacking him were now being engaged from other positions in the woods.

Reaching up to his face with his left hand, Jessie felt the warm, wetness of blood. Working his jaw and neck to ensure he was still functional, Jessie sat up in the ravine and picked up the shotgun.

Breaking the shotgun open and ejecting the two spent shells, he immediately pulled two more from the bandoleer with his right hand, shoved them into the barrels, and slammed it closed, ready to rejoin the fight.

Jessie raised himself up to scan the area for targets of opportunity as the gunfire ceased. The violent struggle that had seemed in Jessie's mind to be occurring in slow motion was now over, having taken place in a span of mere seconds. As his world began to return to focus, Jessie heard unfamiliar voices.

"Clear!"

"Clear here, too!"

"They're all down!" he heard in the woods from virtually all directions.

Turning their attention to him, a voice with a distinctly southern accent called out, "Show yourself! You, in the trench, show yourself!"

Taking a leap of faith that the cavalry had arrived, hoping it was not merely another group of marauders, Jessie stood and held the shotgun out to the side, keeping it in plain view.

"Drop it!" the voice said.

Doing as he was asked, Jessie carefully tossed the weapon aside with the muzzle pointing away from him.

"Hands where we can see them!" the voice called out.

Once again complying with the orders, Jessie raised his hands above his head to see several figures appear from behind the trees in the woods in front of him. He could also hear movement behind him, confirming that he was, indeed, surrounded.

Jessie looked the men over carefully. There was no consistent uniform or method of dress. Each man wore a hodgepodge of camouflage clothing, ranging from old-school woodland BDU's to German Flecktarn, and even the more modern Multi-Cam and Scorpion patterns. Each man had a day pack of one form or another on his back as well, and wore face paint in various colors to aid in concealment.

The only common trait the men seemed to have was they were carrying M4 carbines as their primary weapon, along with load-bearing vests that were well-stocked with fully loaded thirty-round magazines.

"Come on up out of there where we can see you!" the man who seemed to be in charge ordered.

Walking up the sides of the ravine, Jessie stumbled and nearly fell, catching his balance just before tumbling back into the washout. Seeing the men flinch and ready their weapons, he carefully continued up and out of the ravine, standing still and quiet once at the top.

"Name?" asked the man taking charge, who appeared to be in his mid-forties, wearing mostly Flecktarn.

"Jessie," he said, looking the man directly in the eye.

"Jessie, what?"

"Jessie Townsend."

"How did you end up in a tangle with the UF?"

Looking around, Jessie asked, "Who are you with?"

"Don't make me repeat my question," the man said.

Pausing, Jessie thought out his answer carefully, and said, "I ran across a few people in trouble. I helped them, and they've been on us ever since."

Seeing the two men standing directly in front of him look to each other, the man asking the questions turned back to Jessie, and asked, "Who were they? Who were these people you helped?"

"Who are you with?" Jessie again asked.

Seeing the man's patience begin to grow thin, Jessie added, "Look, we all seem to be on the same side of the fence regarding those occupying foreign bastards, so let's stop treating each other like the enemy for a moment."

"All right, I'll level with you if you level with me," the man conceded. "We're looking for some friends of ours. They went out and didn't come back as expected. We're wondering if those were the people you helped."

"It was a man and a teenaged girl," Jessie said, seeing a look of disappointment on the men's faces.

Taking it a step farther, feeling he just might be among friends, Jessie added, "The man had just rescued the girl from the UF."

Jessie could see that statement rang a bell with the men.

"What was his name?" the man asked.

Thinking it over for a minute, and knowing how careful Nate was about revealing his identity to him, Jessie countered by saying, "How far are we from Del Rio?"

"What?" the man replied with both confusion and piqued interest.

"The man I was helping told me to head to Del Rio for help."

"Look, mister," the man said, "I can see you're playing it safe by not wanting to give out any more information than you have to. We get it. But we need you to answer our questions. Who were you helping, and where are they now? Tell us what we need to know, and we'll help you get that cut on your face properly dressed, and you can be on your way."

Seeing concern on the man's face rather than rage, Jessie took a chance. "Nate. His name is Nate."

"Is? Is he still alive?"

"Do you know him?" Jessie asked.

"We may. Now, please, tell us if he's okay and where he's at. Were there others from his group somewhere?"

"I gave you his first name. Now, you give me his last name, and we'll go from there," Jessie countered.

"It starts with an H. His last name starts with an H. That's as far as we're gonna go, not knowing who exactly we're dealing with. Now, tell us where he is and if there were others. Nate is a friend of ours, and so were the other men he was working with. They didn't return when expected, and we're out here to find them. Those UF hunters you encountered were probably looking for them. It was a stroke of luck for us that their attention was on you, which allowed us to move in undetected and engage them while their attention was focused elsewhere."

"Lower your weapons and let's move out of this area before any friends of theirs come looking for them. I'll tell you everything you need to know along the way."

"Along the way to where?" the man asked.

"To Nate, of course," Jessie replied.

Looking Jessie over, the man turned to two of his companions and said, "Search the hunters for anything of use. Get this guy a '74, too. There's only so much he can do with that old shotgun."

Chapter Fourteen

Lying there in the darkness of her subterranean prison, Britney longed for the ability to sleep. She longed for the ability to make her mind stop running through all of the possible horrors that lay ahead of her.

Feeling a breath on her cheek, she flinched, only to feel something brush up against her and quickly move away. Her heart raced as she once again knew she wasn't alone. Was it toying with her? Was it trying to scare her? Or was it interested in her in some other way?

Her thoughts were interrupted by the terrifying blast of the horn used by her captors, and the eerie echoes that reverberated throughout the cave system that followed.

She could hear the figure in the darkness move away toward the entrance to the chamber. Something was different this time. The horn blast came from a different direction than it had when they had come for Greg. It also had a slightly different tone and duration. *Are they communicating with those things?* she wondered.

She waited silently for something to happen, but nothing came. The last time the horn blew, they had arrived quickly to carry Greg away. She assumed this was a good sign, and that the horn didn't mean what it had previously. She had heard the horn blow from that direction before, and nothing had ever happened. Perhaps nothing would happen this time?

She began to hear movement in the distance, somewhere along one of the passages of the cave system. She could hear the rattle of chains and the sounds of heavy footfalls getting closer. Her nerves were on edge, and her senses were heightened to the max as she attempted to paint a picture of what was going on around her with sound alone.

The noise of a scuffle entered the chamber as the sounds approached her. Stopping just short, a thud and the rattle of chains impacting the ground next to her, followed by a moan from a voice that was clearly winded from the impact.

They've got someone else, she thought. *Is it Nate or Jessie? Oh, God, please don't let it be. They don't deserve this. They're only in this mess to help me.*

Once the figures that had carried the new arrival into the room had apparently left, Britney said into the darkness, "Who's there?"

Startled, the voice replied in Russian, "какие," or "what?"

Understanding bits of Russian from her time in the camps with Russian guards, she said, "это нормально," which means, "It's okay." "Do you speak English?" she asked.

"A little," she heard the answer in a choppy accent.

"My name is Britney," she said.

"Yuri," the voice in the darkness replied.

"Are you UF?" she asked.

Pausing, the voice answered, "No concern of yours."

"Well, we're down here together facing the same fate, so what does it matter, now?"

"Fate? What fate?"

Britney explained to Yuri all she knew from her time in captivity in the caves. She explained the horrors Greg had passed along to her, as well as the horrific screams of agony he had made once he was finally carried away.

She listened for a response, but Yuri remained silent.

Them

"Since you won't tell me, I'm gonna go ahead and assume you're UF. Do you have comrades out there looking for you?" she asked.

Yuri again remained silent.

"Look," she protested, "I'm not trying to get some sort of military intelligence out of you. I have an interest because I want to know if there is a chance of your friends finding us before they come for me. I just want a glimmer of hope. That's all. So, stop it with the stonewalling and talk to me."

After a brief pause, Yuri said, "Whoever are these monsters... they killed team I operated with. I am sole survivor."

With that revelation, Britney's hopes for a rescue were dashed. Even though the UF were her enemy, and had proven themselves to be time and time again, including their role in the murder of her parents, she had at least hoped she'd be taken once again as a prisoner of the UF and freed from her underground hell.

Yuri could hear her begin to cry in the darkness. "Why you cry?" he asked.

Regaining her composure, she replied, "That's a pretty stupid question."

After a few minutes of awkward silence, she said, "Just so you know, your friends killed my parents. They took a busload of us to a mass grave and began shooting at us, killing everyone but me. You occupiers are not just invaders, you're murderers. Cold-blooded murderers. You deserve to be down here. You deserve this fate."

"No... No, that not true," Yuri protested. "We are here to restore peace!"

"Oh, yeah, then what were you doing in these woods? You were looking for us, weren't you?"

"Was looking for insurgents," he replied. "Insurgents that attacked bus."

"You can't really be that naïve... can you?"

Hearing no response, she continued, "If you're not that naïve, you're obviously that stupid, or you willfully accept the lies you're told to help you sleep at night."

"No! These words you say are not true! We are here to restore peace!"

"Whatever," she retorted, "And now you're here with me... and him."

"Him?" Yuri asked, confused by her statement. "Who is... him?"

"The one in the darkness that doesn't make a sound. We're not alone in here. I doubt we ever are."

Chapter Fifteen

Once clear of the ambush site, Jessie and the others stopped for a water break after traveling east on foot for about twenty minutes. "Tell me everything," the man who had been questioning him asked.

"Before we get into the details, how about some proper introductions?" Jessie suggested. "You all know my name."

"I'm Q," the man in Flecktarn declared. "It's short for Quentin. This gentleman is Carl," he said, gesturing to the man to his right in Multi-Cam. "The gentleman with the big ol'.45-70 lever-gun is Daryl," Q said as Daryl nodded, tipping his floppy brown leather frontiersman-style hat to Jessie.

Turning to a short, stocky, bearded man in Scorpion Camo, Q said, "This human brick wall is Sam." Turning to his six-foot-tall African-American counterpart, he added, "and this formidable fellow is Tyrone."

"Pleased to meet you all," Jessie said with a nod.

Looking Jessie squarely in the eye, Q insisted, "Now, please, tell us what you know."

Jessie explained to them how he had been traveling east when he stumbled across Nate and Britney, who were being pursued by the UF. He then explained how the trio was traveling together when they were pushed south into the mountains below Highway 411, and how they had encountered the strange, animal-hide-clad individuals and how the beasts had taken Britney. He explained in great detail his and Nate's foray into the cave, and how he had to leave Nate behind to seek help.

Retrieving a topographical map from his jacket pocket, Q unfolded it and mumbled, "Let's see. Okay, Dandridge is here... oh, yes, here is 411. So, you were in this general area?" he asked.

Nodding in agreement, Jessie explained, "Yeah. And we traveled to this area here when our encounters with, um, *them*, occurred."

"Do you think you can find it in the dark?" Q asked, looking at the sun's position in the sky. "We can't get that far on foot with the remaining daylight. We'll have to push hard into the night."

"Yeah. Yeah, sure. I traveled in the dark all night last night. It's the only way I know the area between here and there. But speaking of traveling on foot, did any of you see a dun horse running away from the gunfight? I was leading my horse on foot when those bastards ambushed me. I sent him running to keep him safe."

Looking around, Q asked, "Anyone see a horse?"

Seeing them all shake their heads no, Jessie sighed and said, "Well, let's get going. Nate's been a sitting duck for far too long now.

"Do you guys have night vision?" Jessie asked. "Because those bastards do. It's how they move so well in the darkness of the caves. It's awfully damn hard to work your way through a cave with torches and flares illuminating your position when your opponents can move without being seen."

"So, you're telling me these guys dress up like some sort of cavemen, but use high-tech night vision?" Q asked with a confused look on his face.

"I'm afraid so," Jessie confirmed. "Which also means they'll have it in the dark of the woods, too."

Them

"We've got a hand-held thermal. It's really more of a game tracker than anything else. We're lucky to stay supplied in ammo and weapons. Having night vision for all our guys just isn't workable given our suppressed supply chain." Looking around while he gathered his thoughts, Q asked again, "So, you're sure they all have night vision?"

"We took a PVS-14 from one of them in the cave. I left that one with Nate. While working my way east to find help, I encountered a few more of the bastards; one of which was riding Hank, my horse. I took him down, with Hank's help, of course. He wore a head-mounted PVS-14 like the others."

"The good stuff," Q replied.

"Yep."

"Where's that unit? The one you took from the guy on your horse?" Q asked.

"Unfortunately, it's lashed to the makeshift saddle on Hank's back, which is now running around in the woods somewhere."

Thinking things over for a minute, Q said, "Well, if Nate's in as bad a shape as you said, we can't waste any more time. We'll just have to risk bumping into those freaks in the dark."

Turning and looking to Sam, Daryl, Tyrone, and Carl, Q asked, "Are you guys good with that?"

"Hell, yeah!" Tyrone replied. "I can't stand the thought of Nate sitting out there in the woods alone with those... whoever they are, looking for him."

"That, and the clock is ticking on his injuries," Sam added.

"Let's get to it," Daryl said with eagerness in his voice.

"Alright, then," Q announced, as he turned and began walking due west, "No need to chat about it any further. Off we go!"

~~~~

Awakened by little Zack climbing into bed with him and his wife, Peggy, Nate rolled over, snuggling up next to her. Reaching his arm around her with a yawn, he said, "Well, I guess it's time to get up. I've got a big day ahead of me. I'm supposed to help Evan with that cellar he's working on."

Mumbling, Peggy protested, "No, don't get up yet. Snuggle with Zack and me for just a little while longer."

"How can I resist an offer like that?" he murmured with a smile, cuddling up next to her.

Awakened by the bone-chilling sound of coyotes howling in his vicinity, Nate sat up quickly, causing his head to spin. Feeling the throbbing pain in his leg, Nate mumbled, "Ah, damn it to hell. Oh, how I wish I was still in that dream right now."

As his mind began to clear, Nate looked around and realized it was completely dark. *How long was I out?* he wondered. *Wait, were those coyotes? Ah, hell. Those mongrels must have picked up the scent of my wound on the breeze.*

Thinking things through, he knew if he had to take a shot at one, he'd simply be trading coyotes for their furry two-legged foes. *I'm not sure which is worse,* Nate pondered.

Pulling the headband of the night vision monocular onto his head, Nate positioned the PVS14 in front of his right eye and switched the unit on. Speaking aloud, hoping to scare away his four-legged foe, Nate said, "I bet you song dogs think I can't see in the dark, don't ya? Well, I've got a surprise for your flea-bitten asses. Now, git!" he barked aggressively.

He listened intently, hoping to hear the sound of retreating paws, but the woods were eerily silent. Even the insects and crawly critters of the night seemed to be afraid to make a sound or a move.

Hearing a twig break behind him, Nate smacked a log with a stick he had picked up off the ground, and said once again in a controlled voice, "Git! Damn you!" trying not to be too loud.

Hearing chatter between several of the coyotes in the darkness to his left flank, Nate wondered what exactly it was the dogs were planning. He'd seen their handiwork with the flock of sheep back at the homesteads more than enough to know how well they hunted as a pack. If they were letting you know they were there, it was for a reason.

Scanning the area with his night vision, Nate rolled over onto his left hip to try to see over the log behind him, just in time to catch a glimpse of movement. "You bastards ain't as sneaky as you think. I see you out there. Now, git!" he snarled. "Git before I skin you and make hats out of you! Go on, git!"

One thing Nate knew for certain was the fact that the coyotes back at the homesteads seemed to always know when an animal was injured or lame. They seemed to target the weak, and right at this moment, that was him. They could probably smell the blood and the condition of his wound from miles away.

Although they'd rarely targeted humans in the past, this new world, where unrestricted subsistence hunting had taken its toll on the coyote's regular food supply, had altered the previous norms. Coyote encounters with humans had been on the rise, and given his injured state and the aroma of fresh blood and of his wound, well, they may not pass on the opportunity for a meal.

Thinking of all his options, Nate knew he couldn't continue portraying himself as prey. He had to be a fellow predator. Reaching up and taking hold of a low hanging tree branch, Nate pulled himself upward in an attempt to stand. Pushing with his injured leg sent a searing, burning pain shooting throughout his body. "Holy hell. Grrrrrr aaahhhhh, damn it, that hurts!" he grunted while biting his lip to keep from screaming aloud. Finally getting up onto his prosthetic leg, Nate attempted to stabilize his balance with the tree branch. The pain in his leg was almost too much to bear, but he knew the pain of coyote teeth tearing into his guts while he was still alive would be even worse. He had seen their handiwork enough to do anything it took to avoid falling prey to those filthy beasts.

"I ain't goin' down like that, you damn dogs!" he shouted.

Listening, he could hear spurts of movement all around him. He knew he had been completely surrounded by them while he was asleep, and he also knew the fact they weren't retreating based on his obvious awareness of them was proof an attack was coming soon.

Mustering up every ounce of strength that remained in his body, he slung his rifle around his neck and began pulling himself up into the branches with his upper body strength alone. Feeling the futility of his efforts, Nate took his M4 and hung it by the sling on the broken stub of a branch, and then commenced pulling himself up into the tree, free from the added weight of the weapon.

Hearing snarls in the darkness as the dogs advanced toward him, Nate pulled hand over hand, lifting himself into the dense, and tightly-spaced branches of the pine tree.

Working feverishly to get himself high enough into the tree to be out of reach of the pack of hungry coyotes, Nate felt the crushing jaws of a coyote clamp onto his boot. The dog immediately began thrashing from side to side, in an effort to shake his grip and bring him down from the tree. Swinging his leg and slamming the dog against the trunk of the tree, Nate's rifle was knocked loose from its precarious perch, falling to the ground and out of his reach.

The impact against the tree forced the dog loosened its grip and it fell to the ground. Nate seized the opportunity and reached up to the next branch to pull himself higher into the tree. Just as he began to lift his body upward, he felt another set of teeth clamp onto the back of his thigh, while a second dog grabbed hold of his boot tied securely to his prosthesis.

With the weight of both dogs pulling down while they thrashed about, Nate felt his grip begin to fade, but his prosthetic leg came loose and fell to the ground, taking the dog with it.

Still feeling the crushing, tearing bite of the other coyote latched to his leg, Nate locked his elbow around a tree branch and reached for his knife, drawing it from its sheath. Slashing at the dog, Nate made contact with its face over and over, trying his best to dissuade the dog from continuing its assault.

With a yelp, the dog released its bite and fell to the ground as Nate heaved upward, pulling himself safely out of reach.

Momentarily pausing his climb to rest his shaky arms, Nate looked down with his night vision to see the wounded dog writhing around on the ground in pain. *Yikes, it looks like I got that little bastard good.*

After a few minutes, the rest of the pack moved in closer to the tree, only now, instead of focusing on Nate above them, they seemed to have turned their attention to their wounded pack mate.

When one of the dogs snarled, exposing its teeth, the rest of the dogs followed its lead and began moving in on their wounded pack mate. Once they were within reach, the alpha male leapt onto the injured, blood-soaked animal, with the rest of the pack following suit.

Nate watched in horror as the dogs tore into their pack mate, eating it alive, tearing into its soft belly for the rich tasting fats, intestines, and organs.

That could have just as easily been me, he thought while he stared in revulsion at the gruesome scene.

Chapter Sixteen

"How long?" Yuri asked. "How long have you been in cave?"

"I... I don't know. Maybe a few days?" Britney replied. "I've lost track of time. With no sunset or sunrise, it all blurs together."

"Is one with us, now?" he asked.

"Probably. I don't get how they do it, but they can move very quietly, and without any light at all. They seem to be at home down here."

"I see nothing," he complained.

"Yeah, me neither," Britney agreed. Wanting to break the eerie silence and her haunting thoughts, she asked, "So, where are you from, Yuri?"

"I am with UF."

"That's not where you're from. That's who you're with, now. Where did you grow up? You sound like you're from Russia or something like that."

"I am from Ukraine," he replied. "I was raised by grandmother and lived with her most of life, until joining military."

"What was her name?" Britney asked with genuine curiosity, glad to engage in what seemed to be the beginnings of regular, human interaction.

"Why you ask these things?" Yuri asked. "Why this matter?"

Pausing, Britney said, "I'd much rather spend my time getting to know you than thinking about what's going to happen next. If I just sit here in the darkness, I feel all alone. I think about the horrors I've seen over the last few days. I see my parents being murdered by your friends and hear the screams of

Greg and the other boy echoing through my mind. I... I just don't want to feel alone anymore."

Unsure how to answer, Yuri muttered, "I not join UF. I sent here from my country to work with UN as part of Security Council decree. They put us in UF. We have no way home. We have to stay. We have to serve. They tell us we keep peace and stop insurgents who kill and murder innocent people."

"I'm sorry, Yuri, but it's the other way around. The UF does the killing of the innocents."

"I not see what you see. Only know what I am told," he contended. "The same as most soldiers. Soldiers are told why enemy is bad, then they fight. We do not have luxury of choosing enemy."

After a brief, awkward silence and wanting to change the subject, she asked, "What was her name?"

"Whose name?"

"Your grandmother, silly."

"Her name was Zhanna. My parents died when I was very young. Father went off to fight in Afghanistan. He never come home. My mother was told he died fighting in Kumar Province."

"What happened to your mother?"

"I was still very young. After father dies, mother went off to find work in coal and steel town of Makiivka in Ukraine. She wrote letters saying she would send money home. But never did. She stopped writing soon after. We never find out what happened. Grandmother told me she must have died because mother would not have abandoned us. Makiivka was not good place for young woman. If she not die, probably other bad things happen."

"How old you are?" he wondered. "You sound very young."

"I'm fourteen," she answered.

"Very mature for such young girl," he replied.

"I've had to grow up quickly since it all started falling apart."

"Where you from?" Yuri asked.

"My parents and I were from the Nashville area, which was hit pretty hard during the beginning of the attacks. We've been on the move pretty much since the beginning."

"Ah, music city," he said. "I like your music."

"It used to be," she muttered.

Hearing movement on the far side of the chamber, behind Britney, Yuri asked, "You make noise?"

"No," she whispered.

With the reminder they were not alone, their conversation gave way to silence as both Britney and Yuri listened intently for their watcher. Hearing something slip across the chamber in the darkness, they both wondered if it had left, or had merely changed positions to keep them fearing the unknown of the darkness.

While Yuri lay there chained to the floor, he thought of the suffering he'd seen and experienced in his life. He also reflected on the suffering he'd seen inflicted by governments, using him and his comrades in arms as the source of the pain.

I deserve this, he thought, acknowledging his sins against his fellow man in the name of following orders. *But she does not.*

~~~~

After several hours of silence had passed, Britney could hear movement coming from Yuri's location. The movement was very slight, as if he was trying to conceal his actions.

Hearing their watcher shift across the room, she whispered, "Stop it. They can see you."

The hairs on the back of her neck began to stand on end. She could almost sense that the figure in the darkness was on the move. She felt its presence. Her body tensed up as she felt as if the figure was hovering over her.

With the feeling of the dark, evil presence moving from her, she heard something whistle through the air, followed by the sound of a thump and Yuri yelping.

"What's happening?" she asked. The sounds of a struggle intensified with several grunts and Yuri's chains thrashing about.

She could hear someone choking and gasping for air. The sounds of the struggle began to slow until there was one final release of air, and then silence.

Fearing that Yuri had been killed by their watcher, Britney balled up into the fetal position and began to pray for deliverance from her hell when a hand grasped her.

Recoiling in fear, she heard a familiar voice whisper, "Shhhh. Is okay. Hold still."

Opening her eyes, she saw a momentary and faint outline of Yuri's face in the glow of green light as he donned a night vision monocular he had taken from their watcher during the struggle.

"Hold still. I free you," Yuri said as he worked feverishly on Britney's restraints. Whispering, he explained, "They use night vision to move so well in darkness. I take. Now, I use it."

"Is he...?"

"Yes, this one is dead. Now, we must go before others come."

Feeling the chains fall free from her ankles, Britney sat up while Yuri worked on her wrist restraints. Whispering softly, she asked, "How did you do it? How did you get free?"

Them

"Much training," he replied. "This not first time I find myself in captivity. We prepare for such things. Things do not go well for us when captured by insurgents."

Gently removing the restraints from her wrists, Yuri took her by the hand and helped her to her feet. Her legs were shaky from her prolonged malnourishment, and her muscles and joints were achy from being on the cold, hard, uneven rock surface since her captivity had begun.

Her heart raced as Yuri began leading her through the darkness of the chamber and toward one of the cave tunnels.

"Walk carefully," he said, noting the uneven surface of the cave floor.

Yuri's escape seemed too good to be true. Was this really happening? Was she simply dreaming? Her mind raced as she wondered if Yuri had been an unlikely answer to her prayers.

Nearly tripping on a rock formation beneath her feet, she snapped back into the moment and focused with renewed resolve to do whatever it took to escape this living hell, and to see the light of day once again.

Chapter Seventeen

Working their way through the woods at a relentless pace, the six men of the group, which included Jessie, Q, Sam, Carl, Tyrone, and Daryl, pressed on despite their fatigue.

"How long before sunrise?" Sam asked, breaking the group's silence.

Reflecting the moonlight off his faithful old wind-up watch, Q responded, "About three and a half hours." Turning to Jessie, he asked, "How much farther?"

Thinking things over for a moment, Jessie said, "There's a valley between this ridge and the one to our north. Nate is on the northern side of the next ridge, down near the base of the mountain. We can either cut through the valley and up and over the next ridge, or we can stay on this ridge, which eventually meets up with the other where they form a box canyon. We can then cross over and descend, without having to descend and ascend an extra time. I think that would be best for our making good time.

"I've not been on that route beyond this. I had previously worked my way through the valley with Hank. It's a lot darker down there, though, with the moonlight being obscured by the terrain in many places."

"If you're sure you can get us there without having to make those extra climbs and descents, I think that would be the best way to go. If we're dealing with night-vision-equipped threats, I'd prefer to have all the moonlight we can."

"Agreed," interjected Sam. "Jessie," he asked, "How much longer until we're there?"

"Two hours, maybe three. If we can keep up the pace, that is," he answered.

"I'm good," offered Tyrone. "Let's push on."

"I need the exercise, anyway," added Daryl. "Having Linda's horses at my disposal back home is making me lazy."

"It looks like her cooking is taking its toll, too," teased Carl, gesturing to Daryl's belly.

"She won't let me starve to death, that's for sure," Daryl chuckled.

Speaking up, Q said, "Well, if no one needs to rest, let's push on. Since we know what we're up against, let's move forward as a proper patrol." Turning to Jessie, he suggested, "You know the way and are familiar with who we're up against, so if you wouldn't mind taking point?

"Of course," Jessie quickly agreed.

"Here," Q offered while reaching out his hand. "Take this. It's the FLIR thermal game tracker. Scan the area as you go. There's no reason to stumble into something avoidable."

"Sam, you bring up the rear. Keep back a little farther than normal. Make sure you occasionally hold your position and observe. Keep an eye out for the possible movement of those creepy bastards, then bound ahead and catch up. We'll rotate through the rear position when you need a break to ensure the man in that position stays as fresh as possible, since we'll be moving at a pretty good pace. When you bound forward, make yourself known via our standard protocol.

"We'll distribute our three radios between Jessie at point, me in the center of the patrol, and the other with Sam or whoever ends up in the rear after rotations.

"Maintain silence, using vibrate patterns to check in when prompted by two vibes from me. If you feel the need to request the status of the rest of us, use your own position identifier. Jessie, you're the point man, so you're first in the column. That makes you one pulse. I'm two pulses, being the second radio back, and Sam is three pulses. Transmit your vibes by order of point, center, and rear to eliminate confusion.

"If you need to report something verbally, vibe in with five pulses and wait for a verbal 'go' from me. We don't want anyone speaking up when someone else may be in a potential contact situation. Understood?" Q asked, ensuring Jessie was familiar with their standard patrol comms procedures.

"Simple enough," Jessie replied with a nod.

"If we seem a bit non-standard to the tactics and procedures you may have seen in your past, it's because we aren't following some published field manual. We aren't going by someone's military experience, although we have plenty. We use what has worked for us, based on our own experiences, and the diversity of personnel we have in our group. Not everyone here has the same background. Often, not even close. We need a farmer and an experienced combat veteran to be able to work together with minimal training. We keep things simple, but effective, changing as our environment around us changes."

Handing Jessie the radio, Q looked at him with a serious expression, and warned, "I don't mean to sound rude, but if you cross us, we'll kill you. No question. We've lost too many good men and women already to infiltrators. Treason against us is suicide for the traitor."

Taken aback by Q's sudden cold turn, Jessie remarked, "I get it, but you don't have a thing to worry about from me. Just keep your eyes, and especially your ears, open and focused on what's around you. The real threats here lie in the darkness, not in deception. Are you sure you trust me with your only game tracker?"

"Yes, and no," Q replied. "My gut says I can trust you. My gut says you're a good man with Nate's best interests at heart. But my heart has been broken by traitors too many times to trust anyone completely. Except of course for the folks like these guys here, who've proven themselves time and time again."

Nodding, Jessie said, "I guess we'd better get going."

Giving the signal, Q ordered the group forward. Jessie took the point position as directed, Tyrone fell in behind him, Daryl followed along behind Tyrone, Q fell in at the center, Carl dropped in behind him, and Sam took up a bounding rear guard as directed.

~~~~

Working his way through the darkness with only the moonlight to guide his way. Jessie occasionally paused to scan the area ahead of him with the thermal game tracker. Seeing only the heat signatures of nocturnal wildlife, mostly small game, rodents, and birds, Jessie kept up the pace.

After an hour of steady movement, Jessie felt two vibrating pulses from the radio carried in his left hand. *That's a request from Q to report, I believe.*

Responding with one vibratory pulse, Jessie felt two more pulses, followed by a slight pause and then three pulses. *I guess that's it,* he thought as he continued moving forward.

Realizing they were nearing the point where the two ridgelines converged, Jessie knew they'd be in the heart of hostile territory at any minute—that is, if they weren't already. Coming to a stop at the ridge facing down into the area where he had left Nate to seek help, Jessie scanned the area with the thermal, and then clicked his vibratory alert button five times to request verbal comms.

"Go," Q replied softly after receiving the message and verifying it was safe with the others.

Whispering into the radio, Jessie explained, "Okay, I'm at the point where we start descending toward Nate's location."

"How much farther?" Q asked. "To Nate, that is."

"Maybe a mile or two. It's downhill though, so we should make good time unless we make contact," Jessie responded.

"Everyone good?" transmitted Q.

Receiving the appropriate response vibes, he then commanded, "Let's move."

As they worked their way down the hill, Jessie felt a cold chill run up his spine. Halting his advance, he raised the thermal game tracker up to his eye and began scanning the area. *Where are you, you filthy bastards? I know you're out there hiding in the darkness like animals. C'mon. Show yourselves.*

~~~~

Trailing the group and covering their six, Sam stood atop the rocky ridgeline and watched as the others worked their way down the hill, disappearing from the faint moonlight of the night as they entered the thick vegetation below.

Turning around and scanning the area behind them before joining his brothers in arms in their descent, Sam caught a momentary glint of light. Focusing on the area just behind and to the left where he'd seen the flicker, Sam flipped his M4 from safe to semi and slowly raised the rifle to the high-ready position. Lowering himself behind a rocky outcrop, he reached

Them

for the radio clipped to his belt as he heard a thwack, followed by a heavy, bone-jarring impact to his right side.

Dropping the radio, Sam instinctively reached for the intense pain on his right side and found the shaft of an arrow, embedded deeply between his ribs.

As he fell to the ground, unable to breathe, Sam used his last ounce of energy to reach over and pick up the radio, holding down the vibratory alert key as the moonlight highlighted the silhouette of a large, dark figure standing above him.

The figure heaved an axe high above its head, swinging it down violently onto Sam's arm that held the radio, severing it at the elbow.

Sam attempted to scream to no avail. His lungs simply would not push any more air. As the figure raised the axe once again to deal what Sam knew would be the final blow, he was rescued from the hell of his current world by the sweet, silent loss of consciousness, and death.

~~~~

Feeling the vibration from the radio, Jessie unclipped it from his belt and hunkered down behind a cluster of trees. Waiting for further guidance, he felt the report pattern. Jessie quickly rogered up with his single vibratory pulse, followed by Q's two pulses, and then...nothing.

His heart sank while he anxiously awaited Sam's check-in, but it never came.

Feeling the report pattern vibrate through the radio once again, Jessie replied with his tone, again heard Q's, then nothing. *Damn it to hell, they're here.*

Chapter Eighteen

Arriving at a flooded section of the cave, Yuri looked down to see wear on the soft limestone surface from what appeared to have been a flat-bottomed boat. "I knew I was on boat," he whispered.

Looking into the darkness across the water with the night vision monocular, he added, "It go very far."

"What is it?" Britney asked. "Is it like an underground river or something?"

"No. More like flooded cave. Makes good natural barrier," he explained.

Looking around at the general structure of the flooded chamber, Yuri noted the steep slope of the walls that descended into the water. "Unless filled with stones, water looks deep. We find different way. Boat must be on other side. They may come back while we are in water. If they find us swimming, we would be unable to fight or flee."

"Whatever you think," she whispered.

"We go this way," he decided, working his way toward an area where the cave branched off into several chambers and tunnels.

Leading Britney by the hand, Yuri would quietly give her notice of changes in her footing to help her navigate the varied geology of the subterranean maze. "Watch head," he cautioned, placing his hand on her head, forcing her to squat down. "Object extending from ceiling. Sharp points."

Holding on tightly to Yuri, following his every move, Britney felt him come to a sudden stop. "What is it?" she asked.

Feeling him squeeze her hand, she heard him say in a grim voice, "Bones."

"Bones?" she asked, fearing his answer.

"Bones of many people," he replied. "Is horrible. Bones sorted and stacked in piles. Some bones broken or cut, like they were chopped off. Many teeth missing from skulls."

"Skulls?! she shrieked, squeezing his hand tightly. "Let's go. Please, let's not stay here any longer."

Doing as she asked, Yuri carefully led Britney around the piles and stacks of bones toward the far side of the chamber where there appeared to be a gap.

Reaching the opening, Yuri whispered, "Stay here. I go see."

"No!" she insisted. "Please! Please don't leave me in the dark alone."

"Is okay, we go," he conceded, leading her forward.

When they entered the chamber, the sound of running water could be heard off in the distance, as if it was trickling down the cave's walls. Kneeling down to touch the floor, Yuri felt a shallow flow of cold water following a low, water-worn channel in the floor. Scooping up a handful of the ice-cold water, Yuri took a sip.

"Is good," he declared. "Water running beneath our feet. Is good. Drink. You need to drink. You not get enough when in chains."

Kneeling alongside Yuri, Britney began scooping up the fresh, flowing water with her hands, drinking handful after handful. "Oh, this is good," she said, wiping the dripping water from her chin.

Just then, the sounds of the all-too-familiar horn echoed through the labyrinth of underground chambers and passages.

Britney's heart sank as Yuri said, "They know. They know we are gone. Quickly, we must move."

Leading her through the chamber, Yuri saw where a large, flat rock had fallen from the ceiling sometime in the past. The rock had created an obstacle to climb over to continue down that path, but it also presented them with an opportunity.

Looking down at their feet, Yuri was pleased to see that the small stream had kept the limestone floor free of sediment that would have otherwise highlighted their tracks.

Hearing movement coming from the passage behind them, Yuri pulled her hand and instructed, "Quickly. Climb rocks. Hold onto my belt. Do not lose me."

Scurrying up the fifteen-foot-high wall of rubble, Yuri slipped between several of the larger jagged stones and into a gap in the rubble. "Come," he whispered, taking her by the arm and leading her into the tight confines of the rock slide.

Several feet into the pile of fallen rocks, they found a void created by the debris that was approximately three feet across and four feet high.

"We hide here," he whispered as the sounds of their pursuers could be heard entering the chamber.

Britney's heart pounded in her chest because she knew if they were discovered, there would be no escaping again. They were pinned in with nowhere to go. Yuri had killed one of their own, and that was an act she was sure the barbarians would not let go without severe penalties. If the innocents in their grip suffered so greatly, what would they do to those they saw as having lashed out at them?

Yuri listened to their movements, but he heard no words from the figures in the chamber. He heard what sounded like smacking and pounding on one's chest. Almost as if they were communicating by the rhythm and beat of their hands and fists.

Them

The figures then went silent, as if they, too, were pausing to listen. Britney felt a tingle in her throat. She felt the urge to cough begin to overwhelm her. *Please, God, no.* Struggling to control herself, Britney held her breath, hoping the feeling would soon fade.

Just as the urge to cough became unbearable, she buried her face in Yuri's chest to muffle the sound as the figures once again began to move about in the darkness, leaving the chamber, and departing in the direction from where they had come.

Gently coughing into Yuri's chest, she felt him pat her on the back as if to reassure her everything would be okay. As she embraced him, she thought of the irony of having a man who she would have thought to be a monster, having been with the group that murdered her parents and so many others in cold blood, who was now her potential savior.

After waiting for what seemed like a half an hour or more, Yuri whispered, "We go now."

Taking her by the hand once again, Yuri led Britney out of the rock pile and back down into the wet, damp chamber of the cave.

"We go this way," he said, following the sound of the trickling water.

Chapter Nineteen

Joining up with Daryl, Q whispered, "Move up with Tyrone, and the two of you join up with Jessie. Try to establish a defensible position and wait for the rest of us to join up with you. Carl and I are gonna go back and check on Sam. He's not responding after that odd vibe alert."

"Roger that," Daryl confirmed with a nod, and he immediately began moving forward toward Tyrone's position.

Working his way back to Carl, Q asked, "When's the last time you laid eyes on Sam?"

"At the top of the ridge. When I went over and started down, it looked like he was keeping a watch on our six while the rest of us began the descent."

"Was anything unusual going on?" Q asked.

"No. It all seemed to be business as usual. Why?"

"We got a long, steady vibe alert," explained Q. "I pinged everyone for a response, and Sam's radio has been silent ever since. Something's up. I can feel it."

"Have you tried voice comms?"

"No. I don't want to give away his position if he's in a bind and avoiding contact. Let's work our way back up the hill. Be careful. According to Jessie, we're getting close to where we'd expect to encounter those creepy bastards."

"Roger that, Boss," Carl said as he double-checked the condition of his rifle and began working his way up the hill toward the ridgeline.

~~~~

Them

Using the game tracker, Jessie watched as two human figures approached from his rear. *Look to be the size of Daryl and Tyrone,* he thought.

"Jess," he heard whispered in the darkness.

"Come on up," he replied.

Once Daryl and Tyrone were at his position, Jessie asked, "What's going on?"

"No response from Sam after that tone was received," Daryl explained quietly. "Q sent us to join up with you. He said to get ourselves in a defensible position and wait on him and Carl to show back up with Sam."

Looking around, Jessie said, "This is probably as good as it gets without moving farther away from our path of travel. This cluster of trees is pretty tight and gives us visual cover and makes for a good barrier from several directions. I'll keep an eye out ahead, while you guys split the difference behind and beside us. I'll pass the thermal around so we can each scan our areas systematically. We don't want a friendly-fire accident, nor do we want to be snuck up on by those furry bastards."

"Sounds good to me," Daryl replied.

"Me, too," affirmed Tyrone. "I'll take this side, Daryl," he said, referring to their western flank.

"I've got this side, then," Daryl indicated before turning to face their eastern flank.

Seeing nothing on the thermal up ahead, Jessie handed it off to Daryl, who thoroughly scanned his area as well. "Nothin' here," he noted as he passed it off to Tyrone.

"I see... Oh, wait, that's Q and Carl working their way up the hill," Tyrone said. "Well... I saw them, but just lost them," he remarked when they passed behind some trees and terrain as their path of travel winded its way up the mountain.

Just as Tyrone began to hand the thermal back to Jessie, he caught a glimpse of color to the east of Q and Carl's position, level with their height up the hill and moving toward them.

"Ah, hell," he said. "I've got movement. I don't think it's Sam either. It's way too tall to be him, and it's working its way toward Q and Carl."

"Lemme take a look," Daryl said, reaching for the thermal game tracker.

"That's definitely not Sam," Daryl said confidently. "Well, hell, what do we do? If we key up on the radio, we'll help that bastard zero in on them. I could reach the threat from here with my .45-70 if it weren't so damn dark. I can barely see my front sight in this."

Thinking it over for a moment, Daryl said, "Jessie, if you relay the threat to Q, I'll start pounding the general location of the threat to keep him pinned down while they take evasive action or get into position to fight. I mean... I won't hit anything, but it'll turn the tables, at least, taking the surprise out of the equation."

Scanning the area again with the thermal, Daryl exclaimed, "Damn it, there's two of them! Call 'em!" he demanded as he raised his big .45-70 lever gun, aiming at the approximate area of the threat. Thinking quickly, Daryl held the thermal onto the barrel of his rifle just ahead of the rear leaf sight. "This will give me a better general idea," he mumbled as he quietly cycled a round into the chamber with the gun's oversized lever loop, and said, "Now!"

Picking up the radio and pressing the push-to-talk button, Jessie exclaimed, "Q, you've got movement to your right. Here comes the artillery," just as Daryl let the four-hundred-and-five-grain lead flat point round fly, followed by a steady volley of seven more rounds from the twenty-four-inch barreled reproduction of the venerable Winchester model 1886.

Seeing a muzzle flash from the vicinity of the threats as they fired on Q and Carl's position, Tyrone joined Daryl in laying down a suppressing and diversionary barrage of fire with his M4 while Jessie kept an eye on possible threats ahead of them.

Upon firing his last round, Daryl put the thermal to his eye and scanned the hillside, "I see Q and Carl on the move. They're hustling to the east and back down the hill, away from the threat."

Looking back to the area of the threat, Daryl said, "Well, I'll be damned. I think we lucked out and accidentally hit one of those bastards. I've got one on the ground not moving. The other is retreating to the west. And... he's gone. Lost him."

"Are you sure the other one is down?" Jessie asked.

"He, or it, ain't moving. We'll know in a few minutes if the image starts to cool."

Pointing in the direction of Q and Carl's last known position, Jessie said, "See if you can keep a visual on Q and Carl. We don't want to engage them by mistake when they come upon us in the dark."

"I think we should move," advised Tyrone.

"Come again?" Jessie asked, seeking clarification.

"It's like the old truism, 'tracers work both ways'," Tyrone explained. "If the two we saw aren't the only ones, the rest of them know where we are now. We lit ourselves up with muzzle flash pretty damn well."

"Good point," conceded Jessie. "I'd vote to move toward where we think Q and Carl may be coming from. The sooner we join up with them, the better chance we'll have of repelling another attack. If we stay separated, it may just make it easier for them to pick us off one at a time."

"Sounds good to me," agreed Daryl as he handed the thermal game tracker back to Jessie so he could reload his rifle. Loading one round and then racking it out of the magazine tube and into the chamber with the rifle's lever, Daryl loaded eight more rounds in the magazine tube for a total of nine rounds on tap. "She doesn't hold as many as one of them fancy AR's or AK's of yours, but each shot means something."

With a chuckle, Jessie shrugged, "I wouldn't call an AK fancy. They are forties technology and all. And trust me, I envy you right now. I love a good lever gun. As a matter of fact, I was carrying a Marlin .30-30 when this all started a few days ago. And that .45-70 of yours... well, one of its cousins saved my bacon a few months back. You've got your mind in the right place if you ask me."

"I guess I should have read that about you from that ol' Colt on your side," Daryl remarked, complimenting Jessie's choice of sidearm.

Interrupting with a chuckle, Tyrone said, "You two guys can keep the bromance going later. Let's get on with the task at hand."

"Right on," Daryl said. "What do you think?"

Looking to Jessie, Tyrone reached out his hand and asked, "Can I see the radio Q gave you?"

"Sure," Jessie said, fishing it out of his pocket and handing it to him.

Attempting to reach Q and Carl via the hand-held unit's vibratory alert, Tyrone waited patiently for a moment before attempting a second time. "C'mon, guys," he muttered.

"Nothing?" Daryl asked quietly.

Them

"Nope, let's move. We don't want to risk keying up with voice just yet. Let's get moving. We can't keep sitting here waiting for... um, them, to find us. I'll lead," Tyrone asserted, looking at Jessie. "No offense, but I know all the signals they may use."

"None taken," Jessie replied.

~~~~

Shivering and sweating profusely from what Nate was now sure was a fairly serious infection, he rested across several closely-spaced branches of the tree, looking down at the tattered remains of the coyote had fallen victim to the ravenous hunger of its own pack.

Damn, that's a rough way to go. Those mongrels rip you apart, gut first, while one of them holds your face in the dirt with his teeth. It's like they don't even try to kill their prey like a big cat. They merely hold it down while they eat. Sick.

Although Nate had seen the remains of sheep that had fallen victim to coyote attacks back at their homesteads, Nate had never seen them in action. Before now, he could only surmise what had happened based on the remains and on the trauma to the sheep's nose and face. He now knew that trauma was a result of being pinned down by teeth while being eaten alive.

Oh, thank God that wasn't me down there.

Flipping his night vision on and looking around, he couldn't see any sign of coyotes remaining in the area, but knew if he struggled to climb down the tree in his condition to retrieve his weapon, he'd never get back up to safety. He was growing weaker by the minute. He'd lost a lot of blood, and now infection was setting in. Add to that the hunger and thirst that was taking its toll on him, and he felt the best course of action he could take at this point was simply to stay where he was and hope for the best.

Hearing a thundering boom off in the distance, up the hill and toward the ridge behind him, Nate perked up and quickly turned his head in the direction of the sounds. He could hear a large caliber rifle firing away, thump after thump, followed by the steady cadence of the supersonic cracks from a smaller, high-velocity round.

"What the...?" he mumbled as he attempted to make sense of it all. Almost as soon as it had started, the gunfire ceased. *Something's going down, but what? Is it more of those UF guys getting a run for their money with those monsters from the cave, or... is it the cavalry? Ah, no need to get my hopes up. Just hang on. That's all I need to focus on for now. Not dying, and not falling out of this tree.*

~~~~

Moving in bounds, Tyrone, Jessie, and Daryl stopped momentarily for Tyrone to scan the area with the game tracker. "We don't have a lot of battery life left, guys. I hope... Wait, I've got two on the move. The way they're bounding and moving, I'm gonna put my money on them being Q and Carl."

Attempting the vibratory alert yet again, Tyrone patiently hoped for a response, to no avail. "We've got to assume they've lost comms, or aren't in a position to reply."

Thinking the situation over for a moment, Tyrone said, "You two hold up here. I'm gonna get to a position where I can signal them. We don't want them to head right past us in the darkness.

They don't have one of these fancy thermal toys, and we can't just announce ourselves given our current predicament."

"Whatever you guys say," Jessie replied. "You're a team. You know each other. I'm just the new guy."

"I say go for it," Daryl said in support of Tyrone's idea.

"I'm gonna have to take the thermal, so I can intercept them. You guys gonna be all right here in the dark, blind?"

"We'll live," Daryl answered, patting his friend on the shoulder. "Well, that's the plan, at least," he said with a crooked smile.

Nodding, Tyrone looked up at the sky and noted the clouds forming overhead. "Hopefully we won't lose the moonlight. Well, I'd better get going. Be safe," he said as he slipped off into the darkness in the direction of the thermal images he assumed to be Q and Carl.

Chapter Twenty

Following the steady sound of trickling water through the twists and turns of the vast, underground cave system, Yuri paused abruptly, startling Britney. "Do you feel breeze?"

"Breeze, I... uh," she stammered, momentarily confused.

"Shhh, be still, and feel breeze on face."

"Yes. Yes, I can feel it," she affirmed, beginning to understand where Yuri was going with this.

"We follow. Find where air enters cave," he explained, pulling her along.

Approaching a rise in the cave floor leading up to a small opening, Yuri announced, "Up. We climb up," and he led her to the rock features that lay between them and the opening.

"Here," he said. "Use both hands. Climb up behind me. Stay close."

Doing as she was told, Britney felt with her hands and climbed up the strange, limestone formations. She could feel the breeze getting stronger the higher she went. "That's fresh air," she said, her excitement beginning to build.

When Yuri reached the top, he climbed through the small opening and turned around, reaching for Britney's hand, saying, "Here, I help you."

As Britney reached out into the darkness in search of Yuri's hand, her heart skipped a beat as a large hand grabbed her around the ankle, jerking her violently down the rock formation she had just struggled to climb.

Britney's head bounced off the limestone, nearly knocking her unconscious, and she felt her body slide down the damp stone surface, being pulled by one of them in the darkness.

Them

"No!" Yuri shouted as he quickly climbed through the hole and began sliding down the limestone toward Britney and her abductor.

Scurrying to his feet, Yuri saw a figure to his left through the green image of the night vision. The figure drew back and swung a long object at him. Realizing the object was an axe, Yuri dropped and dodged. Barely getting out of the way in time, he felt the blade graze his forehead, causing blood to spill into his uncovered eye.

Leaping toward the figure to mitigate the risk of the axe by getting in close, Yuri tackled him, taking him to the floor. Grasping the axe handle, Yuri forced it to the figure's neck and began blocking his attacker's airway by bearing down on the axe with all his weight, while his profusely bleeding head wound dripped onto his opponent's face, momentarily obscuring the beast's vision.

He suddenly felt the axe handle lower several more inches into his fur-clad attacker's throat as it weakened from strangulation. Along with the feeling of movement in the axe handle, Yuri felt the distinctive crunch of the figure's trachea, and the fight left its body.

Hearing Britney's screams grow more distant, Yuri stood up, now holding the axe with both hands, and began running through the cavern in pursuit. The water running along the floor of the cave splashed beneath his feet as he ran as hard as he could to her aid.

Hearing Yuri's charge, the large figure released Britney and turned toward Yuri, raising a weapon of some sort toward him. With no time to act, Yuri swung the axe, connecting with the figure just as a deafening blast erupted from the figure's weapon.

Staggering backward, Yuri was stunned and overcome with a burning sensation as he felt a warm, wet substance begin to run down his side.

Hearing his attacker thump onto the cave floor, Yuri snapped back into the moment as he saw Britney's attacker lying still and lifeless. His axe had struck a fatal blow to her abductor's chest, smashing through his sternum and into his heart.

"Are you okay?" Britney shouted, her ears ringing from the report of the muzzle blast in the tight confines of the cave.

"Get gun," Yuri said, wincing in pain.

Quickly picking the gun up off the floor of the cave, Britney handed it to Yuri, who immediately identified it as a sawed-off Mossberg 500 pump shotgun.

"Hurry. We go now," Yuri grunted through the pain as he reached out in the darkness and took Britney's hand.

Pulling her back toward the source of the breeze, Yuri stopped at the body of the figure he had strangled to death with the axe. He started to bend over to inspect the figure, but the pain in his side was too great.

"Search body for weapons, and take optics from head," he instructed, tugging her hand in the direction of the corpse.

Doing as Yuri had asked, Britney knelt down and began feeling around. She was startled at first by the fur that covered the man from head to toe. It felt as if he was a beast of some sort, more than a man. Opening what seemed to be the front of a fur coat, she felt around and located the man's belt. Running her hands around the belt, she located a large, fixed-blade knife in a sheath. She drew the knife from the sheath and placed it on the ground beside the man.

Continuing her search, feeling her way up the dead man's body, she reached his face and was started by his open mouth, and wet, blood-soaked beard. She had no idea the blood was from Yuri's gaping head wound, and simply assumed it was the blood of Yuri's victim.

Reaching the top of this head, Britney removed the headband that held a monocular optic to the man's right eye and handed it to Yuri.

"No. You put on," Yuri urged.

Placing it over her head, Britney found it to be too loose because it had been adjusted for a much a larger person.

"Let me help," Yuri said softly as he assisted her in snugging it tight, then wiped his blood from the lens.

"I can see!" she exclaimed, excited by her first visions since being brought into the cave. Looking down, she flinched from the ominous sight of the large, bearded man whose face was completely covered in blood.

"Come," Yuri said. "You carry knife. Let's go."

Releasing her hand because she could now see on her own, Yuri led her back to the small opening, where they both climbed up and through, into another chamber, deeper in the cave.

"Breeze is coming from this way," he noted as he slid down the limestone slope leading down into approximately two feet of cold water below.

"Is not deep. Come," he said, urging Britney to follow him as she slid down beside him.

Leading her through the tightening confines of the passage, Yuri stopped when he felt the breeze blowing down from above. Looking up, he saw a crevasse that was barely large enough for the two of them to squeeze through and explained, "There. We climb through. Hopefully, it lead to surface."

Struggling through the pain, Yuri began feeling weakened and dizzy from the combined loss of blood and trauma from his wounds. He wasn't sure if he was going to make it, unable to take the time to survey the extent of his injuries, but he knew he couldn't stop until Britney was free from her underground hell.

Boosting herself up to the opening above, Britney climbed feverishly as dirt and debris fell onto Yuri beneath her.

"Sorry," she whispered.

"Is nothing," he replied, attempting to smile.

Once she had climbed several more feet, Yuri heard her say the beautiful words, "Stars! I see stars!"

"Go! Climb free. I follow," he insisted, struggling through the horrific pain of his side and his throbbing head wound.

Once Britney was outside the cave, she reached down and took Yuri by the hand, pulling, trying her best to help him reach the freedom and the fresh air of the surface above.

Crawling free of the opening between the rocks, Yuri surveyed their surroundings, and he heard Britney begin to cry tears of joy. Seeing the relief and pure elation on her face, he looked up and said in his native language, "Спасибо господин."

"What does that mean?" she asked softly.

"Thank you, Lord," he replied.

Chapter Twenty-One

Working their way through the darkness of the woods, Q looked up at the sky and saw that the moon was about to be obscured by a broken layer of clouds that was starting to form.

"Great," he grumbled. "That's the only light we have."

"We'll be okay," Carl responded. "How about we try to reach the others with the radio. We need to link back up in a bad way. I don't like being separated out there."

"Good idea," Q conceded, reaching for the radio. "Ah, hell," he grumbled as he felt around his belt where the radio had previously been clipped.

"What?"

"The damn radio. I... I can't find it. Dammit to hell! I must have lost it back there somewhere when we had to crash through those briars in a hurry."

"Well..." Carl said, pausing to collect his thoughts. "Let's just keep moving. By the way, do you reckon the guys were actually engaging back there, or just running interference for us?"

"I'd like to think they engaged and won," Q replied. "But who the hell knows? Regardless, it got us out of a bind, and I thank them for that." Pausing to look around, he said, "C'mon. Let's go. Just sitting here makes me nervous."

~~~~

Hunkering down between the trunks of two closely spaced pine trees, Tyrone held the thermal imager to his eye and scanned the area until the unit powered itself down due to lack of battery power. "Damn it," he said, shoving it back into his pocket.

Retrieving the radio, he hit the vibratory alert button once again. After waiting a few tense moments, he started to send another alert tone just as the ominous sound of a horn bellowed throughout the woods. To his horror, the horn could also be heard transmitting through his radio. *Shit,* he thought as he frantically clicked the volume knob to the off position. Remaining perfectly still, Tyrone listened as he heard the sounds of movement in the distance behind him. *They heard it. Dammit, they heard that damn radio. And if they've got Q's radio...*

Clearing the thoughts from his mind to deal with his most immediate threat, Tyrone moved as quietly as he could away from his current position. Doing a low crawl to avoid being seen by the night vision of his mysterious foe, he approached the large cluster of briars and curled up against them at their base, attempting to blend in as part of the terrain. He knew they had the advantage of sight, but he also knew the limitations of non-thermal types of night vision, and hoped he could simply remain out of the picture as they searched the area.

Hearing the sounds of movement coming dangerously close, Tyrone gripped his M4 tightly, preparing to deploy it once a threat target presented itself.

Listening carefully and letting his ears paint the image in his mind, Tyrone identified the sounds of two distinct threats moving through the woods as a team. *Come and get me, you bastards.*

Hearing them stop at the base of the trees where his radio had transmitted the sound of the horn, he listened for signs that they were communicating, but heard nothing. The two figures working their way toward him in the darkness were separating from each other, one working its way quietly downhill to his right, and the other working its way across and above him.

Realizing they were trying to box him in, Tyrone decided to take the fight to them before they could get themselves into the positions they sought. Raising his rifle and approximating the location of the threat up the hill from him, as Tyrone began to fire, he heard a large figure crashing through the dead branches and vegetation behind him.

Caught off guard when the blade of an axe came crashing down through the briars, Tyrone rolled over on this back in an effort to employ his rifle against the threat.

Blocking the axe with his rifle, Tyrone nearly lost his grip from the impact as the rifle thumped into his chest, with the blade of the axe missing him by a mere inch.

When the axe-wielding figure raised the axe to take another swing, Tyrone quickly rolled away while his uphill pursuer came charging down the hill toward him.

Hearing the crack of a 5.56 NATO round behind him, Tyrone fired twice at the charging threat, failing to stop him because the attacker was nearly upon him.

Approximating the location of the figure's head in the failing light of the moon, Tyrone quickly fired two more shots, whipping the assailant's head back, and dropping him to the ground.

Scurrying to his knees, Tyrone looked to his immediate left to see that the axe-wielding man was lying face down in the dirt, having been shot in the back by an unknown source.

Hearing the familiar signal from his group, Tyrone shouted, "I'm good!" just as he noticed the other attacker, who had moved downhill, charging toward him.

"I've got him!" Carl's voice shouted from the darkness just before a series of gunshots erupted from both Carl and the attacker.

Momentarily night-blinded by the series of muzzle flashes, Tyrone struggled to focus through the spots in his eyes while the attacker continued his charge up the hill.

Sending six rapid-fire shots into the barely visible figure, Tyrone watched as the large man dropped to the ground with a thud. Immediately turning toward Carl, Tyrone saw no one there.

"Carl!" he shouted, hearing no response.

"Friendly!" Q yelled as he rushed toward Tyrone's location.

Tyrone watched as Q stopped short and knelt down to look closely at something on the ground.

With the spots of color in his eyes from the muzzle flashes in the darkness beginning to clear, Tyrone could see Q and quickly moved to join up with him.

Reaching Q's side, Tyrone dropped to his knees at the sight of Carl's lifeless body lying in a contorted position, having taken a round directly through the neck. "Son of a bitch," he growled as he placed a hand on his dear friend. "He took one for me," he said, wiping a tear from his eye.

"Any of us would have, brother. That's what we do. He died well," Q proclaimed, regaining his composure. "Now, c'mon. This ain't over. More are on the move behind me. We've gotta go."

~~~~

Hearing the sounds of gunfire, Daryl exclaimed, "They're on them. Let's go!" He and Jessie hastily worked their way through the darkness of the thick woods toward what they assumed to be their friends in distress.

"Slow down," Jessie shouted, having concerns about Daryl's emotionally-guided, reckless pace.

Seeing no change in Daryl's charge, Jessie followed, keeping a keen eye out on their surroundings, hoping Daryl's desire to help his friends wouldn't lead them right into the hands of their enemies.

Ducking beneath a low hanging tree branch, Daryl straightened and continued to run, only to feel an arm clothesline him in the throat, taking him off his feet and smashing him to the ground with a heavy thud.

Looking up, trying to make sense of his situation, Daryl saw the reflection of a blade from the moonlight as the clouds drifted on, allowing its light to shine down on them once again. Daryl cringed, expecting the worst, just as he heard Jessie's voice shout, "It's us! It's us!"

"Shit, man!" Q exclaimed, as he pulled back the blade and slid it back into the sheath on his belt. "I almost gutted you," he said, reaching out his hand and helping Daryl to his feet.

Coughing, Daryl grunted and wheezed, "Damn, man. You took the wind right out of me."

"Sorry, but you're a big ol' burly guy just like them. And that beard, well, at a glance in the dark..."

As Jessie joined up with them, Daryl looked around and saw Tyrone standing a few yards behind Q. "Where's Carl?" he asked.

Seeing Q look down to the ground, and reading the look on Tyrone's face, Daryl's gut tightened as he had realized he'd lost his close friend. Taking a deep breath, Daryl pleaded, "Sam?

Where's Sam? Did you see him up the hill before you were turned back down?"

"No, we didn't make it to the top before they rousted us," Q explained. "Thanks for the artillery, by the way. You saved our bacon."

Seeing the disappointed look on Daryl's face, Q insisted, "Sam may still be out there. We don't know anything just yet. Keep the faith, brother."

"Right," Daryl sighed, getting a grip on his emotions.

Looking around, Q said, "We can't keep heading back up the hill and taking hits. We've got a mission, and we'll never achieve it if we keep letting them run us in circles, picking us off one by one. Sam knows the mission. Hopefully, he's working his way down the hill now. I think we need to press on. We'll come back for Carl once we've secured Nate and the girl."

"Right on," Daryl said, nodding in agreement. "You okay, T?" he asked, looking at Tyrone.

"Yeah. I'm fine. Thanks to Carl, I'm fine," he answered in a solemn tone.

"Were you able to get anything off the ones you encountered?" Jessie asked.

"Tyrone checked out one big guy that came at him with an axe, but he didn't have anything of added value. We had to move on too quickly to search the others that are dead deeper in the woods. They were still coming down on us."

"No night vision on that guy, huh?" Daryl asked.

"Unfortunately, no," Q replied.

Turning to Jessie, Q got the men back in the game, saying, "Lead the way. Let's get back on track. We need to move in bounds. Let's double up. Daryl, you move with Jessie, and Tyrone and I will be moving in bounds close behind. One covers and the other moves. We're in the thick of it here. We have to assume there are eyes on us from all possible angles."

"Roger that," Jessie agreed. "You ready, Daryl?"

"Yeah, I'm ready," Daryl replied.

"Okay, then," Jessie explained. "It's not much farther to where I left Nate. We have to work our way down the hill, probably another half mile or so. When it starts to level out, you may come upon a wash. If we follow that wash or at least parallel it as we work our way down, we'll be in the ballpark."

"Are there any other details you can give us?" Q asked. "You know, in case we have to find Nate without you?"

"Yes, of course," Jessie replied. "We made our way to the surface at a large outcrop on the side of a hill. We found a water-carved entrance to the caverns beneath the rocks. Rainwater must have flowed down through the gaps in the rocks and into the hole we climbed out of. We worked our way up the hill and slightly east until we came across a level area where there were several large, downed trees. They looked like they had gone down in a windstorm, maybe a year or so ago. Nate was resting behind the downed trees, just out of sight. You wouldn't see him unless you walked right up on him. The downed trees provided good visual cover and protection from the wind."

"Copy that," Q said with a nod. "Thanks. Now, let's get on with it."

Continuing down the hill toward Nate's location, Q, Tyrone, Daryl, and Jessie covered one another with each bound forward. After advancing, they would stop, listen and observe for signs of trouble before proceeding.

After making progress for what seemed like a quarter-mile or more, Jessie stopped and covered Daryl as he advanced to join him at his position of cover behind a large oak tree. "It's not much farther," Jessie whispered.

Seeing Q and Tyrone move toward them in the moonlight, Jessie motioned them forward.

Once the four men were together, they knelt behind the oak tree, with each of them covering a different potential approach while being back-to-back to one another.

"It's not much farther," Jessie said to the others. "The wash should be down the hill and to the left. If we cross the wash, we should be able to work our way diagonally to Nate's general location."

Pleased with Jessie's update of their progress, Q nodded and said, "Great, let's…"

Interrupted by the sound of a coyote in the distance, each of the men felt a tingle travel up their spines as they looked at one another.

"Something wasn't right about that," observed Daryl, analyzing the howl of the four-legged predator.

"I know what you mean," Q replied. "I can't put my finger on it, but that howl gave me the creeps."

"I'm not used to hearing a lone coyote in the area," Jessie said. "It always seems when there's one, the yips, yaps, and replies from every song dog in the area can be heard rustling up their prey."

"Are we just getting paranoid, or should we be concerned?" Q asked. "I mean, these creepy bastards communicate with horns and such. I've yet to hear one of them speak or yell. Hell, every animal sound we hear out here could be them communicating with each other."

"We can't let every sound we hear rattle us," Jessie insisted. "We've got to keep moving."

Them

"Damn, I wish the sun would hurry and come up," Daryl said. "This has been a damned long night. I'm ready for it to be over."

"You ain't the only one, Daryl," Tyrone agreed. "My nerves are shot. I need a stiff drink."

"We'll have to recuperate with some shine when we get home. Just keep your head screwed on straight for now. Jessie, let's move," directed Q, motivated to keep his men working toward their objective.

Bounding several more times, the group arrived at the wash Jessie had described. "We encountered them in this area when we were tracking Britney." Looking up at the moon, he continued. "It looks like the clouds won't be passing back in front of the moon anytime soon. Let's move as far as we can in this next advance without stopping. Daryl and I will cross the wash while you cover us, then we'll cover you from the other side. After that, let's press on through unless we make contact."

"Make it happen," concurred Q, patting Jessie on the arm.

"C'mon," Jessie said to Daryl, and the two men descended into the wash.

Q watched Jessie and Daryl as they disappeared into the shadows of the rainwater-carved ravine while Tyrone watched his and Q's back. Seeing them emerge out of the wash on the other side, Q watched for Jessie's signal.

"Okay, they're ready for us," Q said, patting Tyrone on the back before he slipped down into the rough, rocky washout. Reaching the bottom, Q stopped and covered Tyrone while he climbed down the loose, rock-strewn side of the wash, joining him in the bottom. "C'mon," he said as he began to climb up the other side.

Hearing the sound of a twig snapping on the ground uphill of their position, Q and Tyrone heard something bounce off of the ground and roll down the hill toward them, through the dead leaves on the ground.

Tyrone and Q both instinctively dove away from the tumbling object. Their time fighting the foreign occupiers had left them wary of grenades and other forms of explosive threats, and to them, anything being tossed their way had to be treated as such.

Jessie and Daryl scanned the darkness of the woods, looking for the source of the object, to no avail. With his safety off and his finger hovering over the trigger of his AK-74, Jessie's heart raced as he waited for the other shoe to drop on them at any second.

Feeling no shockwave from an explosion, Q turned to look at the object that had been thrown at them, which was now clearly illuminated by the moon's high position in the night's sky. His body convulsed with fear, disgust, and outrage when he first recognized the wide-open eyes, and then the rest of Sam's facial features on the severed head.

Suddenly, Jessie heard Q and Tyrone scream and wail as they frantically climbed the loose, rocky sides of the wash toward his and Daryl's position on the other side.

"Nooooooo! Damn you sons of bitches! Nooooo!" Tyrone bellowed.

"What is it?" Daryl shouted, confused by the situation and holding his rifle at the high ready, prepared to engage and a mere flinch away from pulling the trigger.

"Go! Go! Go!" Q grunted in a highly-stressed voice as he and Tyrone rushed past Daryl and Jessie.

Them

Covering their egress from the area, Jessie and Daryl soon turned and ran to catch up with Q and Tyrone, still at a complete loss as to what had just occurred.

Catching up with Q and Tyrone, who had stopped and set up a position of cover for him and Daryl, Jessie demanded, "What? What the hell happened?"

"It was Sam's fucking head!" Tyrone exclaimed as he broke down into a strange mix of tears and rage. "They threw Sam's fucking head at us! They could have shot us. They could have killed us. But instead, they chose to dismember our friend to fucking toy with us!"

Putting his arm around his friend and squeezing him tight, Q whispered, "Shhhhhh. Shhhh, you're right. They did that to get inside our heads. Don't let them in. Shut that evil out and let's get Nate and get the hell out of here. We'll come back with everything we have to eradicate these sick sons of bitches permanently. I promise you that. But we'll do no one any good if we let their sick, twisted mind games rattle us any more than they already have. Let's get moving and find a safe spot for a break."

Chapter Twenty-Two

Blinking his eyes as the sun's morning rays shone through the tree branches above him. Nate smiled a little, pleased to have survived the night, only to wince in pain when he tried to shift his weight in his uncomfortable perch. "Ahhhh..." he groaned while trying to move around to restore proper circulation throughout his body.

Craning his head to get a view of his leg, Nate mumbled, "Damn. That's not looking good." Trying to peel back his bandage to get a better look, he noticed his hand was shaking uncontrollably.

Laying his head back on the branch, he thought about his wife Peggy and son Zack back home. Every minute that went by made him feel less certain that he'd see them again. If Jessie did not return with help, he would die right where he was. If his physical condition combined with the elements didn't kill him, the strange hostiles in the area surely would. No, his only hope was to be rescued by a friendly force, and without Jessie, that just didn't seem plausible.

I've got to get out of this damn tree, Nate thought, feeling the effects of dehydration and hunger. Reaching up and taking hold of a branch directly above him, Nate pulled himself up into the seated position and began to make plans for his painful descent.

Hearing a twig snap, followed by the sound of weeds and brush rustling, Nate froze in fear. Attempting to not move a muscle, Nate scanned the area by moving only his eyes. At first, he saw nothing, and then out of the corner of his eye, he caught movement.

Them

His heart sank when he recognized the camouflage pattern worn by UF soldiers. *Hunters!* he thought. Almost as soon as the fear of the presence of the UF entered his mind, a strange relief swept through him. *At least if they kill me, it'll be with a bullet. I'd rather go out execution-style than die at the hands of those beasts in the cave. God only knows the horrors that would bring.*

Remaining still, hoping they would pass, he remembered his rifle on the ground next to the tree. *Just keep on moving, guys. Nothing to see here,* he mused to himself in an attempt to stay as calm and relaxed as possible.

Just as the six-man team looked as if they would continue and pass through the area, one of them paused and signaled to the others.

Damn it! They see it.

The soldier worked his way over to the base of the tree, looked around at the macabre scene left by the coyotes, then leaned over and picked up Nate's rifle, holding it up for the rest of his team to see.

Still using only hand signals, the group began to systematically scan the area and the man holding the rifle looked up into the tree, making direct eye contact with Nate.

"Howdy. Welcome to America," Nate said, attempting to muster a friendly smile.

Immediately pointing his AK-74M at Nate, the soldier shouted, "Здесь, в дереве!"

A second soldier quickly ran to the side of his comrade and shouted in English up toward Nate's position in the tree, "Throw down weapons!"

"He's got my weapon," Nate replied sarcastically while slowly showing them his empty hands.

"Climb down from tree! Now!" the man ordered in a stilted, heavy accent.

"I'm injured; please be patient," Nate said, pointing to his blood-soaked pants.

"Climb down now, or I'll shoot you down!" the man demanded, flipping the safety lever down on his rifle and aiming directly at Nate's center mass.

"Okay, I'm coming," Nate insisted as he began to work his way down through the branches, gritting his teeth in pain as he went.

Once within reach, the man jumped up and grabbed Nate's boot, pulling him down hard to the ground.

Screaming in agony upon impact, Nate felt his wound tear open and begin to bleed again. "Damn it, ahhh hell!" he screamed as he writhed in pain.

The man shoved his knee into Nate's stomach and forced his shoulders against the ground while the soldier who had found his rifle took both of his hands, extending them over his head and placing flex cuffs around his wrists.

Once secured, the man who'd shoved his knee into him released his pressure and began to search Nate's person for hidden weapons or dangerous objects.

Pulling Nate's knife from his belt, he tossed it aside and said something unintelligible to his comrades. Looking back down to Nate, the man, who was clean-shaven and appeared to be in his early thirties with short, blonde hair, said through gritted teeth, "Where are others?"

"What others?" Nate asked, only to feel the man's hand slap him hard across the face.

"Do not toy with me, insurgent."

Them

"I'm not toying with you. I'm just not sure who you're talking about. Are you referring to the cave people? They'll find us soon enough if you keep yelling like that."

"Cave people?" the man repeated, confused by Nate's statement.

"Yeah, cave people. I don't know what else to call them. I don't know who or what they are, but they're pretty damn vicious. They're like beasts."

"Look, hillbilly, we're looking for UF patrol that went missing recently. If you help us find them, we will do what we can to help you with wounds. If you do not help us find them, we will tie you to tree, cut out tongue so you cannot scream for help, and leave you for wild animals to devour... alive. Now, tell me who you are with, where they are, and what you know of UF patrol."

"Look, pal, I'm being honest here when I say I don't know anything about a patrol, but I do know that the creepy bastards I'm trying to warn you about are more than capable of taking out your patrol, as well as the one you're looking for. They operate in a very unconventional manner. Almost like a pack of wild animals. They hit you before you even know they're there."

Looking Nate over, the man snarled and asked, "Where is leg?"

"I think it ended up right over there," Nate answered, gesturing toward a tall patch of weeds near the base of the tree.

"You carry rifle popular with insurgents. Who are you with?" the man demanded again.

"That rifle? Hell, the AR-15 is popular with all Americans. Its presence doesn't indicate affiliation with a certain group," Nate replied. "It just means I found a good deal at Walmart back before the collapse."

Reaching out and taking Nate's rifle from his comrade, the man looked it over, and said, "This is U.S military issued M4, not civilian AR-15. Where did you get rifle?"

"Look, man. When it all started falling apart, the rules didn't seem to matter much. A lot of former government weapons began circulating around. I just happened to come across this one at a swap meet."

Glaring at Nate, the man declared, "You speak in circles with no truth. I can see you do not want things to go easy for you."

"Look, if you think I'm some sort of wanted outlaw, then please, by all means, arrest me and take me back to your base. They'll sort it all out there. Let's just get the hell out of these woods before they come."

"Before who come?"

"Them!" Nate shouted. "I'm telling you, you don't want them to find you. I'd much rather be arrested by you and charged with whatever crime you want to charge me with than found by them, again."

Standing up, the man walked away from Nate and joined his four other comrades. They discussed something amongst themselves while the younger man who'd found Nate's rifle stood watch over him.

"You need to convince your team to get us the hell out of here," Nate whispered. "You don't wanna be here when they come."

The young man, appearing to be in his early twenties, kicked Nate with his boot to shut him up.

Once the man who appeared to be in charge finished discussing the situation with the rest of his team, he turned and was walking back toward Nate when the sound of a horn could be heard off in the distance, echoing through the hills. The eerie sound triggered the man to stop and listen.

"That's them!" Nate said. "It's too late to run. They'll just pick you off one at a time. I highly recommend you set up a defensive perimeter and prepare to hunker down for a fight. It's coming, whether you want to acknowledge what I'm saying as the truth or not."

Giving out orders in what appeared to be Russian, the man directed his young comrade in arms who was guarding Nate to tie him to the tree Nate had spent the night in.

Grumbling to himself, Nate wasn't pleased with the turn of events. He knew Britney's abductors would soon be upon them, and he did not look forward to being helplessly tied to a tree while the UF soldiers were slaughtered all around him.

The younger man, along with one of the others, stood on each side of Nate and picked him up underneath his arms. As they carelessly dragged him to the tree, Nate gritted his teeth from the pain the rough handling was causing him.

Reaching the base of the tree, Nate's hands were untied and pulled around the tree behind him, where he was re-secured from behind. *This ain't good,* Nate thought as he worried about the possible outcomes of either being attacked or abandoned in his current state. Either way, he knew the deck was stacked against him.

~~~~

"There," Britney said, pulling the bandage tightly around Yuri's head. "That should at least keep it clean until we can get you somewhere to treat you properly. How's your side?"

"Better than before," Yuri said with a smile. "Thank you for taking care of me. Shotgun blast must have merely grazed me. It hurt so badly, and bled so much, I thought it was direct hit. I thought I should be dead by now."

Pausing what she was doing and looking him directly in the eye, Britney said, "You could have just left me there, chained to the floor in that wretched hell hole. You could have easily gotten out of there on your own. But you didn't. You put your own escape in jeopardy to get me out of there. I'll be forever in your debt for that. I haven't had many people in this world I could count on. You... you have no idea..."

Reaching out and wiping the tear from her cheek, Yuri sighed, "If we not meet in cave, you would not like me. You... you would hate me."

"I don't care who you were when you entered that cave, Yuri... um, I don't even know your last name," she admitted, looking him squarely in the eye.

"Kovalenko," he replied with a smile.

"So, as I was saying, Yuri Kovalenko, I don't care who you were when you entered that cave. I don't care what you did, where you're from, or who you served. When you came out of that cave, you arose as my hero. You put your life on the line for me, and I will never forget that or be able to repay you."

Amazed at her statement, Yuri couldn't help but flash back through his memories of the training he'd received about the current state of the U.S. and the insurgency he was here to fight. He thought about the selfless way her rescuers had sacrificed themselves fighting his own kind to get her away from the murderous ambitions of the very cause he had served so faithfully. These insurgents did not seem like domestic terrorists, intent on hampering recovery efforts. The people

Britney had spoken of seemed more like her fellow countrymen, who were heroically coming to her aid.

Unsure about what the truth really was anymore, Yuri looked Britney in the eyes and said softly, "You have already repaid me."

Sitting up, Yuri looked around and declared, "Okay, we go now."

"Go where?" she asked. "I can't go back with you. I can't. I just can't."

"Then we go somewhere else. Somewhere you can be safe," he explained. "I will not take you back to camps. I promise you that."

Looking into his eyes, Britney began to smile as her feelings of elation were quickly doused with fear. She saw Yuri's smile extinguish as his eyes darted around quickly. Reaching for the shotgun with his right hand, realizing it was just out of reach, he shoved her aside with his left hand and dodged to his right.

Britney could feel the disruption of the air as an arrow flew by her face, missing her by mere inches. As she fell to the ground, she saw Yuri charge the fur-covered man who had been behind her, blocking his attempt to nock another arrow.

The large, ominous figure, covered in animal fur from head to toe, kicked Yuri hard in the chest, knocking him backward and onto the ground.

Immediately bouncing back and leaping to his feet, Yuri charged the man again, exposing the broadhead-tipped arrow he had pulled from the man's bow-mounted quiver as he had fallen backward.

As the man tried to draw his knife, Yuri plunged the razor-sharp broadhead into the man's neck, slicing his jugular vein, and sending him crashing down as blood spewed like a fountain from his neck.

Running over and retrieving the shotgun, Yuri made his way to Britney, who was now trying to scurry away in fear on all fours. Taking her by the hand, he helped her up and insisted, "We must run."

Leading her through the thick forest, they hadn't gotten far before hearing the all-too-familiar sound of the cave dwellers' horn echoing through the trees.

Yuri struggled through the pain of his wounds. His confrontation with the archer who now lay dead had torn them loose, and blood flowed freely once again. Catching a glimpse of movement to his left, paralleling their course, but at a distance, Yuri saw a fur-clad rider on horseback galloping across a small clearing.

Yuri knew the rider was likely racing ahead to cut them off, so he began to think of ways to take evasive action, but was unsure how many pursuers they had or their exact locations. He didn't want to make a turn or alter their course only to fall into the hands of someone who awaited them.

Leaping over a log, Yuri's feet no sooner hit the ground than he saw a figure crouching in front of them, aiming a rifle directly at him and Britney. As the stranger reflexively started to raise the rifle, Yuri heard a man shout, "No!"

Seeing that the shout had come from an injured man tied to a tree, Yuri was barely able to make out the silhouettes of soldiers taking visual cover in the brush all around him. They wore the same camo pattern as him. They were UF soldiers.

A feeling of relief swept through his body when he heard a man shouting in his native language to drop the weapon. Doing as he was ordered, Yuri tossed the shotgun to the ground ahead of him, placing his hands on top of his head.

"Raise hands," he turned and said to Britney.

Yuri's feeling of relief quickly gave way to the crushing realization that she had been running from the UF, but she was now once again in their hands, breaking the promise he had made mere moments before.

Britney watched as UF soldiers appeared from the brush, pointing their weapons at both her and Yuri. Seeing Nate tied to a tree, she shouted, "Nate!" just as a hand pushed her from behind, forcing her to her knees.

One of the soldiers approached Yuri and began interrogating him in a language that sounded to her like Russian.

Looking toward Nate, she saw him mouth the words, *It's going to be okay*. She was both relieved to see him alive and horrified that he had fallen captive to the ones who had set out to kill them both. If they knew who Nate was, he would surely be killed or imprisoned. And she had been witness to an unspeakable crime committed by the UF. If they knew who she was, they could never let her go. Her story would create too much of an uproar with the local population.

In their native language, Yuri argued with the man interrogating him. He pleaded with him to turn their attention to defending against the attack Yuri knew was coming at any moment. Looking to Nate, realizing that both he and Yuri had issued the same warning, the man ordered his men to set up a defensive perimeter.

He turned back to Yuri and told him in Russian, "Secure her to tree next to other prisoner. You watch both. Do not let them escape. Do you understand, Sergeant Kovalenko?"

"Yes, Senior Lieutenant Romanoff. I understand," Yuri replied sharply.

Chapter Twenty-Three

Running through the woods at a breakneck pace, Jessie could hear the hounds pursuing him. The UF-trained search dogs were gaining on him, and he knew it was just a matter of time before they caught him, pinning him down for their handlers, or attacking him; either way, it wouldn't end well unless he could find a way to shake them.

Splashing through a creek flooded by recent rains, Jessie attempted to mask his scent, and he ran upstream before continuing away from them. Based on his personal experiences with dogs in the past, he knew he'd have to go a substantial distance to keep them from picking up his trail once again.

As the barking grew louder, Jessie looked back to see that they were now in visual range as the hounds came bounding through the woods, guided by their noses.

Turning and running onto the dry ground on the opposite side of the creek, Jessie began running at a full sprint. The dogs had now picked him up visually and turned to run straight through the creek to intercept him on the other side.

Nearly exhausted and out of breath, Jessie knew he couldn't pull away from them, so he began to climb a pile of slick, moss-covered rocks, hoping it would slow them down long enough for him to get away.

As he climbed the large rocks in haste, his foot slipped, and he fell backward onto the cold, hard ground below. With the wind knocked out of him, he struggled to bring his rifle up to meet the threat of the dogs that were now within ten yards and about to leap onto him with their large teeth exposed.

Just as he was about to pull the trigger, the dogs slid to a stop, growled, and then turned and ran away with their tails tucked between their legs.

"What the hell?" he mumbled, then he heard a deep, heavy growl above and behind him.

Slowly turning around and looking up the rock wall from which he had just fallen, Jessie saw a large black bear standing at the top looking down at him.

Turning to... "Jessie. C'mon man. It's time to get moving," Tyrone's voice said in a low whisper.

Flinching, Jessie awoke and began frantically looking around and behind him.

"Relax, man. It's only me," Tyrone assured him.

Grinning, Jessie chuckled, "And thank God for that," as he yawned, stretched and sat up. "Man, that was the deepest sleep I've had in a long time. I guess knowing you guys had my back allowed me to finally relax a bit."

"That's saying a lot considering our current situation," Q replied.

"So, what did I miss?" Jessie asked.

"Nothing much. After you and Daryl went to sleep, Tyrone and I stayed up. I watched the northern half of our perimeter, and he watched the southern half. All activity seemed to cease for a while. We heard that damned horn sound a few minutes ago, so we figured we'd better get back in the game. It sounded a long way off, but just the fact that we can hear it tells me they're too close. But just remember, the next break belongs to me and Tyrone."

"Absolutely, you've earned it," Jessie concurred as he checked his rifle and readied himself for the threats that still lay ahead.

Speaking up, Daryl said, "Hey, guys? Um, I've got to take care of business."

"Buddy system!" Q quipped. "Jessie, you're Daryl's buddy. Go with him."

"Roger that," Jessie groaned as he stood and stretched.

Walking a short distance from camp, Daryl said, "Okay, man. You stay right there, I'm gonna duck behind that big tree. This ain't gonna be purdy. You don't wanna be downwind of me right now."

"Thanks for the warning," Jessie chuckled.

As Jessie stood there, scanning the area and keeping an eye out so Daryl could tend to the business at hand, he heard Daryl say, "You know, I can't figure out why they backed off. They had us on the run. If they would have kept the pressure up, they stood a good chance of picking us off one by one in the darkness."

"Yeah, I was thinking the same thing," Jessie agreed. "The only thing I can figure is they were taking too many losses themselves. They may have needed to regroup and evaluate the situation. Would killing four of us be worth potentially losing three or four more of their own? We were keeping their cost-to-gain ratio high. Probably too high."

"Yeah, who knows? I'm just glad we were able to catch a break. I was exhausted. My eyes were starting to play tricks on me, and given the stress of the situation, that wasn't good."

Rejoining Jessie, Daryl warned, "You really don't wanna go over there," while gesturing with his hand in front of his face.

Returning to the group, Jessie asked, "So, what's the plan?"

Snugging up his pack, Q said, "The sound of the horn came from that direction. Downhill from us and to the west," he said while gesturing in the direction he described. "Now that the sun's up and you can see better, how far do you think we are from Nate?

Looking around and thinking it through, Jessie replied, "I'd say right about where you're pointing."

Grumbling, Q said, "Let's go. Nate's a'wait'n."

After a half an hour of slowly and methodically working their way toward Nate's last known position, Jessie gave the others the sign to hold and hunker down. Working his way back to Q, Jessie said, "See those rocks over there next to those fallen trees?"

"Yeah," Q replied.

"That's the spot. He was down behind that big fallen oak. Let me work my way over there. I'll signal if it's clear. There's no need for us to walk into a trap. If they found him, they'd know there was a chance I'd be coming back for him."

Nodding in agreement, Q signaled to the others to hold their positions, keep their eyes open, and to cover as Jessie advanced.

Slowly working his way toward the downed trees, Jessie whistled softly to announce his presence if Nate was still there. He didn't want to be shot by a scared and injured friend who would no doubt be a bit jumpy by now.

Not hearing a reply, he moved closer, whistling once again.

Watching Jessie's movements carefully, Q observed as Jessie reached the tree. It was clear to him by Jessie's lack of reaction that Nate was no longer there. He watched while Jessie surveyed the area and finally motioned them forward.

As the others joined up with Jessie, Q asked, "So... what's the story?"

"I left him right here," Jessie said, pointing. "There's blood over here on the ground at the base of this tree. There's a muddle of prints. There's everything from coyote tracks to boot prints. There are at least five or six sets of boot prints, maybe more.

"Those look like Russian, or UF standard-issue boots to me," Q said. Kneeling down next to the tree, Q touched the blood with his finger and rubbed it between his index finger and thumb.

"This is fresh," Q added. "Whoever was here hasn't been gone for long."

"Over here, guys," Daryl said, kneeling down and looking at one point in particular on the ground.

"What is it? Q asked.

"Look," he said, pointing. "These prints are too small to be from a man. They look like sneakers of some sort. And look here—handprints. I'd say someone small was put on their hands and knees right about here."

"Britney!" Jessie exclaimed.

"So, you think the UF has both Britney and Nate?"

"That's the only conclusion we can draw from this," Jessie speculated, unsure whether he was happy or disappointed in the information before them.

"It looks like they went this way," Tyrone said, pointing at a cluster of tracks leading away from the scene to the north, away from the mountains.

"That would make sense," Jessie acknowledged, adding, "The UF guys, if they were hunters, would have been inserted by helicopter, which more than likely would have come from the north where the UF has a greater presence."

Q noted, "They were likely inserted to look for you two. They wouldn't let that hit go unpunished. I'd say the group that had you pinned down when we found you were on the same page with these guys. Nate being in their hands is just as bad as if he were with those... those furry bastards from the cave."

Looking to the sky in the direction of the tracks, Jessie stated, "They're probably moving toward an extraction point, as well as potentially trying to evade those troglodytes, or like you said, those furry bastards from the caves."

"Troglowhats?" Q asked.

"Troglodytes," Jessie replied.

"What the hell is a troglodyte?"

"A primitive or prehistoric cave dweller," Jessie explained. "They fit that category well, almost seeming to be living some primitive fantasy life of a caveman."

"Except for the high-end night vision," Q quickly countered. "That kind of clashes with the whole primitive thing."

"Yeah, except for that," Jessie conceded. "It sure does make getting around in those dark caves easier, though."

"Where the hell would they have gotten those things? And battery power? Where... I just don't get it," Daryl vented, shaking his head.

"Whatever or whoever they are, we need to get moving," Q declared, getting the mission back on track. "If this is where you left Nate, and if there are signs of the girl being here, too, we need to assume the UF has them, and we need to get moving. The last thing I want to hear, as long as we have reason to believe the UF has them, is one of those damned ugly Hind helicopters taking off and flying away. If they make it out of these woods with them, our odds of getting them back plummet."

Chapter Twenty-Four

"Where are we going?" Britney asked as Yuri led her and Nate in the center of the UF patrol as they worked their way to the north.

"Shhh. Do not bring trouble on yourself. Follow instructions," Yuri replied.

Yuri's heart sank in his chest when he saw the look in Britney's eyes at his dismissal. She looked shocked and heartbroken by his willingness to go along with the UF patrol and how quickly he immediately began following orders, acting as her guard.

As a tear rolled down her cheek, Yuri tried to explain, "You not understand. Just go along."

"I understand completely, Sergeant Kovalenko," Britney snarled with ice in her veins. "I get it. You're just doing your job."

Stepping over to Nate, who was clearly struggling and in severe pain, Britney pulled his arm around her and urged, "Here, lean on me."

"I weigh too much for you to carry," Nate protested.

"Nonsense, you look terrible. You're pale and sweaty. You're not well, and I'm getting worried about you."

Turning back to them from near the front of the patrol, Senior Lieutenant Romanoff snarled, "Silence them, Sergeant Kovalenko!"

"Do as he asked," Yuri pleaded.

Turning away from him and refusing to acknowledge his voice, Britney held on tightly to Nate while they worked their way north.

Hearing the sound of a horn echo through the woods again, Senior Lieutenant Romanoff grumbled, saying, "Is probably insurgents trying to fool us. Mind games not work this time," he boasted with a grin, while a few of the others chuckled along with him.

Tripping over an exposed tree root, Nate fell to the ground, nearly taking Britney with him. "Ahh, damn it," he grumbled, punching the ground out of frustration.

Senior Lieutenant Romanoff turned and stomped his way back to Yuri and barked through gritted teeth, "I give you simple task! You guard prisoners and keep them moving! I'm starting to see why you aren't with your patrol. Maybe you abandoned post?"

"Not true!" Yuri snapped. "My patrol was ambushed. Everyone was killed but me. I told you. They took me prisoner, and I escaped. That is what happened."

Drawing his sidearm from its holster, Romanoff pointed the gun at Nate's head, and seethed, "I should just kill this one now to speed up the patrol. He is dragging us down. I have every legal right. He is insurgent. He is hostile enemy combatant and I am officer of Russian Federation and as such, I am formally recognized by Unified Forces as legal authority in all matters concerning keeping of peace and security. As insurgent, he is threat to both."

"No!" Britney cried, only to be backhanded by Senior Lieutenant Romanoff.

Watching Yuri's reaction, Romanoff stepped to within inches of his face, and said, "You do not like that, do you? Pick up pace or I will make much worse things happen. Do you understand?"

"Yes, Senior Lieutenant Romanoff," Yuri replied sharply.

"Very well. I expect to not have to question your loyalty again. Do I make myself clear?"

"Yes," Yuri replied.

Romanoff stood there for a moment, reading Yuri's eyes, and then turned and walked back toward the front of the patrol, getting them moving forward once again.

~~~~

"Q" Daryl whispered as he approached Q's position.

"What's up, Daryl?" Q asked.

"Jessie and I spotted a UF patrol up ahead. Jessie altered course to parallel their track, just up the hill from them. He's confident we can stay out of their sight while shadowing them from our elevated position."

"Do they have Nate? And the girl?" Q asked.

"We're not sure. Jessie asked that you and T move on up with us. He's afraid if we're too spread out, we won't be able to react quickly enough if engagement is required."

"Of course," Q replied. "Let's go."

Moving up to Jessie's position, Q asked, "What do we got?"

"Exactly what we're looking for," Jessie reported. "I see Nate, and the girl is with him."

Handing Q the binoculars, Jessie pointed, saying, "Over there. Beyond that big forked oak tree."

Adjusting the binoculars and scanning the area, Q confirmed, "Yep. I've got'em. I see seven UF guys. That's an odd number. They usually patrol in teams of six. I've never seen them deviate from that."

"Maybe they're training a new guy," Tyrone joked.

Replying with a chuckle, Q shook his head, "They don't put new guys on the hunter teams. Anyway, now that we've got their location, let's practice a little optical discipline. We don't want a glint of light from a lens giving us away."

"Good thinking," Jessie remarked. "What else do you recommend? You know these guys."

"Let's keep on working alongside them just like we're doing now until an opportunity presents itself. There's four of us, and seven of them, so we've got to hit them at just the right time to keep our numbers from being a disadvantage. The hunter teams are sharp. They're all damn good shots, too. We need two of them to hit the ground before their comrades engage if we expect to get the best of them."

Hearing a long blast from a horn in the distance, Daryl said, "Damn it to hell, I wish they would just get the hell on with it."

"Get on with what?" Tyrone asked.

"Whatever those creepy bastards are up to. The wait, the unknown, it's killing me."

Raising an eyebrow at Daryl's statement, Q said, "I appreciate your enthusiasm, Daryl, but the waiting is not literally killing you. When they strike, at that point, they may be literally killing you. Let's not wish such things into being."

"Sorry, boss. I'm just tweaked by those bastards. I can look at a UF soldier and know exactly what I'm facing and can mentally deal with it like it's all business. But this... it's like a weird ass-movie. A weird-ass movie that would have me yelling at the screen, throwing my popcorn."

"Jessie," Q whispered, getting Jessie's attention.

"Yeah," Jessie replied softly.

"Considering the fact that we're facing threats from two foes, let's work in two-man teams, maybe twenty meters apart. That's close enough to act and communicate, but far enough away for one team to react and provide cover fire if the other team is hit. In each two-man team, one man monitors the movement of the UF guys, and the other searches the area around us from threats from your troglodyte buddies."

"Roger that," Jessie concurred.

Turning to Daryl, Jessie asked, "Which do you want? Commie bastards or troglodytes?"

"I'll keep an eye out for those troglowhatevers—the cavemen. You just keep doing your thing."

With a nod from Q, Jessie and Daryl worked their way forward, giving Q and Tyrone the spacing they desired.

After hand-railing the UF hunter patrol's path of travel for approximately twenty minutes, Jessie noticed they seemed to have ceased forward movement. "Hold up," he whispered to Daryl.

Turning back to Q and Tyrone, Jessie gave them the signal to hold their position while he observed. Unable to see exactly what was going on due to the thickness of the trees between them and the hunter patrol, Jessie explained, "Wait here. I'm gonna get a little closer and try to see what's going on."

"Roger that," Daryl affirmed. "I'll boogie back to Q and Tyrone and brief them.

Patting Jessie on the shoulder, Daryl warned, "Hey, be careful, man. Like Q said, those guys can shoot. They earn their place on these teams. They aren't just assigned. Those aren't your average convoy escorts or grunts."

Nodding, Jessie smiled and slipped off into the trees, disappearing in an instant.

Steven Bird

Working his way back to Q and Tyrone, Daryl whispered, "The patrol seems to have stopped. Jessie is going in for a closer look."

"I hope he doesn't give us away," Tyrone grumbled.

"Naw, I've been watching him work," Q assured them. "He's not like an experienced special ops vet or anything, but the man's head is on straight, and he moves through the woods easier than most. He'll be fine."

Within what seemed like ten or fifteen minutes, Jessie reappeared and joined up with Q and the others.

"What do we have?" Q asked, anxious for an update.

"We were right; there are seven. They have an officer with them. Is that normal?"

"An officer?" Q asked. "Are you sure? I've never heard of anyone senior to a master sergeant being on a hunter team, and it's usually a senior sergeant that fills the lead role."

"I'm more familiar with the Russian Federation's Ratnik gear than I'd like to be," Jessie explained. "None of them are wearing any logos, patches, or insignia, which is to be expected during an operation such as this, well out of view from the public's eye. All but one of them are wearing no insignia, that is. One of them has three small stars in the shape of a triangle on his bump helmet."

"Small stars? That's a senior lieutenant in Russki ranks if I remember correctly," Q noted.

"Yep, and he's acting the part. I'd imagine the rest of his team aren't too happy having him along. One guy, in particular, stands out. He's apparently got guard duty over their prisoners, Nate and Britney."

"What makes that guy stand out, other than having the bitch job?" Q asked.

"The lieutenant looks at him differently. I can't put my finger on it, but something's just not right."

"A little inner turmoil may work to our benefit when the time comes. Especially if the team is stressed or thrown off by having a staff jerk along."

"They may be tired of having their hunter teams go missing," Jessie explained. "I mean, they've taken their share of lumps lately. This guy may be along for that reason. He may be along to personally supervise a team and bring back some information for the brass back at the UF regional outpost."

"Whatever it is, having a mismatched cog in the machine may just work to our advantage," Q predicted with a crooked grin. "What's their current setup?"

Drawing on the ground with a twig, Jessie explained, "Nate and Britney are here, seated with their backs against a tree. Nate's got his head on Britney's shoulder. He doesn't look well. The odd man out is standing watch over them, here," he said, drawing an X in the dirt to show the man's position.

Continuing, Jessie explained, "They have a perimeter set up with men here, here, here, here, and here," he detailed, forming a circle around the group, "with the lieutenant and what I assume to be a senior NCO-type, probably the senior or master sergeant you spoke of, closely liaising with each other. The lieutenant seems to be the bossy, authoritative type, but for some reason can't leave this guy's side."

Scratching his chin, Q speculated, "What if Tyrone and I move in from this direction, and you and Daryl work your way around to the other side. Four simultaneous shots would bring the odds in our favor quick."

"How can we synchronize four shots without radios? Didn't you lose yours?" asked Jessie.

"We'll give everyone time to get into position, Tyrone and I will call out our two targets on our side, and you and Daryl do the same. Hold your sights on target until the crack of my rifle. As soon as you hear my report, drop your man and move in. Tyrone and I will focus on the two senior men, while you take out the sad sack with guard duty. If it doesn't go down exactly as planned, we'll still have the element of surprise, because they clearly don't know we're here. Hopefully, that will bring our numbers into the advantage column on the scoresheet rather quickly."

"Well... that sounds like a good plan. Now, let's go see what really happens," Jessie said with a smile.

"Exactly," Q replied. "But ya gotta start somewhere."

Chapter Twenty-Five

"Sergeant Kovalenko," Britney said with contempt in her voice.

Feeling like he'd been punched in the gut by her disdain, Yuri replied, "Yes. What can I do for you, Britney?"

"Nate here is very sick. Can you get me a cold, wet cloth of some sort?"

Nodding in reply, Yuri turned to Master Sergeant Popov, the team's senior NCO, and when on a routine patrol, the team leader, and asked, "Master Sergeant, may I borrow a hand towel? My gear was lost when taken captive."

Looking to Nate and Britney, Popov answered, "You are not prisoner's servant. You are prisoner's guard. What has happened to you, Junior Sergeant Kovalenko? I knew your team leader well. Senior Sergeant Vasiliev was a fine soldier. He ran an outstanding and very successful hunter team. If not up to task, you would not have met his standard for superior NCO's and would have been replaced... or simply left behind. He had ways of avoiding hassles of administration."

Nodding, Yuri replied, "I am good, Master Sergeant. Just shaken from losing team."

Yuri returned to Nate and Britney and said, "I am sorry. There are none to be spared," before turned and walked back to an old log where he took a seat to watch them from a distance, unable to stand for long periods of time due to his weakened and injured state.

"Five more minutes and we move," Senior Lieutenant Romanoff proclaimed. "If the prisoner does not have strength to walk, we will dispose of him. I will not jeopardize my team for insurgent."

Squeezing Nate's hand tightly, Britney said, "You're going to make it. I'll help. Don't worry."

With a chuckle, Nate said, "It's a long walk out of these woods. Don't worry if anything happens to me. Just take care of yourself. You'll make it out of here and be okay. I can feel it."

As she leaned in and rested her head on his shoulder, Nate asked, "So, what's with that UF guy, Kovalenko? How did you end up with him, and why do you seem so hurt? It's like your puppy died or something."

"The horrors I faced in the cave are something I don't care to relive," she explained. "It was worse than any nightmare I could possibly imagine. It was a true horror movie. Two other captives…"

"There were more?" Nate asked.

"Yes, two young men were down there with me, at first. They didn't make it, and their deaths were something that will haunt me for the rest of my life. Anyway, Yuri, or Sergeant Kovalenko, was captured after his unit was ambushed by…them. He was the sole survivor and was brought into the caves and held prisoner with me. I would have been next to go. They seemed to have an almost ritualistic method about how they did things."

Pausing to regain her composure, she continued, "Anyway, Yuri fought one of them and killed him in the darkness. He could have left me. He could have made his escape much easier, but he didn't. He freed me and led me out of that living hell, but not before facing more of them and being injured himself.

"Once we were free of the caves, he still didn't leave me. He promised me he would not allow me to be sent back to the camps. Once the cave people found us, he fought and killed another of them, and while we were running from the others, we ran into this group and found you."

Them

"He seems to have lost his allegiance with you, now," Nate speculated.

Shaking her head, Britney confessed, "I don't know. It's heartbreaking. I don't know who to trust or believe anymore. You and Jessie were the only two people, other than my parents, that I've been able to trust without hesitation for as long as I can remember. I thought Yuri was one of those people as well. But..."

"It's okay," Nate interrupted, seeing that she was losing her composure. "You've still got me, and Jessie is out there somewhere. He won't leave us."

"I hope you're right, but forgive me for questioning my faith," Britney mumbled as she wiped her nose.

"I promise you..." Nate began to say before being interrupted by Senior Lieutenant Romanoff.

"Kovalenko, get the prisoners ready to move," he ordered.

~~~~

Quietly working their way around to their assigned ambush location, Jessie and Daryl found a suitable spot behind thick briars and vegetation to provide visual cover, as well as a large, old tree stump to act as physical cover if they were to become pinned down. The stump was about forty meters from their targets and looked as if it were the gravestone for a tree that had once stood tall and proud, much larger than the trees that currently populated the area. *This must have been logged long ago,* Jessie thought.

Whispering to Daryl, Jessie said, "I'll take the stocky fellow on the left. You take the tall guy on the right. Q and Tyrone will most likely take their counterparts on the far side.

Nodding in the affirmative, Daryl took aim, and held his sights on his chosen target, patiently awaiting Q's initiation of their attack.

Doing the same, Jessie placed his sights on his man and thought to himself, *Okay, Q. Any day now.*

~~~~

Lying prone and taking cover behind an old, rotting log, Q turned to Tyrone and asked, "Who do you want?"

"The guy on the left, the one who looks like he's carrying an RPK-74, looks like the best choice for me. That, and it takes out their light machine gun at the same time."

"A fine choice, my friend," Q acknowledged. "I'd like to smoke that lieutenant first, but our best bet would be the soldier with the mustache to the right. After we smoke these two, you go for the number two man, and I'll take out the lieutenant."

"Yes, sir," Tyrone whispered as he placed his sights on his selected target. "I think I may just take that RPK back home with me," he added, only half joking.

"Take whatever you want, my friend," Q responded with a sly grin.

"Crap, it looks like they're getting ready to pull chocks and move," Q grumbled as he saw the officer giving orders and pointing in their previous direction of travel.

Placing his sights on his target, and preparing to initiate the attack, Q slowly eased his finger into position only to see his man flinch and stumble backward.

What the...? he thought as he saw the man stagger and place his hands around an arrow sticking out of his chest.

Them

The fatally wounded man's plight went unnoticed by his comrades, and he fell forward and onto the arrow, shoving it through his body and out of his back.

Before Q could react, gunfire erupted from all around them.

Hearing hoofbeats through the woods behind them, Q and Tyrone looked over their shoulder to see a fur-clad man race past them on horseback, only to be taken off his horse by a barrage of automatic fire from the RPK-74.

Hearing a primal scream behind them, Q rolled quickly to his left to see one of the troglodytes running at him at full speed and wielding a spear. Unable to bring his gun around in time, Q heard a deafening shot ring out from beside him as Tyrone placed a round into the man's lower torso.

When the large, fur-covered figure fell forward, still clutching the spear, it pierced the ground next to Q, grazing his side and opening a deep laceration in his flesh. The large man fell on top of him, knocking the wind out of him with his nearly two-hundred-pound body.

Unsure of the extent of his wounds, Q struggled to push the man off, then he felt Tyrone roll the body to the side.

"C'mon!" Tyrone shouted as he reached out his hand to help Q to his feet.

On the far side of their intended targets, Jessie and Daryl watched as a swarm of the cave dwellers ran through the woods toward the UF hunter patrol, Nate, and Britney.

"Holy hell! How many of them are there?!" Jessie shouted as he and Daryl scrambled to their feet, each of them engaging one of the attackers while they tried to get a mental grip on what was going on around them.

Jessie watched the UF soldiers fighting feverishly to repel the attack. *Nate!* he thought as his attention turned to the tree where Nate and Britney had been kept. "C'mon!" he shouted to Daryl, and they ran toward their captive friends.

When one of the attackers came rushing out of the woods to Daryl's right with a large, Damascus-bladed knife, Daryl used the length of his .45-70 to his advantage and smashed the stock into his attacker's face, knocking him backward. Swinging the large rifle back around, he gripped the rifle firmly and let one of the hotly-loaded 405-grain flat point bullets fly, smashing into the man's face, exiting the back of his skull, and taking most of his head with it.

Seeing that the UF soldiers were busy fighting off their mysterious attackers, Jessie ran to the tree to find Nate laying on his side.

"Nate!" he shouted.

"I can't get up!" Nate cried out, having succumbed further to his wounds.

Daryl ran up alongside Jessie, and Jessie shouted, "Grab an arm!" as they dragged Nate away from the melee.

Getting him a safe distance from the heat of the battle, they laid him back against a stump and Jessie said, "Hang in there, buddy."

"What the hell is going on?" Nate asked, confused by Jessie's arrival during the attack. "Daryl! Holy hell, Daryl!" Nate exclaimed with excitement when he recognized his friend. "Where are the rest of the guys?"

Turning to Daryl, Jessie shouted, "Get him a weapon!"

Doing as Jessie had asked, Daryl retrieved a pump-action shotgun from one of the dead attackers and placed it in Nate's hands.

"Where is Britney?" Jessie asked.

"I told her to run and never look back. She went off in that direction," Nate moaned, pointing. "We had no idea you were here. We thought it was just those bastards from the caves. I didn't want her taken by them again."

Patting Nate on the shoulder, Jessie assured him, "I'm gonna go after Britney. Daryl, you stay with Nate. Nate, Q and Tyrone are here also, so be careful who you shoot at."

Nodding, Daryl said, "Take care, brother," as Jessie turned and ran off into the woods in the direction Nate had pointed.

Daryl spun around to scan the area for attackers, but the attack seemed to be ending almost as quickly as it had begun. Hearing Q shout in the distance, Daryl looked to Nate and told him, "Q and Tyrone are still in the fight," with excitement in his voice.

Hearing no reply, Daryl shook Nate but got no response. "Nate! Nate, buddy. Hang in there," he pleaded, shaking his friend.

Checking Nate's pulse, Daryl found it to be weak, but present. "I'll be right back, buddy.

Working his way toward Q, Daryl shouted, "Friendly!" as he approached Q and Tyrone while they held their rifles on two of the surviving UF soldiers.

Looking around, Daryl saw several dead fur-clad attackers, along with the dead master sergeant and two other UF soldiers.

"We've got five here," Q called to Daryl. "Where are the other two? Where are the lieutenant and the guard?"

"I don't know," Daryl responded, replaying the events that had just happened in a blur through his mind.

"Where are Jessie, Nate, and the girl?" Q then asked.

"Nate sent the girl running. Jessie and I dragged Nate over there," Daryl reported, pointing. "Jessie then ran off in pursuit of the girl. Nate needs help, bad. He just lost consciousness."

"How bad is he hurt?" Q asked.

"I dunno," Daryl shrugged.

Turning to the two UF soldier, who now sat on their knees with their hands behind their heads, Q shouted, "English!?"

"Yes. Some," one of the soldiers answered.

"Do you have any medical gear? First aid? Medicine?"

"Yes. Master Sergeant Popov kept it in pack. Is over there," he stated, pointing, and then quickly returning his hand to the top of his head in fear of the rage he could see clearly in Q's eyes.

Gesturing to Daryl, Q directed, "Grab the pack. Tyrone and I will lead these two bastards over to Nate. We don't know where the other two UF guys are or if any more of those furry bastards are still around. They seemed to disappear like ghosts. We can't let our guard down."

"You'd better take a look at that as well," Daryl insisted, pointing to Q's blood-soaked side.

Chapter Twenty-Six

Running through the woods, and attempting to follow Britney's tracks as best he could, Jessie recognized the boot prints of a UF soldier heading off in the same direction. *Damn it to hell. Those bastards never quit, do they?*

Considering the fact that the soldier might be lying in wait ahead, ready to spring an ambush on whoever should come after the girl, Jessie slowed his pace and visually scanned the area intently.

Reaching a small stream, Jessie waded through the four-inch-deep water, pausing to cup his hand, taking several drinks before crossing over to the other side.

Inspecting the damp ground along the edge of the creek, Jessie saw that both sets of tracks led off together. *Is he pursuing her, or does he have her and is forcing her along with him? If he's pursuing her, I'm gonna have a hell of a time catching up to them. If he has her captive, I've got a chance.*

Continuing to follow the trail left behind by Britney and her pursuer, Jessie resolved to not give up until she was found.

~~~~

Running frantically through the woods, Britney's heart pounded in her chest and her lungs burned with exhaustion. She hadn't eaten a real meal since Jessie had fed her prior to her capture, and in her weakened state, her legs were quickly growing shaky and tired.

Stopping momentarily to rest, Britney brushed her long brown hair out of her eyes and looked around, terrified of the threats she might face next.

Hearing a twig snap behind her, Britney spun around to see Senior Lieutenant Romanoff standing there with a MP-443 Grach Yarygin 9mm pistol in his right hand, pointing it directly at her stomach.

"You little bitch! You have caused me more trouble than your life is worth. I should just kill you now," he snarled, gritting his teeth with anger and rage. "Do you know how many UF soldiers died in pursuit of you and your insurgent trash comrades? I should just take your head back with me as prize."

Shaking in fear, Britney wanted to turn and run, but she knew her tired legs could not carry her away from this menace.

Pointing with the pistol, Romanoff ordered, "Lay on ground. Face down."

Doing as he asked, Britney began to cry uncontrollably. She had endured more than any fourteen-year-old girl should ever have to face. Her soul and her spirit were nearly broken.

"Hands behind back!" he ordered, taking a length of paracord from his pocket and hogtying her hands and feet together tightly behind her back with her legs folded.

Picking her up and throwing her over his shoulder, Romanoff looked at his wristwatch and muttered, "Is not too late for extraction. If you fight, I will kill you."

~~~~

Still hot on Britney and her pursuer's trail, Jessie came to a place where it appeared a scuffle of some sort had recently occurred. Both Britney and her pursuer's tracks moved about, and there were signs that someone had been on the ground in the prone position. It appeared to Jessie to be Britney, based on the size of the imprints.

Moving farther forward, Jessie could only see the UF boot prints. Britney's tracks had stopped at the scene of the scuffle. He spent a moment looking around in all directions to make sure her course hadn't merely been diverted, but he could find nothing.

"That bastard's got her," Jessie snarled, and he took off running once again, following the soldier's boot prints.

Running for what seemed like another half mile, Jessie felt an impact on the back of his left leg, squarely in the middle of his hamstring, followed by the crack of a gunshot and an intense burning sensation. Stumbling and falling to the ground face first, Jessie struggled to roll over as quickly as he could to face the threat that was clearly behind him.

"Do not move," a voice insisted in a choppy, Russian accent.

Still lying face down, Jessie ceased his struggles and watched as the boots he'd been pursuing walked around and in front of him, then their wearer knelt down, holding a pistol to the back of his head.

"I have questions for you. If you do not answer, I will kill you as enemy combatant. Do you understand?"

"Yes," Jessie begrudgingly replied, attempting to buy some time to think his way out of his predicament. "Where is the girl?"

"She is safe for now, although that is none of your concern," the man answered. "I am Senior Lieutenant Romanoff of the Ground Forces of the Russian Federation, acting on behalf of the Unified Forces, the current governing authority of this area. I have complete legal jurisdiction over you. Do you understand?"

Playing along, against his true beliefs, Jessie nodded in the affirmative, muttering, "Yes, I understand."

"Now. What unit are you with, and where are your insurgent comrades?"

"I'm with the Southern Alliance," Jessie said, avoiding giving the man the actual affiliation of his friends. "I was part of a QRF sent to rescue the girl. An extraction force is on its way."

"And how and when will this extraction force arrive?"

"They're arriving from the north. That's all I know. They give us very limited information in order to prevent our missions from being compromised in an occasion such as this."

Thinking through Jessie's statements, Romanoff looked to the north, which was his intended path of travel for his own extraction. "You lie," he said, pushing the gun firmly into the base of Jessie's skull.

Jessie sternly declared, "I'm not lying. I..."

Interrupted by a strange voice, Jessie heard another man with a Russian accent shout, "Romanoff!"

Stepping out from behind a tree directly in front of Romanoff was Junior Sergeant Yuri Kovalenko. "Where is the girl?" he demanded, pointing an AK-74 at Senior Lieutenant Romanoff.

"You traitor!" Romanoff shouted. "Lower your weapon immediately or I'll have you hanged, or shot before a firing squad!"

"No! No, you will not!" Kovalenko insisted. "Tell me where girl is, or I will kill you."

"Yuri!" Britney shouted, still bound and tied, hidden behind a clump of trees.

Them

When Yuri's attention was momentarily diverted to Britney, Romanoff raised the pistol from the back of Jessie's head and fired a hastily-aimed shot, striking Yuri in the left shoulder.

Returning fire as he fell backward, Yuri's rounds missed their mark, but sent Senior Lieutenant Romanoff running off into the woods to escape the barrage of bullets.

Picking himself up off the ground, Yuri ran toward Jessie, who scrambled to retrieve his own weapon, which lay in front of him. Prepared to engage the man, Jessie rolled to his side and raised his rifle, but the man ran straight past him to Britney, who was bound behind the tree.

Although he couldn't see what was going on behind the trees, Jessie could hear in Britney's voice that she was relieved to see the soldier, and that he, too, was happy to have found her, alive and in one piece. Struggling to his feet, using his rifle to help him stand, Jessie limped over to Britney and the soldier.

Once the soldier cut the cord that held Britney's hands and feet, she hugged him, and then she turned and ran to Jessie, hugging him tightly as tears of joy flowed down her cheeks.

"I'll go after Romanoff," the stranger said to Jessie.

"No! Yuri, don't go!" Britney pleaded. "He's still a threat," Yuri insisted.

Looking Jessie in the eye, Yuri nodded and said, "Take care of her," and then turned and ran off into the woods in pursuit of Romanoff, struggling through the intense pain of his now numerous wounds.

Chapter Twenty-Seven

Tyrone began administering medical care to Nate using the medical supplies obtained from the master sergeant's pack, while Daryl stood guard over the two UF prisoners and Q kept a keen eye out for threats.

Waving smelling salts below Nate's nose, Tyrone mumbled, "C'mon, buddy. Wake up. We need you to keep up the fight."

Inhaling, then wheezing and coughing, Nate's eyes opened wide. "Hey, buddy," Tyrone said, patting him on the cheeks to get him to focus.

"What the...?" Nate gasped, trying to catch his breath.

"Just relax there, buddy. We gave you some antibiotics and a few other things to keep you going until we get you home."

Reaching up and putting his hand on Tyrone's face, Nate said, "I'm so glad to see you guys. Britney? Where's Britney?" he demanded, quickly snapping back into the situation at hand.

"Jessie went to find her," Tyrone assured him.

"How long have they been gone? How long have I been out?" Nate asked.

"About a half an hour," Tyrone replied. "Q and Daryl are here with me, too.

"Hey, Nate!" Q said with a grin, happy his friend was awake.

Turning his head and seeing Daryl's large, bearded face, Nate mumbled, "Hey, Daryl. How did you convince Linda to let you in on this?"

"She was just as worried about you as I was," Daryl replied. "She wouldn't have forgiven me if I hadn't come."

Them

Confused as to why there were only three of them, Nate wondered, "Just three of you? Why? We've never operated with less than five."

"We started out as five," Tyrone admitted solemnly.

Laying his head back on the ground, Nate sighed, "Awww, no. Damn it, no. Who? Who was it?"

"Sam and Carl," Tyrone said with his eyes beginning to water. "They both went down swinging."

With thoughts of regret and loss swirling around in his mind, Nate looked over to Daryl to see that he was holding his rifle on two of the UF soldiers. Still unsure of what exactly had occurred, Nate asked, "What the hell happened? How did it all go down?"

Q explained, "Just as we had set up what we felt was the perfect ambush, those furry bastards got the same idea and attacked the hunter patrol. They hit them hard, and luckily, they didn't see us hiding in the bushes, also poised to attack. We didn't go unnoticed forever, though, and ended up getting into the mix."

Begrudgingly, Q continued, "Unfortunately, two of the UF guys got away. At this point, we don't know whether they're on the run, engaging Jessie, or watching us this very moment. We're just sitting and waiting, for now."

"How the hell are we gonna get out of here?" Nate lamented. "I'm jacked up. And you guys can't carry me all the way back. If they send more hunters in search of yet another missing patrol, we're screwed."

Interrupting after overhearing the conversation, one of the UF soldiers offered, "If you let us go, we will lie and lead them in wrong direction."

"Shut your pie hole!" barked Daryl.

"Sorry, comrade. That's just not gonna happen," Q added. "What I was going to say before we were so rudely interrupted, was that..."

"Shhh!" Daryl whispered. "I heard something. Uphill, to the south."

As Q and Tyrone started scanning their surroundings through the sights of their rifles, Daryl kept a nervous eye on the prisoners.

From just uphill of their position, they heard a voice shout out, "Friendly! Hold your fire!"

A smile grew across Q's face as he stood and said, "I'd recognize that old voice anywhere!"

Just then, Pastor Wallace and others from the Blue Ridge Militia appeared from the woods wearing camouflage and well-outfitted load-bearing vests, ready for a fight.

"Holy hell... uh, I mean, heck," Q rejoiced, reaching out to shake Pastor Wallace's hand. "What are you doing here?"

"Remember, I was Gunnery Sergeant Wallace before I was Pastor Wallace. I just couldn't let them come without me. Especially knowing an innocent young life was involved. What kind of shepherd would I be if I didn't do my part to protect the flock?"

Over the next half hour, Q, Tyrone, Daryl, and Nate caught Pastor Wallace and the others up on the events that had transpired. They shared laughs and tears as they detailed their victories, their adventures, and their defeats and losses.

"We're gonna find Sam and Carl," Pastor Wallace vowed. "We're gonna get them home where they belong for the proper burial and final respects they deserve. I promise you that."

"Thanks," Q said, patting Pastor Wallace on the arm. "That's important to all of us."

Them

Looking around, Q announced, "It looks like we've got enough guys here to hold down the fort. I'm gonna go look for Jessie and the girl."

"Me, too!" shouted Daryl.

"You're not leaving me behind, either," insisted Tyrone.

"Are you sure you guys don't need to rest?" Pastor Wallace asked. "There are plenty guys here that can go looking for them."

"No, we've got this," Q answered confidently. "You just keep an eye on those two," he said while pointing to their prisoners, "and take good care of Nate. Also, don't let your guard down. This is still a hot zone as far as I'm concerned. Nate can catch you up on anything we've not already explained about the threats we face."

~~~~

Moving quickly through the woods in search of Jessie and Britney, Q, Tyrone, and Daryl moved in bounds, covering each other as they went. After having already suffered losses at the hands of their mysterious foe, they were determined to keep each other safe while carrying out what they saw as the final phase of their mission.

Crossing the creek and stopping to get a drink before reevaluating the trail and moving on, the men barely spoke a word. Their focus was intense. They'd gone through far too much to come up short now.

Looking down at the ground, Q found the same signs of a struggle that Jessie had, and, he, too, noted how Britney's tracks no longer went on from here. One thing he did notice, though, was that Jessie's did.

"Jessie was on the guy," Q concluded. "Let's move."

Continuing through the woods and following the trail, Q, Tyrone, and Daryl passed by a fallen tree only to hear a familiar whistle, followed by the words, "Over here, guys."

"Jessie!" Q blurted with excitement as he ran around behind a fallen tree to see Jessie and the young girl well hidden from view.

"You found her! What happened? Are you hurt?" Q asked with a barrage of questions.

"The UF officer ambushed me and shot me in the back of the leg. Luckily, it was just a 9mm and not a rifle round. Then, the craziest thing happened."

"Yuri saved us!" Britney exclaimed.

"Who?" Q asked.

"The guard," Jessie answered. "The odd man out. The seventh soldier. It's a long story, but not only did he save us both from Romanoff..."

"Who?" Q interrupted.

"Romanoff, that's the officer's name," Jessie replied.

"You exchanged names?" Q questioned with a puzzled look on his face.

"Let's just say he's proud of his title," Jessie answered. "But anyway. The guard, who was on a hunter team that was ambushed by the troglodytes a few days ago, was taken captive as the sole survivor of his unit. He ended up in the caverns with Britney. That ordeal is a heck of a story all by itself, but to make the long story short, he fought and won their escape. According to her, he repeatedly risked his life to save hers."

"Where is he now?" Q asked.

"He chased Romanoff into the woods that way," Jessie said, pointing in the direction that Romanoff had fled.

"We have to help him!" Britney exclaimed. "He's hurt!"

Them

Quickly working it all out in his mind, Q said, "I'll see if I can find him. Daryl, you and Tyrone get Jessie and Britney back with the others. Oh, and Jessie, the cavalry has arrived. Nate's safe and sound with them."

"Thank God," Jessie whispered. "Thank you, God."

~~~~

Tracking Romanoff as he worked his way through the woods toward a clearing on a high spot up ahead, Yuri knew he had to stop him before he got out into the open. If Romanoff was able to reach the extraction helicopter, a manhunt like he'd never before seen would be sent out after him. As a traitor against his own people, they would never relent in their search for him. An example would have to be made.

When he knelt down to inspect a fresh set of boot prints on the ground before him, Yuri heard the ominous sound of a horn blow up ahead.

His heart sank in his chest, and he resolved to take his own life before he'd let those monsters drag him underground again. From his perspective, he had no future anyway. He would be a wanted man in a foreign land where he was seen as an oppressor and an invader by the local population, and as a traitor by his own kind. No, there was no future left for him.

Catching a glimpse of movement up ahead, Yuri ducked down behind a large rock outcrop and surveyed the scene. *It's Romanoff!* he thought as he saw how the once brave officer was now frozen in his tracks at the sound of the horn. He watched as Romanoff looked around frantically in all directions, trying to decide what move to make next.

Yuri placed his rifle on top of his hand which rested on a large stone in front of him. Carefully moving the AK-74's safety selector down to the semi-auto firing position, he gently placed his finger on the trigger, took aim, placing his sights squarely on Romanoff's back, and took a deep breath, preparing to fire.

Just as he began to apply pressure on the trigger, Romanoff twitched and spun around, exposing an arrow embedded deeply in his thigh, mere inches from his crotch. Romanoff's hand had barely enclosed around the arrow when one of the cave dwellers appeared out of the woods, running fiercely toward Romanoff, wildly swinging a large club.

Connecting with Romanoff's back, the man beat him ferociously until he struggled no more.

Joining alongside him, another of the cave dwellers appeared, and the two picked Romanoff up before carrying him away and out of sight.

Afraid to move, unsure if there were others in the area, Yuri sat perfectly still, listening and observing.

After what felt like thirty or forty minutes, Yuri was satisfied that the two he had seen attack Romanoff were gone, and he stood to turn and walk away.

To his horror, Yuri saw an insurgent militiaman standing behind him, having slipped up on him while his attention had been on the scene before him.

As Yuri began to raise his weapon, the militiaman shook his head and warned, "No. Don't do it. Lower your weapon."

Yuri's heart pounded in his chest, knowing the man clearly had the advantage over him with his weapon already pointed directly at him. Yuri sighed, "My fight is over. Just let me go."

"Go where?" the man asked.

Them

Pausing, not knowing what to stay, Yuri confessed, "I... I do not know."

"You're coming with us," the militiaman insisted.

Just as Yuri prepared to raise his weapon and go down in a hail of bullets, he noticed the man remove his finger from the trigger and begin to lower his M4 rifle. The man then reached out his hand, offering it to Yuri, and said, "We'd like you to come with us. As our friend."

Stunned, Yuri took the man's hand and shook it. With his eyes watering, a flood of emotions he hadn't felt in a very long time rushed to the surface.

Chapter Twenty-Eight

While Jessie, Nate, Britney, and Yuri flew along at tree top level in a former news helicopter turned militia asset on their way to Del Rio, Tennessee, home to Nate and the others, Jessie looked back to see the shadow of the former police Bell Jet Ranger helicopter that followed along behind, carrying Q, Tyrone, and Daryl.

He couldn't help but think about how young Britney, who had been through so much and had lost everyone and everything important to her, was flying along in a helicopter with three men who would have, and almost did, make the ultimate sacrifice to rescue her and give her a new chance at life.

The rhythmic thump of the helicopter's rotor beat seemed to sooth the young girl to sleep as she lay her head on Nate's shoulder, closing her eyes and truly relaxing for the first time since Jessie had met her days before.

Looking at Yuri, Jessie could see uncertainty in his eyes. The man had literally given up everything, and due to his actions, if word somehow got out, he would not only be a wanted man here in America, but would likely never see his home across the ocean again. In their post-collapse world, a global government would be the only group with the assets and freedom to make transoceanic travel possible anytime in the foreseeable future, and even if he did make it home, chances were the charges of his treasonous crimes would follow.

As Jessie's mind wandered through all that he had experienced since losing everything and leaving his homestead high in the Rocky Mountains, he wondered what his search for his sister would bring. Would he find heartache or happiness?

He feared the former but held out hope for the latter. Either way, he was getting close, and his nerves were becoming frayed with anticipation.

Looking across at Nate, whose eyes were locked onto his, Jessie grinned, "You're almost home! I'm sure they'll fix you up real good and have you back up and about in no time."

Smiling, Nate sighed, "Hell, I don't care if I'm up and about. I just want to be home with my wife, Peggy and our son, Zack. I'll gladly take a long, painful recuperation as long as I wake up to their smiling faces every day."

"Sheriff Jessie," Nate interjected, looking at Jessie with his head cocked off to one side.

"What? What is it?" Jessie asked.

"I told you my full name. I told you right before you went off to find help. But you never gave me your full name. How the hell do I not know that by now?"

Laughing, Jessie answered, "I guess we've just been a little too busy to worry about the little things. It's Townsend. Jessie Townsend."

"Nice to meet you, Jessie Townsend," Nate greeted him with a smile.

Reaching out his hand as well, Yuri said, "Yuri Kovalenko."

"It's a pleasure to meet you properly, Mr. Kovalenko," Jessie replied, taking his hand.

"Nate Hoskins," Nate said, shaking Yuri's hand as well.

Looking out the window, Nate announced, "We're almost there. They'll land just outside of town in a small pasture, then they'll truck us on in from there."

When the helicopter touched down, several militia members, from nurses to security personnel, rushed out to meet them. They were led over to a livestock trailer that was hooked to a well-used John Deere 2355 farm tractor.

"Climb on in," one of the security officers urged over the noise of the helicopters taking off and disappearing over the tree line.

As they drove, their accompanying security detail changed clothes in the back of the trailer, donning worn out denim jeans, Carhartt jackets, and other such farm-related attire.

When the trailer was pulled into town, Jessie was shocked to see what appeared to be fifty or more happy townspeople gathered around to welcome their heroes home.

Pulling to a stop in front of the Del Rio Baptist Church, Nate was quickly carried out where a tearful woman and a young boy anxiously awaited, running to Nate's side at first sight.

Jessie's heart welled up with emotion at the sight of such a wonderfully happy ending to the painful saga they had all just endured.

Britney and Yuri were then led into the church, where they would both be cared for and provided for until more permanent accommodations could be found.

Just as Q turned to Jessie and began to speak, he was interrupted by a dark-haired man in his mid-forties with a peppery gray beard who ran up to shake Q's hand.

"Q! Thanks so much for bringing Nate home!" the man exclaimed. "Nate's mom Judith is on her way down from the homestead with Molly and Jason now. She's desperate to see him."

"Jessie, this is Evan," Q said, introducing the two.

"Did you say, Molly?" Jessie asked, shaking the man's hand.

"Yeah, my wife, Molly Baird," Evan responded.

Seeing confusion on Jessie's face, Q asked, "What's wrong?"

Them

Turning back to Evan, Jessie said, "Where is your wife from... originally?"

"Colorado. That was a long time ago, though. Why?" Evan wondered.

Jessie's heart began to pound in his chest. Could it be? Could he finally be at the end of his long, difficult struggle to find his last remaining family member?

Turning to see a woman in her sixties running into the church with tears in her eyes, Jessie heard Evan shout, "Jason, over here!"

Looking to the man Evan had referred to as Jason, Jessie saw a woman, a few years younger than he, standing next to him. He hadn't seen his sister in many years. They had been separated by a bitter divorce at a young age, and Jessie and his sister had simply drifted apart. Sure, they had written the occasional letter or sent a Christmas card at times, but as the years went by, they had seemed to go their separate ways with their divided family. And once the attacks that had driven the country into collapse began, they were completely lost to each other.

Even after all those years and all the changes each one of them had gone through, Jessie recognized Molly, and could see her as the young girl he remembered so fondly from his childhood.

Her eyes instantly locked onto his. Neither of them could believe it. After all these years, miles, wars, and turmoil, brother and sister were reunited in the most unlikely way, thousands of miles from where their journey had begun.

Chapter Twenty-Nine

One week later...

Sitting on the front porch of Evan and Molly's homestead, Jessie rocked back and forth in an old antique rocking chair, with his bandaged leg propped up on the porch railing while he sipped a cup of coffee, watching as the fog burned off to reveal the beauty of the mountains surrounding Del Rio.

Seeing several men work their way up the road to the home on horseback, Jessie stood up and limped to the door, saying, "You've got company."

Joining him on the porch, Evan looked at the riders through a riflescope and said, "That's Pastor Wallace and Daryl. They also have another horse in trail."

As Pastor Wallace and Daryl rode up to the house, Jessie was stunned. His ornery old lineback dun quarter horse, Hank, was with them, being led along tied off to Daryl's saddle.

Waving them up, Evan quickly retrieved a cup of coffee for each and invited them to join them on the porch.

"Hey, Jessie!" Daryl said with a smile. "We thought you might know this handsome fellow."

Letting go of the porch railing, Jessie limped off the porch and hobbled over to his beloved horse. "I don't believe it," he said. "How is this possible?"

Dismounting, Daryl explained, "My wife, Linda, has always been a lover of all things horse. She's got herself a good little business going these days training and caring for horses, in exchange for barter and trade.

"A feller she deals with from the Newport area was out on a supply run when he ran across this fine specimen. Linda is always particular about where horses that come our way are obtained. We don't want any part of the horse thievin' business. Anyway, she trusted the guy, and his story added up to being in the general area of Chestnut Hill. The math just seemed to add up with what you had told us."

Stroking Hank on the neck, Jessie asked, "What do I owe you? What did you pay for him?"

"Don't you ever insult me with a question like that again," Daryl declared, handing Jessie the lead rope tied to Hank's halter.

Jessie tied Hank to the porch railing and joined the other men on the porch, once again taking his seat and propping his leg up on the railing. "Doctors orders," he stated, trying not to seem rude.

"So, all things considered, how are you settling into things here in the great state of Tennessee?" Daryl asked.

"I'm loving every minute of it," Jessie replied as he shook Daryl's hand. "And now that I've got Hank back, well, I can't complain at all."

"Mr. Townsend," Pastor Wallace greeted with a nod, shaking his hand as well. "We didn't get a chance to make proper introductions back there in the woods."

"Yeah, there was a lot going on, to say the least," Jessie replied. "So, you were Gunny Wallace in a previous life, I hear?"

"Previous, and sometimes present life, when need be," Wallace admitted. "The old me has had to show his face a few times as of late."

Changing the subject, Pastor Wallace said, "In addition to bringing back the horse, I figured Jessie still had a lot of unanswered questions swirling around in his mind that I may be able to answer about what happened back there."

Seeing Jessie's interest pique, Pastor Wallace gestured to the chairs and suggested, "Please, gentlemen, let's all take a seat."

Once they were all settled, Pastor Wallace explained, "Well..." he began, unsure of where to start. "Our boys roamed the entire area, and based on the intelligence you gave, we found the cave system where the girl was taken. Since we had adequate men and supplies, we made entry into the cave. I must say, that was some setup. They could have remained hidden out there forever if they hadn't given us a reason to come looking for them.

"Anyway, we engaged several more of... them... whatever they were supposed to be, killing the remaining few. We thoroughly cleared every chamber and passage of the entire system. You can trust me when I say, we got the last of them."

"What about that UF officer who Yuri said was taken by them?" Jessie inquired.

"Oh, we found him, too," Pastor Wallace asserted, raising an eyebrow. "Well, some of him, anyway."

"So, he's dead?" Jessie queried, desperate for confirmation.

"He's very dead," Pastor Wallace replied. "They seem to have eaten him."

"What!?" Evan exclaimed.

"I'm afraid that's the fate many others had met, as well. And I'm sure Yuri and the girl would have, too, if he hadn't fought so hard for their escape."

"Wow," Jessie shuddered, leaning back in his chair, just trying to soak it all in.

"There was some truly sick, evil stuff going on in there," Pastor Wallace added. "The crazy part is, we still don't know who they were or where they were from. We combed through that place like a crime scene and couldn't find one written word. To our knowledge, no one had heard them speak a word, either. Did you?"

"No, I didn't," Jessie confirmed. "And as a matter of fact, the only communications of any sort that I heard were those horn blasts."

Continuing, Pastor Wallace explained, "We found one of the horns. It resembled a Viking war horn. I don't think they're related in any way, though. There was nothing else 'Viking' about them. If one dug deep enough into a library of the macabre, I'm sure a culture or belief system they were trying to emulate could be found. Or hell, some sick psycho may have just wanted to start his very own end of the world cult. Who the hell knows? All we can do now is be thankful that every last one of them has met his maker."

"Did you see any other UF activity in the area?" Jessie asked.

"A few of our boys, bringing up the rear on our way out, saw a helicopter off in the distance. They believe it was a Mi34, but couldn't be sure."

Slapping his thigh, Daryl proclaimed, "This sure is one screwed-up world we live in."

Smiling, Jessie agreed, "Yeah, but it's got some exceptionally wonderful people left in it, so maybe there's hope for it, after all."

"So, what now?" Daryl asked.

"What do you mean?" Jessie asked, seeking clarification.

"Now that you found your sister, what'll be your next adventure?"

"I'm staying right here. As far as I'm concerned, I've found my new home, and the only adventures I'll ever partake in again will be whatever unfolds right here in these hills."

~~~~ The End ~~~~

A Note from the Author

First and foremost, let me take a moment to thank you for buying and reading *Them: Society Lost, Volume Four*. This is my twelfth book, and I'm thankful beyond what words can express for each and every person who has bought and read my books along the way. Your support has been life-changing for my family and me, to say the least.

Your support over the past year or so has been especially important to me. As anyone who follows me on social media knows, my life is spread pretty thin. I'm the chief pilot/flight department manager of a corporate flight department for a nationwide electronics retailer, a farmer, a husband and father, a homeschooler, and a writer. I can't remember the last time I woke up and wondered what I was going to do that day. The question in my mind is more like "of all the things I have to do, what will I be able to get done?" At least I can't complain that I'm bored.

People often ask me how I find the time to write. Whew, that's a good question, but it's a passion that I just can't let fall to the wayside, and again, your support keeps me going.

This book was very fun to write. It takes place in my neck of the woods after Jessie's long, cross-country journey, as well as blending with my first series, *The New Homefront*, bringing those beloved characters back for more adventures. I've had a lot of people asking for more from the folks from *The New Homefront*, though they may not have expected to see them here. From a timeline perspective, this book would take place after *The Resolution,* unofficially making it the sixth book in the series.

As you may have noticed, Jessie's journey throughout the *Society Lost* series has run the entire gamut. It started out as a homesteading/prepper, post-apocalyptic story, followed by a vigilante justice western, and has somehow evolved into a horror, all with a little comedy sprinkled in (some of you may debate the comedy part). Maybe I've just got a dark sense of humor. It's been quite the ride to say the least. When I think back to all of Jessie's adventures, I just think, wow, what a journey it was.

What's next for me? I've got several things in mind. Often times, a book just jumps into my head and refuses to get out until I put pen to paper…uh, I mean…key to electronic signal. Over the course of the next year, I really hope to address all of them and get at least four, and hopefully six new novels out. Don't hesitate to let me know what you want to see next.

Thanks again for taking time out of your busy life to read this book and to let a piece of my imagination into your world. May God bless you and your family now, and in any future we may face.

Respectfully,

Steven C. Bird

About the Author

Steven Bird was born and raised in the Appalachian coal town of Harlan, Kentucky, where he grew up immersed in the outdoors. After graduating high school, he joined the Navy and moved to the Seattle area, where he served on active duty for eleven years, eventually retiring out of the reserves at just over twenty years of service.

Upon leaving active duty, Steven began working as a charter pilot and a flight instructor. Eventually finding his way into a turbo-prop airline, and then on to a jet airline, he acquired thousands of hours of flight experience before leaving the airline industry to fly for one of America's largest cellular retailers.

Steven's writing career didn't start off with a degree in English and a background in literature. It was during his time with the airlines that inspired his writing with his first book *The Last Layover,* which was written mostly on an Android smartphone. Since then, Steven has published eleven additional books and has discovered writing as his true calling.

Steven and his wife, Monica, live on a farm/homestead in rural Tennessee on the Cumberland Plateau with their three children, Seth, Olivia, and Sophia. They raise cattle, horses, donkeys, sheep, chickens, ducks, and turkeys, in an effort to be as self-sufficient as possible, while exposing their children to the real world that surrounds them.

Steven's passion for the concept of individual liberty shines through in all of his works, as it does in his daily life. Join him in the stories he weaves through the following books and series.

The New Homefront Series:

The Last Layover: The New Homefront, Volume One
The Guardians: The New Homefront, Volume Two
The Blue Ridge Resistance: The New Homefront, Volume Three
The Resolution: The New Homefront, Volume Four
Viking One: A New Homefront Novel

The Society Lost Series:

The Shepherd: Society Lost, Volume One
Betrayal: Society Lost, Volume Two
The Tree of Penance: Society Lost, Volume Three
Them: Society Lost, Volume Four

Erebus: An Apocalyptic Thriller

Jet: Dangerous Prey

The Edge of Civility

Them

Free Preview of EREBUS: An Apocalyptic Thriller – Available Now!

Winner of the 2018 Audiobook Listener Awards Thriller of the Year!

Them

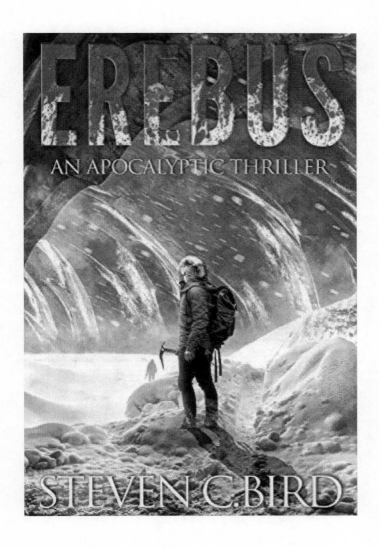

Them

Introduction

In 1841, when the British vessel H.M.S. Terror first charted Antarctica under the command of explorer James Clark Ross, the crew laid eyes on a volcano reaching 12,500 feet above the surface of the frozen ice of Antarctica. Ross and his men saw the huge white plume rising from its crater at the summit, and it has been erupting ever since. Mount Erebus, as it was later named by explorer Ernest Shackleton, was named after the Greek god Erebus, the god of primeval darkness. To anyone who has visited the mountain and its incredibly harsh environment, this name is found to be more than appropriate.

Today, on the steep and icy slopes of Mount Erebus, can be found a rugged team of scientists, researchers, and mountaineers carrying out their work in one of the harshest and most remote parts of the planet, at a facility known as the Mount Erebus Volcano Observatory, or simply MEVO. These professionals, tough enough to brave the extreme climate of Mount Erebus, include experts in the fields of gravity and magnetotellurics, volcanology, geophysics, and even astrobiology. These doctorate-level professionals travel each year from several major universities such as Cambridge, Missouri State, the New Mexico Institute of Mining and Technology, and the University of Washington in order to study Erebus, as well as the unique environment it has created for itself in one of the most remote places on Earth. They are assisted by a professional mountaineer, as well as graduate students from their respective institutions who study under them.

The researchers at MEVO, when not on the mountain at the research camp simply called the Lower Erebus Hut, are based out of McMurdo Station. Mac-Town, as McMurdo Station is fondly referred to by its residents, was founded by the U.S. Navy in 1956. What was initially called Naval Air Facility McMurdo is now simply McMurdo

Them

Station. McMurdo Station is currently run by the United States Antarctic Program and is governed by the Antarctic Treaty, signed by forty-five world governments. The Antarctic Treaty regulates daily life at McMurdo, as well as the research conducted there.

In many respects, the inhabitants of McMurdo Station are on their own on the vast and remote continent of Antarctica. This is especially true during the winter months, when most of the station's one thousand residents return to warmer climates, leaving behind a skeleton crew of only two hundred to face the rigors and potential horrors of life at the bottom of the world—alone.

Chapter One

Mount Erebus Volcano Observatory (MEVO)

Holding on tightly to the core sample drill as it bored into the side of one of the massive ice towers that reach high into the sky, Dr. Hunter focused on his task at hand with relentless determination. Standing over him like giants from ancient-Greek mythology, the ice towers, formed by condensing air as it vents from one of the many fumaroles on Antarctica's largest and most active volcano, Mount Erebus, reach as high as sixty-feet above the ground.

With the frigid arctic winds atop Mount Erebus pounding his body, his coat buffeted violently as he struggled to maintain his footing. His beard, nearly full of ice and snow, clung to his face like a rigid mask as he wiped his goggles, attempting to see the drill as it bored its way into the ice before him. The season's expedition was about to come to an end, and he could not afford to leave without the core samples he desperately needed in order to complete his research.

"Doc, we've got to get moving," Mason yelled through the howling winds, placing his hand on Dr. Hunter's shoulder as if to urge him away from his work. "If the storm gets any worse, we won't be able to see well enough to make it back to the hut! It's already damn near zero visibility."

Ignoring the plea, knowing his task was nearly complete, Dr. Hunter yelled, "Got it!" as he pulled the core sample gently from the tower of ice. Without saying a word, he patted Mason on the shoulder, and they began their hike through the pounding weather to their snowmobiles, to return to the Lower Erebus Hut before the mountain claimed them, as it had tried so many times before.

~~~~

Them

Entering the Lower Erebus Hut, Mason slammed the door shut as quickly as he could to keep the fierce frigid winds at bay. Everyone in the room turned to look at the two ice-and-snow-covered men. Having just returned from the summit with Dr. Hunter's core samples in hand, they placed them gently on the floor and began to dust off the fresh snow that covered them, in preparation for removing their heavy outer layers of protective clothing.

"I was starting to worry about you two," said Dr. Linda Graves, a forty-four-year-old astrobiology researcher with the University of Washington.

"So was I," replied Mason, as he began peeling off his balaclava and removing his many layers of clothing. Mason, or Derrick Mason to be exact, was a graduate student of geochemistry at the New Mexico Institute of Mining and Technology (NMT).

As a student of Dr. Nathan Hunter, the Principle Investigator for the expedition and a professor of geochemistry at NMT, Mason had been hand-selected to come along on this year's expedition to Mount Erebus. Dr. Hunter not only chose him for his academic prowess, but also for his abilities as a seasoned mountain climber and avid outdoor adventurer. Mason was an experienced hunter, long distance hiker, mountain climber, and most importantly of all, a survivalist at heart. There were plenty of students academically up to the task, perhaps even more so than Derrick Mason, but Dr. Hunter refused to let his research be slowed by having to babysit a graduate student who wasn't physically up to the extreme conditions that Antarctica, and specifically, Mount Erebus, thrust upon those ill-suited for the challenge.

With Derrick Mason, however, he had a stout, twenty-eight-year-old outdoorsman that he knew could be counted on when things became challenging and treacherous on the volcano.

Peeling off his gloves, Dr. Hunter quipped, "If we were gonna leave without one of our critical core samples, what would be the point of coming? I'm not waiting until next year to come back just to fill in the gaps, and I know you didn't come all the way from Seattle to leave just yet either—all things considered. Caution is wise, but risk yields rewards."

"That it does," joked Mason, rubbing his face in an attempt to return warmth to his skin. "But it's days like this that remind you of the fact that Shackleton named this mountain after the Greek god Erebus, the god of primeval darkness."

"Did you get what we were looking for?" Dr. Graves asked.

"I think so," Dr. Hunter replied. "I still want to get down as far as I can into the fumarole on the north side of Tramway Ridge and get a sample before we leave. But today's cores contain some of the material we were looking for."

Changing the subject, Dr. Hunter looked around the room, and asked, "Any word from Mac-Town?" referring to Antarctica's McMurdo Station.

"The first helicopter will be here in the morning," answered Jared Davis, a volcanologist and a junior member of the research team from NMT. "We'll have them available through the end of the week, but after that, Mac-Town will be buttoned up for the winter. The last Air Force C-17 leaves Saturday. If you've not done what you need to get done by then, you'll either have to leave it behind until spring or be stuck here with the wintering-over crew at Mac-Town."

"I suppose so," Dr. Hunter replied. "Now, getting back to the important business at hand, what was for dinner and is there any left?" he asked, looking around the crowded and cluttered living area and seeing dishes piled high in the kitchen sink. "It looks like we missed out on whatever it was."

Brett Thompson, a Homer, Alaska native and the team's mountaineer and safety specialist, spoke up and said, "Neville made us a pot of his famous Worcestershire stew."

"He made what?" asked Mason with a confused look.

Neville Wallace, a tall, lanky, curly-haired British graduate student who had accompanied Dr. Gerald Bentley, the Co-Principle Investigator and volcanologist from the University of Cambridge said, "I simply concocted a basic vegetable stew from what was left of the fresh produce, before it spoiled. It was already getting a tad bit long on the shelf, so I opted to put it to good use. To mask the rather dismal condition of the ingredients, I kicked it up a bit with what was left of the Worcestershire sauce. It wasn't anything to write home to mum about, but it filled the void."

In a deflated tone, Dr. Hunter replied, "Wasn't? I assume that means it's all gone."

"I told Lester and Ronald not to go for seconds until you had returned and eaten your share, but you know how those two buggers can be," Neville said, poking fun at the two men who had finished off the rest of the soup.

"Oh, well... we'll survive," said Mason as he plopped down onto the only empty spot on the old, worn-out sofa. "I was in the mood for some sort of canned meat anyway. As a matter of fact, I'm so hungry I could go for one of those one-hundred-year-old cans of mutton still on the shelf in Shackleton's Hut."

Tossing him a can of pickled herring, Dr. Hunter said, "Here ya go. It's not century-old mutton, but it'll do. We're scraping the bottom of that sort of thing, too," he said as he searched for food in each of the nearly empty cabinets.

"If something happens and the helicopters don't show up soon to give us our ride back to Mac-Town, we may have to decide who we're gonna eat first," chuckled Mason, as he peeled open the can.

"I vote for Lester and Ronald then, since they ate the last of the soup," said Dr. Jenny Duval, the official camp scientific assistant. "It only seems fair."

"Hey, now!" replied Lester Stevens, an engineer brought along as the team's lava-lake-imaging technical guru.

Lester Stevens and Ronald Weber were the resident non-scientific technical experts, and though they had never met before traveling to Antarctica, the pair often seemed as if they were long-lost brothers. The others frequently joked that they spent way too much time in the hut and needed to get out on the mountain more. They often teased about the two having a fictitious mental condition they called *MEVO Fever* from being isolated on the mountain for too long. If anyone in the camp had it, it was truly those two jokers.

As the rest of the group settled into their nightly routine of watching old black-and-white science fiction movies, Dr. Walter Perkins, a researcher from Missouri State University who specialized in gravity and magnetotellurics, stood and waded through the tired bodies strewn about the floor. The researchers lay about the hut with their heads propped up on boots, jackets, or whatever they could find to help them see the television. To an outsider, it would appear to have been the scene of some apocalyptic movie where the dead lay scattered on the floor wherever they had fallen.

Approaching Hunter and Mason, he asked, "Dr. Hunter, would you like me to put your samples away in the cold room while you two finish your five-star cuisine?"

"Thanks, Walt, but we can get it," Dr. Hunter replied. "There's no reason for you to get the chills after warming up from your day out and about. The two of us are barely thawed, so we won't even notice."

Looking to Mason, watching as he devoured his canned meal of compressed fish, he said, "Actually, Derrick, I can get it. I'm hitting the sack after that. Get your stuff together and be ready to accompany me to Mac-Town in the morning when the helicopter comes. We'll get our samples on the next transport and then head back up to the summit when we return tomorrow afternoon. I saw something interesting that I want to check out."

"Yes, sir," Mason replied sharply. Taking another bite of pickled herring, he turned and asked, "What did you see?"

"We'll talk about it in the morning; it may be nothing."

"Roger that," Mason replied, turning his attention back to his half-eaten can of fish.

~~~~

Early the next morning after the weather had cleared, Dr. Hunter looked off into the distance, scanning the horizon for the arrival of the helicopter that was scheduled to transport his core samples back to McMurdo Station. Once at McMurdo, they would arrange to have the samples loaded onboard a U.S. Air Force C-17 for transportation back to the states where he could continue the analysis of his samples in a proper laboratory environment.

"There they are!" shouted Mason over the howling winds of the clear, arctic morning.

Looking at his watch, Dr. Hunter replied, "It's about damn time! We're cutting it close. We barely have time to get them on today's flight. We haven't got time for delays."

Upon landing, Dr. Hunter and Mason loaded the crate of core samples, as well as some other gear that was packed and ready for shipment, on board the Eurocopter AS350. Once everything was securely lashed to the floor, the pilot was given a thumbs-up and they were quickly on their way.

During the flight, Mason couldn't help but look across the frozen continent, thinking of how, strangely, he would miss it during their time back in New Mexico. Antarctica, a place that to a casual observer may seem to be merely empty, cold, and harsh, somehow endears itself in the hearts of those who spend time there. There is a beauty and peace about the frozen continent that feels like home to a wandering soul, and a wandering soul he was.

As the helicopter approached McMurdo Station, a research base that more closely resembled an industrial mining town than an environmentally-friendly research facility, Mason's mind switched gears as he chuckled to himself, thinking, *then again, I could use those warm New Mexico nights right about now.*

After landing, Dr. Hunter and Mason quickly unloaded their core samples and placed them on a forklift for transportation to McMurdo's Ship Off Load Command Center.

Walking into the facility behind the forklift, Dr. Hunter and Derrick Mason were immediately greeted by George Humboldt, a logistics specialist at McMurdo. Pulling his scarf away from his mouth, George said, "Dr. Hunter, I'm glad you made it."

"Have we missed it?" Dr. Hunter impatiently inquired.

"No, but unfortunately, the flight is delayed until tomorrow due to mechanical issues." Pointing at the crate on the forklift, he asked, "Is that the samples we spoke of?"

"Yes. Yes, it is," Dr. Hunter replied with tension in his voice. "I can't stress enough how these samples need to remain frozen at all times. They contain...well, they contain material that is critical to my research. I just can't do without them."

"Don't worry, Doctor," George replied. "It's no problem at all. I don't think I need to point out that transporting ice samples is a fairly routine task for us here at McMurdo."

"I know. I know," Dr. Hunter replied. "Forgive me, but I believe I'm onto something special and if my samples are lost for any reason, it will be a setback that will require me to wait until next year just to catch back up."

"Every sample from every research team is important, Doctor. But you have my word that I will ensure that exceptional care is given to yours. By this time tomorrow, your samples will be well on their way back to the U.S., and will be in good hands."

Patting Dr. Hunter on the arm, Mason interrupted by saying, "C'mon, Doc. George has a handle on things here. Let's get some lunch before we head back out to MEVO. I've been looking forward to a hot meal after what we've been down to for the past few days."

Nodding in agreement, Dr. Hunter said, "Yes, of course. Thanks, George," as the two men turned and began their walk toward the station's cafeteria.

~~~~

Completing the paperwork for Dr. Hunter's shipment, George watched as Mason and Dr. Hunter left the facility. Turning to see Vince Gruber approaching with the forklift, he chuckled, placing his clipboard on top of Dr. Hunter's samples.

Them

Stepping off the forklift, Vince said, "They always wait until the last minute. Every year, it's the same damn thing."

Patting Vince on the shoulder, George smiled, saying, "Yep. They all think their work is more important than everyone else's, too. You'd think these ice samples were tubes of gold the way that guy acts. He's one of the worst. He's always uptight about his stuff. He could carry it on the plane his damn self, if it were up to me."

Pausing to look around at the vast amount of cargo they had yet to load, George continued, "Oh, well. You'll be home in Florida soon, and I'll be back in Philly eating a real cheesesteak, not the sorry excuses for a sandwich they have here. Let's just get on with it and mark our last few days of the season off the calendar."

~~~~

Arriving at the station's cafeteria, still referred to as the galley due to McMurdo's roots as a naval facility, both Mason and Dr. Hunter grabbed a plastic tray, a large and a small plate, and silverware as they began working their way through the hot food line. Plopping a heaping scoop of barbecued pulled-pork onto his plate, Mason said, "Man, I've been looking forward to this."

"I know what you mean," replied Dr. Hunter. "MEVO is like a second home to me, but when provisions begin running low, it's not like we can run out and get more. Being based on the side of a major volcano has its inherent limits."

As the two men sat down and began to eat, they were approached by Dr. Raju Tashi, a particle physics researcher from the University of Wisconsin. "Dr. Hunter, may I join you?" he asked.

"Of course, Raj," Dr. Hunter replied. "And this is one of my best and brightest graduate students from NMT, Derrick Mason," he said, gesturing to Mason. "Derrick, this is Dr. Tashi. He's one of the particle chasers out at the IceCube facility. They're researching neutrinos. Pretty exciting stuff for a particle chaser."

"Pleased to meet you," Dr. Tashi said to Mason with a smile as the two shook hands.

"Likewise, Doctor."

"How are things going at IceCube?" Dr. Hunter asked.

With a look of excitement on his face, Dr. Tashi replied, "Excellent. Our experiments with the high-altitude balloon went very well. We're excited to get back to Wisconsin to study our results in more detail. We have wrapped up our operations for the season and are all awaiting transportation back to the states. And yourself? How are things at MEVO?"

"Excellent as well," he replied. "Although I wish I could say we've wrapped things up as you have. No matter how much I accomplish, I always feel a step behind the mountain. There is so much to learn. So much to explore. And of course, as soon as you're on to something good, Erebus throws you a curve ball and a critical piece of equipment gets smashed by a crater bomb or the like."

"Well, at least you haven't been smashed by a crater bomb yourself," Dr. Tashi said with a chuckle.

"He came close a few times," Mason said, looking to Dr. Hunter with taunting smile. "Last week, a crater bomb the size of a Volkswagen almost nailed him.

"Is that so?" asked Dr. Tashi with a raised eyebrow.

Placing his glass of tea on the table while poking around at his tray for the next bite of food, Dr. Hunter responded, "Let's just say Erebus doesn't give up its secrets without you having to earn them."

"I don't envy you for that," Dr. Tashi replied. "At IceCube, all we have to contend with is the cold."

"Well, gentlemen," Mason said as he pushed himself back from the table with a satisfied look on his face. "I'm gonna grab dessert. Can I get anyone something while I'm up?"

"Frostyboy is down again," Dr. Tashi said in a tone of frustration, referring to the cafeteria's famous soft-serve ice cream machine.

"No! Ah, damn it," Mason said, exasperated by Dr. Tashi's news.

Them

Patting Mason on the back, Dr. Hunter laughed and said, "Don't fret about it. By next week, you'll be getting yourself a scoop at Cold Stone Creamery from that cute blonde who has her eye on you back at NMT."

With that, Dr. Hunter stood and said, "It was great seeing you again, Raj. Are you coming back next summer?"

"That has yet to be decided," Dr. Tashi replied. "If not, keep in touch. I'm sure we'll cross paths again. We may not be in the same field, but science is a small world."

Shaking his hand, Dr. Hunter smiled and said, "You take care. And yes, yes, it is."

Chapter Two

Mount Erebus Volcano Observatory

As the helicopter touched down near the Lower Erebus Hut, snow and ice crystals swirled around them as the twenty-five-mile-per-hour wind gusts pounded the craft. Shoving open the door and holding it against the violent winds, Mason signaled for Dr. Hunter to exit the still-running helicopter. Once Dr. Hunter was clear and on his way to the Lower Erebus Hut, Mason shut the door firmly and signaled to the pilot that they were clear. Before the two men reached the door of the facility, the helicopter pilot had lifted off and was on his way back to McMurdo Station and the comforts it provided.

Closing the door securely behind them, Dr. Hunter looked around the room and asked, "Where is Linda?"

Looking up from his work of packing up some of the team's sensitive data-recording equipment, Ronald answered, "Linda? Oh, Dr. Graves. She and Brett went back up on the mountain this morning just after the two of you took the helicopter out to McMurdo."

"I hope they hurry. It's getting late. There isn't much daylight left as it is," Dr. Hunter said with a noticeable uneasiness in his voice.

"They'll be fine," Mason replied. "Brett is a top-notch mountaineer. I wish I had just half of his climbing skills."

"You find your way around the mountain pretty well," Dr. Hunter said as he walked over to the coffee maker.

"I'm an outdoor junkie, but I'm your average outdoor junkie," Mason replied with a thankful smile. "But Brett—he's hardcore. That's why I know they'll be fine. Besides, Dr. Graves is a fitness freak. She can scurry up a vertical ascent and be looking down at us from the top, while the rest of us are stopping to catch our breath a quarter of the way up."

Them

With a chuckle, Ronald added, "And Doc, you know better than to let her catch you uttering words of concern about her. She'll rip you a new one."

Smiling as he took a sip of hot, black coffee, Dr. Hunter said, "You're right about that, Ronald. She's not one to tolerate a male counterpart's acknowledgment that she's a lady."

~~~~

Opening her eyes and seeing nothing but darkness around her, Dr. Graves realized she was lying flat on her back. With her head pounding from the impact, she paused for a moment before she attempted to move when she heard Brett yelling down to her from above.

"Dr. Graves!" he shouted. "Dr. Graves, are you okay?"

With his words echoing off the walls throughout the ice cave, it was disorienting and difficult for her to tell from which direction his shouts were coming. Sitting up, she felt herself become dizzy and light-headed as she replied in a weak, shaky voice, "Yeah. Yeah, I'm fine—I think."

"I can barely hear you!" he shouted. "Are you okay?"

Mustering the strength to shout back, she yelled, "Yes! Yes, I'm okay!" She instantly regretted her efforts as the intensity of her throbbing headache increased with each word she uttered, as if the words were bouncing around inside her head.

"I'm coming down!" he shouted.

Struggling to get to her knees, Dr. Graves reached for her headlamp, only to find that it had been irreparably damaged in the fall. Pulling her hand-held flashlight from her pocket, she flicked it on, only to discover in amazement that the walls of the cave around her contained traces of grayish microorganisms, unlike anything she had ever seen.

Hearing a rope bounce off the wall behind her, she turned and pointed her hand-held flashlight skyward and into the small, tubular vertical fumarole shaft from which she had fallen into this previously undiscovered chamber deep beneath the ice. Seeing Brett's climbing rope, she shouted, "I've got your rope. Come on down. I'll belay you from here."

Within a moment, Brett Thompson, the MEVO research team's professional mountaineer, appeared above her with his feet dangling as he descended into the dark chamber. Brett, still an Alaskan at heart, had been in and around large mountains his entire life. Standing six-foot-two with a slim build and sandy brown hair, Brett had always been popular with the ladies. However, his heart belonged to the extreme environments created by the mountains.

After working as a guide on Denali since his mid-twenties and having climbed the likes of Everest, Kilimanjaro, and the Matterhorn, Erebus seemed like the next logical place for his mountaineering career. It had yet to disappoint him in that regard.

Dropping into the chamber in front of Dr. Graves, he said, "You scared me half to death. That fumarole has to be at least one-hundred and fifty feet nearly straight down."

"Thank goodness for helmets," she said, tapping her gloved knuckles on her head. "That, and I tried to ball up the best I could to create drag on the sides of the ice tube to slow my descent. That way, it wasn't really a fall so much as it was a slide—at least until I reached the opening in the ceiling here. That part was a free-fall."

"Either way, I'm amazed you're up and walking," he said, scanning the chamber with his headlight.

"Hand me one of your sample containers," she said, reaching out to him as she began to look closely at the life-forms that appeared to be thriving on the chamber walls. "We've stumbled across something special here. It's hard to tell exactly, given the conditions, but I don't think we've documented microbes such as these before."

Handing her the container with the lid removed, Dr. Graves took it and immediately began collecting specimens with her Zero Tolerance brand folding pocket-knife, a gift from her brother that she carried with her at all times. "These walls are almost wet to the touch. What temperature is it in here?"

"I'm showing thirty-three," Brett replied, looking at his thermometer with his headlamp. "It's almost warm enough to remove a few layers of gear."

"Don't," she quickly replied. "These chambers have all sorts of gasses flowing through them, and we don't have any O2 with us. We may find ourselves having to egress in a hurry, and you won't have those few precious seconds to spare."

Screwing the lid back onto the container, Dr. Graves said, "Turn around. Let me put this in your pack, if you don't mind."

"Of course," he said, allowing her to stow her precious sample safely in his pack.

"Do you hear that?" she asked.

"What?"

"Nothing," she replied with amazement. "It's so quiet down here. Everything is so still. In most of the caves and tunnels created by the fumaroles, you can see the light shining through the walls and ceiling from the sun above. You can hear the wind pounding the mountain. But here, there's nothing. It's silent."

Looking around, he said, "Amazing, isn't it? I'm not sure we've ventured this deep before."

"Of all the trips we've made into the ice caves, I've never noticed that particular vent."

"The one you fell into?" he asked.

"Yeah. It's like it simply appeared."

"The heat from the mountain mixed with the cold ice above can do some crazy things," he said. "Helo Cave, and others like it that are close to the surface, appear steady to us because they have the cold to keep them solid. This far into the volcano, though, who knows what hot gasses come and go, cutting a swath through the ice only to have it fill in and refreeze later before we've had a chance to discover it."

Walking over to Brett's climbing rope that dangled into the chamber, Dr. Graves asked, "Do you have your ascenders?"

"Yes, ma'am," he replied.

"Get them set up while I take a few more samples. We'd better get going. Who knows when the next blast of hot gasses will come rushing through."

~~~~

Looking impatiently at the clock that hung on the wall in the Lower Erebus Hut, Dr. Hunter began to speak when the door opened, allowing a rush of frigid arctic wind to enter, blowing papers off the table in front of him. "Linda, so glad you two are back. How did it go?" he asked, attempting to mask his concern.

"It's a long story," she confessed, "but it's one you'll want to hear."

****I hope you enjoyed this free sample.****

Made in the USA
Columbia, SC
05 October 2020